I0585977

BEYOND HIS STATION

THE SUMMERS CHRONICLE   BOOK ONE

PHILLIP ROSEWARNE

Published in Australia by Sid Harta Books & Print Pty Ltd,

ABN: 34632585293

23 Stirling Crescent, Glen Waverley, Victoria 3150 Australia

Telephone: +61 3 9560 9920, Facsimile: +61 3 9545 1742

E-mail: author@sidharta.com.au

First published in Australia 2022

This edition published 2022

Copyright © Phillip Rosewarne 2022

Cover design, typesetting: WorkingType (www.workingtype.com.au)

The right of Phillip Rosewarne to be identified as the Author of the Work
has been asserted in accordance with the Copyright, Designs and Patents Act 1988.

This book is a work of fiction. Any similarities to that of people living
or dead are purely coincidental.

All rights reserved. No part of this publication may be reproduced,
stored in a retrieval system, or transmitted, in any form or by any means without the prior written
permission of the publisher, nor be otherwise circulated in any form of binding or cover other than
that in which it is published and without a similar condition being imposed on the subsequent
purchaser.

Phillip Rosewarne

Beyond His Station

Book One

ISBN: 978-0-6484916-6-8 (pbk)

978-0-6456825-7-1 (ebook)

pp286

Phillip Rosewarne has lived and worked in various places on the east coast of Australia, his first job being for a shipping company. After working in New Guinea, Phillip was a project clerk for the Australian government in Canberra and the Northern Territory, where he worked in Katherine and Darwin, initially  for the Commonwealth Department of Works, and then for three years as head storeman for Woolworths in the Darwin area, two years either side of Cyclone Tracy. Phillip bought a cattle property in Queensland, which he operated for four years.

After returning to Canberra, he spent the next twenty-five years at the Commonwealth Department of Primary Industries, as it was then known. During that time, he worked in a science bureau within several primary industry sections. He gained a Certificate of Horticulture from the Tafe College and an Applied Science Degree from the University of Canberra.

Phillip always had a desire to write novels as opposed to scientific papers. He began writing shortly after leaving school, and the passion to write never left him. It was only later in life that he had the opportunity to write fiction on a more permanent basis.

Phillip is currently retired, and lives in the Northern Beaches region of Sydney.

This book is the first of a trilogy of vast disparity and apparent disconnection, but coming together in the third. It is dedicated to my wife Patricia, who inspired so much of what has been written.

CHAPTER 1

A man is born a hostage to his fate, abandoned and alone it seems to fulfil a destiny that is preordained. Sometimes though, a man can ransom an escape by an act seemingly unforeseen by fate and be born anew, almost as if recreated to open a new page in the book of days. By this means, he may escape the struggle and misery of the human condition. It rarely occurs, but when it does, blessings may flow because predestiny has been abrogated. John Summers cheated providence of its low intent by an unsuspected act that flooded his remoulded existence with favours. These truths confounded John all his days and it bothered him to be seemingly so blessed because of one act. It could not repay the past, but he had prepared for the future.

John Summers was nearly fourteen when he was told he would no longer attend school. It was the year 1953. Late autumn had sullenly descended over the undulating pastoral valleys and exposed hills of the western plains of New South Wales. A misty, insipid sun crept above the shrouded horizon, instilling a somnolent atmosphere over the frosty farming properties. John would now replace the long-serving, retiring farm hand, old Jack. John was a little disturbed to be given this news, especially as he was starting to succeed in his studies. It showed his lowly position in the family's hierarchical arrangement. However, he would not miss rising in the dark in the early winter, the long trip into town in the rickety bus, and the late returns home, arriving as he had left—in the dark.

This had all arisen now because the Merritts had made no provision for much-needed labour, even though everybody knew Jack would one day soon have to depart. Jack had finally and reluctantly retired after lifelong service as the leading farm hand but had succumbed to the effects of a hard-working life and had been forced to move away to the coast where it was warmer in the winter. This had created a problem for the Merritts as times had been tough for them, and they were not in a position to replace him but still needed a farm labourer. John was not only a strapping, solid lad, but also competent at the many and varied occupations station life presented.

Old Jack had been a strong influence on John, and he would miss him terribly, as they had spent a lot of working time together. Jack's energetic wife, also from the country, had been kind to John and understood how he had missed out on so many Merritt family activities. Because of this, old Jack had shown much kindness and given many hours of his time to John. Old Jack was handy with bush crafts, especially leatherwork, and often made John gifts, as the Merritts were lousy with finding things for John. Jack had the impression that John was condescendingly tolerated as a family obligation to his long-dead parents but didn't know the whole story. Over the years, Jack had made leather belts, dog collars, a knife pouch and a pocket watch pouch for John, but the thing he treasured the most was a whip with a stout leather stock and a short thong; just long enough for a small boy to use and learn to crack. Jack had spent hours crafting this whip for John. It was a full twelve-plait handle with eight-plait kangaroo hide that Jack had made seven feet long, just as the stockmen used. John spent hours playing with it and learned to become quite dexterous.

Henry and June Merritt ran the property, but technically it still belonged to Henry's mother, Mrs Vera Merritt, who had survived her husband, Claude. Vera had been Nan to all the children but held a special place in John's life. She had favoured him over her other grandchildren and overtly treated him kindly and considerately.

The property's problems stemmed from the sad reality that Henry was not a good manager and the place was not returning as much income as a property of this size should. The Merritt place was located in prime sheep and wheat country on the central slopes of New South Wales. It was a wonderful property and should have been returning a huge income while wool was so valuable. The price of sheep and wool had risen dramatically and had stayed buoyant since the war, and graziers had never had it so good. Alas, not the Merritts. Henry also had a propensity to gamble on the horses and was fond of an occasional drink; though not to the point of alcoholism.

The property was located in an area that contained some of the richest and most productive agricultural and grazing land in the state. It was not far from the town of Parkes. The Merritts inherited the property through Henry's side of the family, who had arrived in the early pioneering days when the early settlers followed the discovery of gold in the district. Some of June's relatives, the more prosperous members, were more than a little peeved that Henry got hold of the place at all, especially following his subsequent displays of inadequacies as a manager. At first they were in favour of their daughter and sister marrying into such a pioneering family, but subsequent events dampened that approval.

The mismanagement of the property was a quiet family joke outside the immediate confines of June's hearing. June, Henry's wife, recalled the days when money was no object and still tended to be unrestrained in her spending habits. She had come from a similar landed-gentry background, and the others in her family who still operated grazing properties were in good shape as they managed their affairs very well. The Merritt's three children also regarded themselves as belonging to the landed gentry and aspired to live as such. They had never been taught the benefits of moderation.

As the twig is bent, so is the tree inclined, as Vera used

4

to say. John, on the other hand, for some reason, was very careful with money and saved any that came his way. This was probably a throw-back to his canny father, who was legendary when it came to making and enjoying money.

John was Henry and June's nephew and a cousin to their three children. John's parents died in October 1939 when he was only three months old. He had been told that they lived in a posh flat in North Sydney. Vera, Claude, Henry and June would regularly visit before the war, especially before Henry and June's children were born and, for a time, while they were infants. John's mother was Henry's sister, and the Summers were really Henry's friends but Claude and Vera also got on well with the Summers.

Henry and June still had fond memories of carefree days spent in the company of John's parents, with luxurious parties and slightly naughty days over at the beaches near Manly, especially Freshwater. Freshwater was the beach next to the suburb of Harbord and before the war was frequented by the more risqué set or those not yet required to be seen in only the right places.

In the bygone days, the Merritts felt that some of the activities in which the Summers partook were slightly illicit, especially at the racetrack.

The Merritts still attended church every Sunday, and it was a longstanding family ritual that attendance was considered compulsory. The local district church was once the social centre of their lives, but this influence was now waning. While the family was staunch Church of England

and the children attended Grammar schools in Sydney, this aspect of life was diminishing as more of the young people moved to the city.

Harbord was noted for its less-than-salubrious working-class status; the sort of place the Merritts would not normally visit. It had a reputation for licentiousness in the early days when it was officially known as Freshwater. Many of the more solid local residents petitioned to change the name to Harbord in the 1920s to distance themselves from the reputation associated with the name of Freshwater. Confusion reigned ever since as parts were still known as Freshwater and parts as Harbord. This dichotomy reflected John's ambivalence to his new circumstances.

John's parents and Henry and June Merritt had wonderful carefree outings to the casual beach areas. John's father was a self-made man who was definitely on the rise but still knew how to have a good time. He knew how to make a lot of easy money, mainly at the racetrack, where he befriended all the right people and knew all the jockeys and trainers by name and reputation. Vera sometimes spoke of it to him, fondly remembering his parents and awakening deep emotions within him about his parental deprivation. Henry and June, however, never mentioned it and could not be drawn into remembering those days; it was simply not discussed. John surmised it was too painful an experience for them to recall those happier times.

Their three children appeared not to know anything about it either, though they never tired of reminding John of his sullied background, especially the youngest, Eleanor. John did not suspect that there was a much deeper and more sinister reason.

There was one other matter that rankled with John and was utilised as a weapon at moments of sibling and inter-family rivalry. John, through his father, was descended from an assistant surgeon who arrived on the First Fleet. It was shameful enough that John was descended from a First Fleeter, notwithstanding his relatively exalted position in that group. As far as the Merritts were concerned, all First Fleeters were tainted with the social stigma of convict ancestry. Due to the few women available, the earliest settlers took an ex-convict as a wife out of necessity. Even in the 1930s, after one hundred and fifty years of settlement, possessing convict blood was a severe social stigma. This was the topic of occasional light banter between the Merritts and Summers in the early days, then developed into a smear against John when the Merritts had their own family.

All the animosity covered the fact that the Merritts, through June, descended from an officer of the Second Fleet. These military officers were suspect by the very nature of their being assigned such low duties as guarding felons at His Majesty's pleasure in such a backwater. This period in the history of the earliest settlement of New South Wales coincided with the height of the Napoleonic wars between England and France. Any officer worth his salt eagerly sought promotion and glory in that endeavour, not accompanying felons on domestic duties to the colonies.

June's military ancestor profited because of his powerful

position in the early colony's controlling body, taking up extensive selections and grants of the choicest agricultural land when they crossed the Blue Mountains after 1813. However, his immediate offspring consisted entirely of five female children, and the name would have disappeared completely except that all the descendants bore a hyphenated name announcing their renowned link to the past.

This habit was a constant source of irritation to John, and he gradually despised the affectation. It affected him so that he became annoyed by this pretension; it coloured his attitude toward the bearer, especially later in his youth when the Merritt children invited friends to visit the property also bearing this, by now, despised badge.

The Merritts raised John with their children. Still, they never accepted him as an equal, primarily because of his parent's background and profession and partly because of the age difference between him and his three cousins. On his arrival at the property at three months of age, the Merritt's youngest child, Eleanor, was seven, while the middle boy, William, was ten, and the eldest, Arthur was twelve. They were kind and pleasant enough to him, but when the crunch came, he still wasn't one of them. The three Merritt children were sent to the best boarding school in Sydney from the beginning. With their limited income, this had proven difficult for Henry and June, but it was considered the minimum they could provide their children. While they spared no expense in educating their children, they drew the line at John, sending him to the local state school thirty-five miles away on the government bus. He was now asked to forego any further schooling to accommodate the poor management practices of Henry Merritt.

John was initially included in the Sunday activities, especially the ritual of attending the local Church of England. John didn't attend church long enough to gain much benefit, but a few aspects lingered in his mind.

Being told to leave school was another example of the different treatment he attracted. The Merritts now also asked John if he would mind vacating his homestead room and moving into the old quarters that Jack and his wife had recently vacated. They wanted to free up his room for visiting friends of his cousins and acquaintances from the expensive Sydney boarding schools, who were constantly being invited to the property to stay over during holidays. The Merritts encouraged their children to foster these interactions to get the best possible outcomes and connections for them in the future. John would occasionally be invited back to the main house for evening meals, but he was mostly asked, even at this young age, to look after himself.

Vera was a wily old lady, forced to keep an eagle eye on the financial management of the family's affairs, knowing that her son was loose with his money and enjoyed the occasional bet. This was where John partly fitted in with the Merritt family. As a professional punter at the racetrack, John's father had accelerated Henry's propensity to indulge in this form of gambling. In fact, John's father regarded it as a legitimate lifestyle and was preparing to become a bookmaker. This occupation required good knowledge of the racing industry, good connections, and a solid bank balance. Vera and her husband Claude began to have reservations about mixing with this crowd but marvelled at how good John's father was at it. He called it 'the science of odds'.

Henry was a man who was easily led astray by money matters, and John's father was evangelistic regarding racetrack science. Together, they had amassed a few good wins, especially John's father. In fact, he had managed to accumulate a sizeable sum of money stored in a safe deposit box in a Sydney city bank, which he had revealed to Henry in a moment of family familiarity after a substantial success. He was hoarding this money to elevate himself eventually to the position of bookmaker.

On the death of John's father in a car accident near the racetrack in 1939, Henry was first to the bank with the key, which was kept in a wallet in the North Sydney flat rented by John's father. Henry claimed the considerable sum of money for himself. Not known for his initiative, this was an uncharacteristically adventurous manoeuvre by Henry. He even amazed himself at this stroke of cunning and deceit. He convinced himself that he had only borrowed the cache, even though without consent, consoling himself to advise John what he had done for him in due course. Unfortunately, the money was quickly heading towards dissipation by the time he could make amends. It would be ironic that John would benefit from Vera's discovery of the event years later. She knew that Henry's reckless ways would soon squander any ill-gotten gains. So understanding that she would keep his dark secret, she appropriated a sizeable amount of the remaining loot. She invested it, mostly in government bonds and blue-chip shares. Henry always felt guilty about robbing John of his inheritance, but not enough to mention it to him.

Determined to guard this income during her later years, Vera had accumulated it in the form of cash in the station office safe. She had learned from John's father that the surest way to safeguard your assets was to control the results yourself. To prevent Henry from squandering any funds, she maintained control over all the assets and locked the safe. She rather eccentrically carried the only key around her neck tied on a long piece of leather bootlace. This disreputable family history partly influenced the actions the Merritts were imposing on John.

John was a solid lad and quite strong despite his young age; he would one day fill out to be a big man if he kept up the hard labour of station life. He was tall for his age, and he could easily pass himself off as much older. He was not a particularly good student, didn't miss going to school, and preferred the outdoors life of working on the land. However, John could clearly see the Merritts were not good managers as Henry was more of a veranda cocky, shying away from hard work or any work for that matter, but liked the accompaniments of wealth rather than actually accumulating it.

Jack's departure left John with little guidance in the day-to-day operations and was mostly left to his own devices. Luckily, this suited everyone. John knew all the routines and arranged his working life to priorities, keeping the property running, repairing the run-down fences and maintaining the dilapidated sheep yards around the sheering shed. Then there were the regular jobs of shearing, jetting or dipping the sheep, and crutching and worming. He was a competent driver of all the property vehicles, a good horseman and could muster the sheep on his own with the aid of the farm dogs.

Henry had long ago abandoned any attempt at growing wheat or other crops as there was more than enough to do without that complication, despite the country being admirably suited to cropping.

John loved the open paddocks, especially the small remnant bush areas of the property where he often escaped, wandering alone, watching the wildlife that lived within its bounds. On the wetter days, he'd spend his free time observing the activity of the wild struggle of life. If he saw a wedged-tailed eagle flying high in wide lazy circles in the heat haze, he would stop, trying to spot its mate and wonder at their freedom. To him, this freedom was a two-edged sword. The eagles, and indeed all the hunting birds on the property, were fearsome-looking creatures, but they failed to understand the fear their appearance caused. They were free because of their obligation to work all the daylight hours, and toiled incessantly to feed themselves and their offspring nesting high in the nearby mountains. Freedom had a price—this was a lesson not lost on him. He tried to appreciate the condition of his lowly circumstances and endured any disrespect for the certain comforts offered in compensation. He was not a Merritt and he knew they could easily release him from their employment, which would be difficult for him.

On leaving school, John had chosen a pup from a litter of dogs bred on the property. He called her Kelly and trained the puppy, and in return, she accompanied him everywhere. He hoped she would be a companion for him for many years.

John could never convince Henry to spend any money on maintenance of the capital items, especially the fencing. This caused constant problems with wandering sheep and marauding dogs. He also could not convince Henry to attend to the increasing weed problem on the property or the incessant rabbit plagues that dogged their property management schemes. Henry paid a poor salary and was usually very late—sometimes months late. This riled John but he had an ally in Nan Vera. Being an excellent money manager and accumulator, she understood its value and the need for promptness and honesty.

John wondered if he might be invited up to the house for Christmas, as Christmases at the Merritts were always huge affairs with all invited, including any workers on the property. It was the one time of year that he felt slightly more involved with the family, and sometimes they even gave him a small gift.

The regular visits of John's cousins' former boarding school acquaintances became a source of irritation, as they were often unpleasant—at least towards John. He would confide in Nan that they always seemed to look condescendingly upon him and were what he usually described as "up themselves".

The other family children gradually grew apart from John

as all their lives took different courses. As old Vera Merritt's health slowly deteriorated, she needed closer attention. The family asked John if he would mind looking after her when they travelled to Sydney for the Royal Easter Show or to Manly for holidays. During these periods, Old Mrs Merritt realised that John was much more sensible and reliable than the others regarding managing her finances. Each month, she liked to go to the bank, withdraw her cash allowances, allocate them over different envelopes, and place them in the safe. She stowed neat bundles of ten-pound notes and, sometimes, special bank exchange twenty and fifty pound notes, secured with rubber bands. As with most people of her generation, she still had memories of bank closures in the Depression and losing all her savings held in those banks.

As soon as it was possible for him, John obtained his driving licence. This had several advantages, including relieving Henry of the necessity of replenishing the property hardware and supplies. Henry could now devote even more time and thought away from the farm. As it became more difficult for Nan to travel into town, she began to rely more and more on John to deposit her occasional debenture cheques, withdraw her income in the form of cash from the bank, and return it to her. There she would sort out the returned money, add it to her bundles, and neatly stack them in the safe. John had no idea how much was in there, but he knew there would be a significant amount.

Nan was a short, stocky woman and had gradually developed diabetes, which prevented her from walking much.

As her mobility declined, she became more house-bound. The disease also affected her vision, and she became more short-sighted. The more she dealt with John's sensibilities, the more she came to rely on him to assist her with her routine of money handling. The large safe, with its heavy door, was in an awkward position in the station office, behind the desk in the far corner. Nan found accessing and operating it with her arthritic and aged hands more difficult.

When John turned sixteen and could drive, she entrusted him to do the withdrawal banking alone. Back at the homestead he would help her to bundle up the notes, and eventually, with her ailing health, John would deposit the envelopes in the safe.

The first time John opened the safe, he was astounded. He tried not to appear too interested, but it shocked him at the immense accumulation of money neatly stacked on the safe floor. The safe had a top section, separately lockable, and John had no idea what was in it. He assumed it contained things such as the wills, deeds and other important papers concerning the family. The amount of money had disturbed John. Firstly, there was the neglect of the property. Secondly, there was the thought that he could make better use of some of this cash himself; thus, he might become less of a hostage to fate and chance.

It was the year of the Melbourne Olympics, and Easter fell on 1 April. The Merritts were preparing for the Royal Easter Show in Sydney with much excitement. John, who would soon be seventeen, knew an invitation would not be extended to him to attend, and they would ask him to look after an increasingly ill Vera. The knowledge of all that cash secreted away in the large station safe raised dark thoughts—thoughts he tried to discourage.

Thoughts and plans took shape in his imagination of ways he could take some of this money for himself, and the germination of a plan formulated in his mind. As part of this careful planning, he bought a Land Rover station wagon that was fully enclosed in the back. This he paid for with the small amount of savings he had put aside over the last few years of low-paid work on the farm. Ostensibly, it was for station use and ideal for the work, but he bought it with other motives. It was a couple of years old and in good condition. He got it at a good price, as all the graziers were flush with money while the wool prices were so high, and they were constantly upgrading their equipment.

John had the opportunity to execute any number of the plans circulating in his mind while the family was in Sydney.

The family would be away for at least one week, possibly two. That gave him plenty of time to find the right moment to deal with the safe. Old Vera was by now quite frail, but still sharp as a tack in her mind. Any heist must be well planned to be executed successfully. John spent hours going over the ideas in his head and preparing for any circumstances he could conceive of as arising. He took a large discarded suitcase from the storage shed and a roll of heavy weatherproof canvas and hid it in his quarters. The shed also had some discarded old keys, and he found one that approximately duplicated the size and weight of the safe key Vera hung around her neck. He carefully tied this onto a length of leather bootlace to replicate the real one.

During the family's absence from the property, John moved back into the homestead, usually to his old room, to look after Vera. This made the execution of his plan much simpler. He was nervous, as he sensed that his opportunity would arise this time, and he hoped he would have the courage to go through with it.

Vera, now bound to a wheelchair, was quite unwell on the third day, and after dinner, John pushed her to her downstairs bedroom. As usual, after heaving herself with difficulty onto the bed, she removed the key strung on the leather bootlace from around her neck and hung it on the bedpost. Usually, Vera was a restless sleeper, but she snored heavily when she was in a deep sleep. About eleven o'clock that evening, when he heard her snoring, he crept into her room, replaced the safe key with the fake one, and crept out.

The station office was at the other end of the house, near the kitchen. With fumbling fingers and trembling hands, he stood nervously before the huge office safe. Though it had a combination lock, the key was more convenient for a person with age-related issues. John inserted the large iron key and slowly unlocked the safe as he had done many times before for Vera. The door was heavy but swung silently. Before him was the large stash of neatly bundled cash that she had accumulated for years. He methodically removed them from the safe, only taking those that contained the notes of the highest denominations, mostly tens, a few twenties and some fifty pound notes.

It took some time to repack all the bundles neatly into the suitcase, but finally, it would hold no more. Quite a few piles remained in the safe. John closed the safe, relocked it and headed to return the key. Vera was still noisily asleep as John crept back into her room; he swapped over the two keys and backed out of the room as she continued to sleep fitfully.

He lugged the heavy case to the back of the Land Rover parked by the front door, threw it on the prepared mattress in the back, covered it with the canvas and closed the door. John initially thought of burying it at once, but as no one was around, he hoped to do that the next day. He retreated to the house and tried to get some sleep.

About mid-morning the next day, after attending to Vera and trying not to appear too anxious, he drove the Land Rover to a predetermined spot about four miles away from the homestead. After much searching across the property, it was a site he had decided on as a suitable hiding place for the case. It was located away from the main grazing areas, on a knoll overlooking the valley between large boulders. It was too rocky for crops and the perfect place to bury the case. He carefully removed the top layer of grass, dug a hole about two feet six deep, and placed the case wrapped in the heavy weatherproof canvas into the hole. He replaced as much soil as would fit and dumped the rest in a drum. Then he carefully returned the grass to give the appearance nothing had happened there and drove back to the homestead to check on Vera. She was dozing in the sunny back room where he had left her. *So far, so good.*

The trick now was for John to carry on as usual and pretend all was normal. Vera was the only person with legitimate access to the safe, which worked in his favour. He believed that no one else had any concept of what was in there, and her mobility and eyesight were now so restricted that hopefully, she would be none the wiser. His plan was to remain on the property for a few months and then arrange a pretext to leave.

The next morning, Vera was still unwell but he gleaned that all had gone as planned for him. He was attentive to her needs and a little less agitated than he had been for the last few days.

He hoped he could carry on and not betray any guilty behaviour when the family returned home from Sydney. It was a relief to him when they finally arrived home, and he could leave them all to discuss their exciting time away. He was happy to be back in his quarters alone and mull over the events that had occurred in the last week or so.

John carried on working away from the homestead and trying to avoid the family. He was slowly accumulating a litany of minor annoyances to use as excuses for his impending departure. He began dropping hints that he was thinking of trying out in Queensland. He was genuinely becoming frustrated with the lack of support for station work that urgently needed doing. He could speak of it to Nan, but she was physically deteriorating now and unable to pull Henry into any form of agreement on property expenditure.

John was also slowly accumulating the few objects he felt he could honestly take with him. There were a few tools, a couple of wooden ammunition boxes he used as toolboxes and some clothes. He made sure to take all the beautiful leatherwork items that old Jack had made for him over the years. He found a safe hideaway along the inner roofline of the rear canopy to lay the short stock whip where it would be secure but also available if he ran into snakes. The weeks slowly drifted by in monotony, and winter finally showed signs of abating. All the time, John remained as low-key as possible.

After the long winter, spring was in the air, and the station work would now increase in earnest. It was five months since John had buried the suitcase full of money. He felt the time was coming when he could make his move. The Merritts were all planning to be away again in Sydney in September, so that would be an excellent time to depart quietly.

It would be difficult to leave his sick grandmother in the lurch, but that was the price of his path and the guilt he must carry. John considered she would probably not live for much longer.

On the chosen day, John drove his laden Land Rover up to the front door of the big house. Kelly was sitting on the passenger's seat, looking expectantly at him and then out the window, her tail giving away her excitement. Patting her on the head, he told her to stay and went into the house to find Vera sitting at the kitchen table where she usually spent most of the day. She was patiently waiting for him so they could have a morning smoko together. John prepared himself for what he knew would be unpleasant news for Vera.

'Nan', he said, 'I have something to tell you. I have decided to travel a bit up north and am leaving today.'

'What do you mean, dear?' she asked.

'Well, I want to travel a bit, so now is the time to go.'

'What do you mean, dear?' she said again. 'I don't understand.' Her tone was a little more concerned now, as though the message was sinking in. 'But have you got enough money to look after yourself? And what will you do? And, oh John, I'll miss you terribly. What will I do? Who will be able to do all my business as you've been doing for me? What's brought all this on all of a sudden, anyway?'

John could see her colour changing and her demeanour becoming more agitated. He tried to speak calmly and softly to her as he continued with the bad news.

'It's not all of a sudden, Nan. I've been thinking about it for a while now.'

'Is it because they all went off to Sydney again without you, as usual?' she asked, growing angrier.

'Well, not really,' he replied. 'It's a big combination of things.'

'Has he not been paying you again!' she exclaimed. 'How long is it this time since he paid you?'

'About six weeks,' he replied in a soft and calm voice. 'But it's not only that. I get a bit annoyed when they all traipse off to Manly for a week, staying by the beach, but can't find the money to fix the tractor properly or repair the yards or the faulty gates that cause us so much trouble. I don't want to say too much about them as they did take me in as a baby, remember.'

'That wasn't all that wonderful, you know. It's not been the hardship you've been led to believe it is, John,' she said. 'They collected a pile of money from your dad's security box in the city. By rights, that money should have been for you.'

'What d'you mean?' John asked, a little surprised.

Old Mrs Merritt realised that in her shock and anger at her useless son and the now imminent departure of her only confidante, she might have said something she would rather not have said and might regret later on. She lowered her tone and changed tack. 'Suffice it to say, you came here with more than just yourself.'

John thought that was a strange thing to say. Then he remembered all those weird digressions he overheard during the years that did not always seem to make sense—whispers and asides between people that would suddenly dry up when he came near. Suddenly he felt a distinct twinge of minor relief and less sense of guilt. Maybe he was not quite as wicked as he imagined. This thought he fostered more in hope than in any reality. He knew what he was doing was wrong—no matter how much he justified it. Nevertheless, he recalled a couple of whispered comments that troubled him over the years – comments about all John's money in the flat, or safe or somewhere. That was all of little consequence right now, however.

'Look, Nan, they'll be home this afternoon to look after

you, and I just want to be gone, and think about looking for a job in Queensland.'

John could see her eyes were getting a little teary. Vera Merritt was a strong character and not ordinarily prone to emotions. He placed the tea on the table near her and some cake on a plate. She took a couple of sips and replaced the cup. She sat in awkward silence for several seconds.

'I'm certainly going to miss you very much. I can't believe this,' she said again.

'I'll miss you too, Nan.'

'Look, I want to give you some money to help you out, John,' she finally said.

John was already feeling pretty squeamish thinking about all the cash he had stashed away and still buried up among the rocky outcrop. Then there was the Akta-Vite tin full of notes he had hidden in the Land Rover.

'No, truly Nan, I'm really all right … really. I've been saving for years, and now is a good time for me to go.'

It was an awkward farewell for them both. John knew he would probably not see her again. He finally extricated himself from this difficult position and left her at the table. When he arrived at the front gate, he stopped the Rover and cast his gaze towards the rocky ridge and the buried suitcase full of notes. He hoped to be back in the future to retrieve it.

He walked over to the large wooden letterbox for what he hoped would be the last time and checked for any mail. The box was empty. He leaned on the fence next to the box and contemplated for several minutes the windless, sunny day warming the spring air and the slowly greening paddocks in the valley for the last time. He was thinking about how they would all react to his sudden departure. Then he turned determinedly, strode to his Land Rover, and drove off.

CHAPTER 2

John headed for Queensland, but he knew he would probably not like the humidity of the sub-tropics. He had yearned to visit those parts of Sydney that Vera had spoken of in connection with his parents. As a reward for his evilness, John had promised himself that his first destination would be Manly to see North Sydney and Harbord where his parents had frequented. He headed off in the direction of Sydney.

John did not travel too far the first night away from the farm. He found a quiet location by a small stream along the highway and stopped early. He wanted to sort out the Rover and prepare for a long period travelling. Besides, there were no reasons for him to hurry, he was his own boss and had enough money to do exactly as he pleased. He found that a strange position to be in after all those regimented years at school and then working all day on the property. He gave Kelly an affectionate two-handed rub over her ears.

It took John two days of dawdling to finally reach Manly. The Land Rover was a slow vehicle with a low top speed. He was also travelling in unfamiliar territory, following Razorback Mountain before he reached the outskirts of Sydney. Once in Manly, he found a flat to stay in and went straight around to Freshwater Beach.

John quickly discovered that he preferred the country and felt uncomfortable in the city. Yet there was a certain excitement and thrill being in all the bustle. He feared it, yet loved it. He spent a few days exploring Harbord, Manly and North Sydney, and sitting on the beach. He found that he was quickly tiring of that existence and was beginning to hanker after his preferred life. Doing nothing indefinitely did not appeal to him.

After nearly a week on the beach he decided it was time to go to work. Before he departed, there was one more thing to do, and that was to catch the Manly ferry.

The Port Jackson and Manly Steamship Company operated regular ferry services from Manly across the harbour to Circular Quay in the city. John wanted to experience the vibrancy of a huge city before he departed for the bush again, just to taste its flavours. He boarded the rickety old ferry at the wharf mid-morning, avoiding the rush of regular workers who used this method to travel to work in the city. It was still well patronised but not as crowded as the peak hour ferries. John had never been on a boat before and he felt like a child with all the excitement of this novelty.

The ferry had to cross Sydney Heads after leaving Manly and before turning westward up the harbour to the Quay. It was when the ferry began to rock from side to side as it encountered the swell penetrating the harbour through the Heads that John was suddenly struck with a peculiar sensation that chilled him somewhat.

For some unknown reason, John thought about his neglected and socially despised ancestor, the assistant surgeon who had sailed through the Heads over one hundred and fifty years ago. The difference was striking. His ancestor, whose first name John did not even remember, had just sailed thousands of sea miles through mostly unchartered waters in a tiny ship smaller than this ferry. John was empathetic to his plight, arriving into this wild and uncivilised barren harbour. John looked at the harbour with a trained bushman's eye. He knew country and what to look for. The whole place was a low rocky heath set upon almost sterile sandstone. It must have been devastating to come upon so much infertility. John thought that the best thing to do was to build houses on it. It was no wonder they were at Parramatta within days, trying to find suitable country.

Botany Bay was even worse. According to the map, Botany Bay was a huge shallow exposed bay with nothing but sand hills. Sydney Cove might be a safe harbour, mooring many ships, but as for establishing a settlement here, it must have seemed almost useless. John stared at the harbour with all its attractions and could not remove the thoughts about the enormous struggles his ancestor had to endure to survive in this inhospitable place as it must have been then. John felt himself getting quite emotional at the contemplation of his forebears. This inevitably led into the present where he could occasionally descend into melancholy at the thought of his own parents and their demise when he was so young.

Enough of this sadness. John snapped himself out of this dreaming and contemplated the excitement ahead. He could not entirely remove the thoughts about his ancestry, however. Somehow, it seemed to fill him with inspiration to achieve. John decided to depart from the urban confines and begin his quest to discover his future. After returning to Manly that afternoon he prepared his Rover for the trip north to search out country for himself.

John turned the Rover north and headed for New England. He hoped to look at real estate as he headed up the highway. John's intention was to try to buy a small property for himself and run it as he knew he could. He was looking for a smallish place – not too much work, but enough land to keep him busy. He also loved the bush and wanted a place that had some bush left on it and its own creek. These sorts of places existed in New England and maybe around the northern rivers. He also had a preference for country that would run cattle. He knew very little about cattle but thought they would entail much less work than sheep. He loved the sheep work but it was so constant and depended on so many others, especially the shearers.

He would avoid the western areas, as the stations out there were usually large. He wanted a small enough place that he could manage himself. He also understood that a choice property such as the Merritt's in prime country was less realistic for him to aspire to. It would of necessity be in a region close to where he had just left and he realised that his young age might arouse suspicion if he turned up and purchased top country.

Every time John came to a major town such as Tamworth, Armidale, Tenterfield or Glen Innes, he would stop and inspect the real estate windows, even sometimes talking to the agents. On a few occasions he inspected properties that were appealing. He kept a notebook on all the areas he drove through and properties he saw. He also made notes on his impressions of the country.

John spent up to two weeks in some centres looking at real estate and getting a feel for the area. He spent long periods in the New England region and especially the Darling Downs. The trouble with the Downs proper was that it was such rich country that it was all developed – no virgin country left. They even seemed to plough up to and under the fences. The country around Nambour was much more to his liking, mostly dairying, but the land was good with plenty of rainfall and some of it still uncleared.

By the end of October, John decided to head right up north just to see what it was like. He headed for Mt Isa. It was flat, dry and hot, and the cattle and sheep stations were usually very large – not suitable for what he had in mind. He headed back towards the coast and up to Cairns. This was the wrong time of year to be in the tropics. The heat was oppressive but the humidity was even worse. He clung to the coast as best he could. It was so uncomfortable that he began heading south again.

From November to Christmas he drifted slowly south to end up in Noosa Heads by the end of December. After the Christmas and New Year close-downs, John was finally able to contact some more agents when he arrived in Murwillumbah. He then spent until the middle of February exploring the north coast and especially Grafton, which was particularly appealing to him as there were large tracts of country with untouched bush still available for purchase.

To be complete, John decided to drive all the way down to Eden on the south coast of NSW to see what was available. The south coast was very attractive and still mostly undeveloped. This area was also appealing to him. He reached Eden in the middle of March – just when the cool weather was about to commence.

It had now been about six months since he had left home. All the images and impressions of his long travels were swirling around in his mind. He constantly consulted his notepad for his comments and thoughts at the different spots he had visited. He now felt that he had given the east coast a fair going over and his favoured choices were firming in his mind. He liked the area around Nambour and Gympie in Queensland. He also was impressed with the New England region. He liked the Kyogle area. All things considered, however, he was still favouring the Grafton district as it had so much bushland left.

John sat on the wharf at Eden watching the fishing boats coming and going. He decided to head back up north via the Southern Tablelands.

Winding his way slowly up from the coast via Brown Mountain, John arrived in Cooma.

Cooma was located on the Monaro Plains in the Southern Tablelands and was the major town for the Snowy Mountain Scheme and the gateway to the Kosciuszko snowfields. It was a renowned sheep grazing region but John had never been there and knew little about it. He parked his Land Rover in the main street and got out for a walk. He had planned to head north from here through Canberra and back up to northern New South Wales where, so far, the most suitable land seemed to be.

At the far end of town was a small real estate agent's shop and he looked in the window to see what was on offer. There were the usual farming properties and rural holdings in the window, but unusually, one caught his eye. It had obviously been there for some time as it was a little faded and hung crookedly by an off-centre pin. The feature of this block was that it was completely vacant, run down but of considerable size – about 4,000 acres. It was relatively cheap as only about 1,000 acres were grazing land. John was peering at the photograph and description in the window and did not notice the arrival of one of the agents.

'Just looking?' the agent asked.

'Yes, really just looking,' John replied, turning to look at the owner of the voice.

Tom Grady was an ex-farmer who had moved into town

when he could no longer do the hard work of farming. He used his rural skills and knowledge to sell real estate. Tom held out his hand and introduced himself.

After some introductions, John said, 'I'm interested in the large grazing block with all the trees.'

'I wouldn't even take you out to that mate, it's pretty crook. No fences, overgrazed, and too many trees. Not to mention the rabbits. We have a couple of other places though that are good buying. Are you interested in a grazing property or cattle?' Tom asked.

'I'm really looking for something a bit smaller than that but I'd rather like to see it if possible. If you give me directions, I'll go there myself if you like.'

'No, I'll take you there on the way to a couple of others. Can you go now?'

'Sure. Can I take my dog?' asked John, and Tom nodded. 'Is it freehold?'

'Yes,' replied Tom. 'Most land here is freehold.'

Tom was quite personable and explained some of the local areas to John. For some reason, he disliked the property that John wished to see. It turned out that the owner was in a bit of financial trouble and was very keen to sell. He had flogged the place and done no fencing for years, and had let the rabbits get a little out of hand. He owed both the bank and the stock agency a lot of money as well, firstly by getting out of sheep and then through injudicious trading in cattle.

Tom showed John two other places first, but John had no interest in them. He had never considered grazing on the

Monaro, so these did not appeal to him. They were in settled country with bitumen road access amidst flat, featureless plains. But where Tom was now driving seemed to John to be isolated and still largely unsettled. The road was quite rough, even for bush country. It was hilly, treed, and the grazing stock were in good condition. About thirty-five miles out of Cooma, Tom slowed down on the dirt road.

He stopped in the middle of the road and said, 'The bloke that owns the place lives over there.' Tom pointed to his left front. 'He also owns all this country in here on the right adjoining the place you're interested in. As you can see, he's flogged it a bit and owes a lot of dough around, agents and the like. The boundary starts a bit further ahead but you can't see all the country once you get there because of the ridge that rises away from the road. There are no fences on this boundary and the rest are as bad as these here in the front. The block runs straight up there into the timber and includes all that timber over there.' He pointed generally to his right front. 'The gate is just up ahead.'

Tom drove a mile or so up the road and pulled into the right to a tired old metal gate barely hanging on the post. John got out and opened the gate. Tom drove in and John closed it. They drove in silence up a bush track through thick trees. Shortly, they came to a fork that led either further into the timber or to the right out into the open paddock.

'As you can see, there is not much grazing on this block because of all the timber,' said Tom.

'How big is the block?'

'This block is about four thousand acres. It runs for about two miles along the road but about three miles back into the timber country.'

'This is good country though,' said John. 'I mean, look at the beautiful soil and the quality of the timber.'

'Yes,' replied Tom. 'It's granite country and ideal for sheep, but old Frank got into cattle and debt and hasn't looked after it much.'

They headed down to the creek that ran through the property. John asked, 'And this is all freehold?'

'Yes.'

'And this is a permanent creek?'

'Yes.' They got out at the creek and John wandered about kicking the soil and pulling out grasses. When they returned to the gate and onto the road, John asked if Tom could show him where he thought the boundaries were.

On the way back into town, John did not say much but he was certainly thinking a lot. He really liked the place and could imagine himself living there. It was now late in the afternoon, so John decided to stay in a motel in Cooma for the night. The next morning, he got up early and walked around the main part of town, something he always did in any centre that had appealing properties. *A good local town is a real asset when looking at farming.* He then drove around the facilities, looking at the hardware stores, the metal factories, and building and timber yards; all things he would require if he bought a vacant block.

In the afternoon he decided to drive out again to look at

the place. The sun began to sink in the west below the stark mountain silhouette.

'Pink at night, shepherd's delight', Vera always said. He wondered if that was a good omen. He briefly thought about her, then he returned to Cooma and spent another night in the motel.

The next morning, Tom was in early and John asked to go back to the vacant block, get a feel for it, and walk the boundaries.

'Could you ask the owner if I could camp on it with my dog for a night or two to get a better look?'

'Sure,' said Tom. 'I'll ring him now if he's there.'

Tom went over to his desk and, looking up a desk pad, began dialling a number. After a short delay, John could hear Tom saying, 'Morning Frank, it's Tom Grady from Cooma Stock Agents here. How are you? That's good. Listen Frank, I've got a young bloke here who's interested in your place and was wondering if it would be okay to drive over it and maybe walk about a bit. You sure? Could he camp there a night or two with his dog? You sure? No worries. Many thanks, Frank. I'll be in touch.'

Tom put down the receiver.

'Yeah, that'll be alright, John. Frank said you can camp there if you are really interested in the place.'

'Great. I'll go back and have a good look around and get back to you.'

After gathering his things from the motel and provisions

from the general store, John was soon back on the road and heading for the block.

On the first visit with Tom Grady, John had noticed that the track that led out of the timber into the paddocks emerged onto a gently sloping expanse of cleared grazing country. He thought this would be suited to a future dwelling, be it a shed or a house. Nearly the entire block was hidden from the road by a small rise that gently sloped up from the road to a small crest then slid away across a long gentle valley with a creek in the middle distance before rising again to culminate in the much higher timber-covered country at the back of the block. The distant timber could be seen from some of the road but not until the road was well past this block. John considered this a favourable aspect from a security viewpoint and for privacy.

He drove through the gate and into the open paddock. Travelling down the slope towards the creek, he was able to find a picturesque spot close to the creek and the timber, but clear enough to camp in. He studied the position of the sunset and sunrise to determine the best possible site for a shed and noted the wind directions.

John found the weather to be favourable. Autumn on the Monaro was possibly the best season, as the days were mild, the howling hot westerlies of summer were usually gone and the nights were cool enough to sleep comfortably. He spent the next two days exploring as much of the property as he could cover and wandering over the paddocks. It was eerily silent except for the occasional harsh calls of the gang-gangs, the sulphur-crested cockatoos, and the white-tailed black cockatoos; the latter two flocks in their erratic flight patterns as they jerkily glided the long distances between their feeding trees scattered about the country. He would wonder at their ungainly, almost prototypical flying techniques, as if they were some of God's earlier, and not quite perfect, attempts at flighted creation. He said a silent prayer of thanks when he heard the familiar jocular call of the kookaburra, a sign of good luck according to his nan. There were a lot of familiar smaller birds and a few that he did not know. Time to learn all their names in the future, 'God willing', as Nan would say.

After three days of camping on the block, John planned to go into town to see the agent and if possible, the bank. Just after 10 am, he went into the bank and asked the teller if it were possible to see the manager. The manager was interviewing another customer, but would be available in about twenty minutes. After a short wait, John was ushered into the manager's office. Mr Petty was an elderly, quite dapper gentleman. He extended his hand, introduced himself, and asked John to sit down.

'What can I do for you, Mr Summers?' he asked.

John spoke slowly and deliberately. 'I'm interested in a property outside Cooma and wondered if I might discuss finances with you, Mr Petty.'

Mr Petty nodded.

'I've had a look at a place on Bull Flat Road. It's a bit run down and needs a lot of work, but I might be interested if I could arrange a small loan to help me,' said John.

'Not the Dougherty place?' asked Mr Petty.

'You know it, Mr Petty?' John asked, a little surprised.

'Let's say we are familiar with the property.'

'Anyway, I rather like it as it has possibilities,' said John. 'I was thinking of making an offer on it and wondered how I'd stand with you for a small loan to help me with it. I have some savings here in your bank, but not quite enough.'

Mr Petty leaned onto his elbows and said thoughtfully, 'What are you thinking about?'

'I thought I'd make an offer of eight thousand pounds,' said John.

'What's it on the market for?' Mr Petty enquired.

'He's asking nine thousand five hundred pounds.'

'Ah yes,' responded Mr Petty. 'Now I remember. I don't think we can go below eight thousand five hundred.'

John was a bit confused but did not show it. He was thinking quickly. Tom had said that Dougherty owed a lot of money to the bank and the stock agent. *It must be this bank.* In that case, he had just learned that his offer of eight thousand pounds might be just short of the bank's requirements, but nearly sufficient to swing the sale if the bank has any say.

'If I can raise about six or seven thousand would you be prepared to lend me say, fifteen hundred pounds?' asked John.

'I'd probably be agreeable to that suggestion.'

'Thank you, Mr Petty.' John stood up and effusively thanked the bank manager for his time and advice.

John went back to the estate agent's office and asked for Tom Grady. 'Hello Tom. I've come to see you about that block.'

'Ah good. What do you think?'

'I'm prepared to make him an offer of eight thousand three hundred pounds.'

'That's a bit low.'

John said firmly, 'Make the offer.'

'All right, John. I'll see what I can do. Can you come back later?'

'How about on Thursday?'

'That should do it.'

John left the office and collected a few items around town then headed back to the property faithfully accompanied by Kelly. Tom Grady tried to contact Frank, but was unable to during the day. He rang Mr Petty at the Commercial Bank and told him of John's offer.

Mr Petty sighed and said, 'The cunning blighter, Tom. He's offered less to give himself some room to move as he knows that we can't accept less than eight thousand five hundred.'

'He seems like a nice lad, Mr Petty.'

'Yes, I liked him. If you get on to Frank, I'd press him hard to accept eight thousand five hundred.'

'You'd accept that offer would you?

'Yes.'

'It'd be one in the eye for Quiggin too, you know. That bloke is keen to snap up Dougherty's place if he can get it for a song.'

'I didn't know that, Tom. He's carrying a lot of debt too you probably know, so it would be a strain for him to buy.'

'Well, good luck to Mr Summers if he wants it. I will contact you soon.'

John spent the next two days walking over the property while he waited for a reply to his offer. On the second morning, thick grey cloud began to bank up to the west and the day grew colder and dark. That afternoon John found himself sitting on the creek bank in a small clearing in the bush near the eastern boundary. He was staring at his shoes deep in contemplation when he heard a noise in the bush on the opposite side of the creek. When he looked up, he was startled to see a strangely dressed man with his hand on the head of a small boy. The man was short and stocky, wearing khaki-coloured moleskins and had a thick beard. On his belt he wore leather pouches for knives and a watch. He looked like a miner or a timber cutter from last century. The young boy, about nine or ten, was dressed in shorts and long socks with a distinctive red leather belt and a silver buckle.

'Who are you?' John asked.

'I be Albert,' replied the man in a broad accent that was from Cornwall, or Yorkshire, or even Scotland, John thought. 'And the lad be here to tell yee that he's oright and he'll be awaitin' fer yee.'

John was completely confused and a little apprehensive. 'I'm not sure I understand you Albert, er, mate,' stammered John. There was another noise behind him. He looked around. With the dark overcast weather, the native animals were coming out earlier than normal and John assumed the noise was one of them. When he turned back the apparition had gone.

'*Who the hell was Albert?*' wondered John. '*And who was the lad "waiting for me"?*'

40

It was getting quite dark in the bush as late afternoon drizzle began to fall. John went back to his Land Rover to prepare for the night. He did not think much more about Albert, in fact he was so confused by the event that he wondered whether he had nodded off and dreamed it. He was still mindful of the placid appearance of the calm little boy who stared intently but almost knowingly at him through the misty drizzle. John had been struck by how dry and bright, almost dazzling, he appeared, even through the rain.

Then another strange thought occurred to him. It was now over a year since he buried the suitcase of money. That meant that the Royal Easter Show must about be on again. It would be strange if he went back to retrieve the money when that was on again. He knew that this year it was later; about the end of April instead of the beginning. That also meant it would be getting cold there now. He had a sudden melancholic thought for his ill nan and wondered if she were still alive.

John was feeling quite nervous about this venture. He was even wondering if this was the right move or the right place or even the right region.

On the appointed day, John drove out of the property for what he thought could possibly be the last time. He paused deep in thought, meditating uncertainly about the future, which now hung on the next few hours. *Ah well, whatever was meant to be – "God willing", as Nan would say.*

He closed the struggling gate, latched it to the protesting post, and drove off to Cooma with Kelly in the front seat.

Tom was in the office early again, so John approached him with nervous apprehension.

'Good morning John,' greeted Tom cheerily. 'How are you this morning?'

'G'day Tom,' proffered John with an air of reticence. 'I'm good,' he said. 'But a bit out of condition after all that driving about and doing no work. I found all that walking wore me out a bit. Anyway, how did you go Tom?' he asked. Tom had seemed pleased to see him, which John took as a good sign.

'Yeah, pretty good John. We've convinced the vendor to accept your offer, if you can just raise it by two hundred pounds. The next move is up to you now.'

John sat down in the chair in front of Tom's desk. Tom had a contract all ready for him to sign if he wanted to go ahead.

'Goodness!' exclaimed John. 'This is serious.'

John thought about it for a minute. He then asked Tom for some advice. John wanted to go ahead but it really depended on being able to retrieve the loot he had stashed away back on the Merritt's farm. Some of his conversations with Vera now began to come to mind. He recalled that she had said when buying real estate, there were a few pointers to be aware of. John now needed time to retrieve the money and to ensure a few things were in order.

'Can I have this deal dependent on gaining access to my finances, which are a bit tied up at the moment?' he asked.

Tom was prepared to have it signed 'subject to finance' and confirmation that all the surveys were in order. John would also have to reconfirm with Mr Petty, the bank manager, that a small loan was still available. John thought this might arouse less suspicion than an outright cash sale; especially as he was conscious that he was so young to be handling such large sums of money.

When all this was tied up to everyone's satisfaction, it only remained for him to successfully retrieve the suitcase full of money that was hopefully still awaiting his return. He had enough cash on him to pay the deposit but did not want to spend all that he had without first retrieving the rest hidden back at Merritt's. He drove back out to the property after signing the papers and confirming the arrangements with the bank. All that remained was to plan the pickup.

In order to arrive at the Merritt's at about midnight, John would have to leave Cooma at about four in the afternoon as his Land Rover had a top speed of only about fifty miles an hour and it was at least an eight hour trip to the farm in the central west. It was a cloudy, drizzly afternoon late in April and the days were getting quite short and cool. He went to Bathurst and Parkes via Canberra and Yass, and arrived at the far side of the property just after midnight. Hopefully, as it was a week night and raining lightly, no one would be around and he could enter the old fire track without being noticed. It was a twenty-minute crawl along the fire track in the wet when he arrived at the spot he was after.

He turned the Land Rover around to face out the way he had come in and grabbed his moleskin coat to keep the rain off. He tied Kelly with a chain to the seat base as he could not afford for her to run off or start exploring in the dark. He walked up to the spot where he had buried the suitcase wrapped in heavy canvas. When he was satisfied that this was the spot he went back to his truck and retrieved the post-hole shovel and a rake. He walked carefully back to the spot and began to remove the top layer of grass and to set it aside to replace it. Once he had done this, he dug forcefully into the damp soil and piled it up on the side. After a few minutes he felt the resistance on the shovel of the desired package. Another ten minutes and it was successfully retrieved. He felt pretty happy.

John half dragged, half carried the awkward bundle to the back of the truck and placed it in the prepared space covered with a small tarpaulin to protect it from the wet and mud. He then grabbed the four hessian bags of soil he had brought with him and dropped them one at a time into the hole to replace the bulk of the parcel he had removed. He quickly filled in the rest of the dirt, placed the grass back and gave it a quick rake to try to minimise the appearance of any disturbance. It was raining, which would cover any tracks.

He gathered up his tools and had one quick look around to make sure he had left nothing and went back to the Land Rover. He removed his soaking coat and hat and climbed back in and started it up. In twenty minutes he was back at the gate to the fire track. The time was just after 2 am and it was still lightly raining. John drove for about two hours and decided he would pull over onto a large road-side clearing and get some sleep as he was now getting tired.

The morning dawned cold, bleak, and still misting with light rain. The familiar call of magpies and the activities of the smaller birds twittering about his Rover had awoken him early. Kelly was also restless and keen to explore all the new disturbances. Although he was still quite tired, John felt very happy indeed. It would be at least another six or seven hours before he would reach the property near Cooma. He stopped once for some breakfast in Yass and a couple of times for petrol, but otherwise made good time. In Cooma, he bought some supplies before heading out of town.

It was just before midday, in cloudy damp weather, that the Land Rover pulled into the gate at the property. He drove slowly up to his camp site and got out of the car. He had a good stretch and a short walk about. He would probably have to eat what he had cold as he thought there would not be much chance of finding any dry wood.

He had decided to rebury the suitcase, but before he did, he retrieved a bundle of notes from it to pay for the balance of the property and buy equipment that he would now need. He made sure no one was visible, then unwrapped the parcel. He was very pleased to cast his eye over the booty and ensure it was still there. This was the first time he had actually seen the money in daylight. He was a little horrified to pick up a neat bundle of ten pound notes. He wondered if anybody had ever seen so many ten pound notes. Then there were also some twenty pound notes and a few rare fifties. Luckily most seemed to be tens. He grabbed a big bundle of tens. Vera was a tidy, methodical person, and each bundle was neatly tied with a rubber band in bundles of two thousand pounds. He thought five bundles would do for the moment.

John never used the word 'steal' as he considered it partially his money anyway. He then dug a hole by the tree line and buried the case wrapped back up in the tarp. He placed a large boulder over it to help mark the spot. John spent the rest of the day trying to find some dry kindling and wood in the branches of the trees and storing it under a tarp.

The next day was a Thursday. After shaving and cleaning himself up, John drove into Cooma to see the estate agent and, hopefully the solicitor. As it was about forty minutes to Cooma from the property, John left at 8.15 am to arrive at the agent's about 9 am.

Tom arrived at the office at 9.05 am to find John waiting for him. Tom arranged to meet the solicitor after John had seen Mr Petty at the bank. When the bank opened at 10 am, John walked in and asked the teller if the manager were available.

Mr Petty agreed with the deal and organised John's fifteen-hundred-pound loan. John went back to the agent and together they saw the solicitor and the final exchanges were successfully carried out.

CHAPTER 3

Now that the property was finally his, John could think seriously about moving onto it and about all the items he would need. He thought the first thing to do was to go around to the dealer off the main street and buy a strong tandem trailer to cart the things he would be buying out to the farm. He could also now finally go to the engineering yard and order that shed he had been so keen on. After buying the trailer, he bought some more supplies and headed back 'home'.

This time, turning into the obscured, overgrown gate entrance, John felt a deep sense of inner comfort. For the first time in his short life he felt in complete control and in charge of all events. He had an air of self-esteem that was a new experience for him. He tried to remain calm and not get too excited. Dragging the trailer behind the Rover, his first purchase as a landholder, he drove into the open country at the edge of the timber and pulled up. He glanced around in the direction of the buried money to assure himself that it was still there. Kelly got a thorough pat and a rub on the head and he enquired of her if she liked her new home. He unhitched his new trailer and made himself a fire so he could have a cup of tea and think about things.

In the hope of not jinxing this enterprise, he had not prepared too much in the way of a list of things he would need. He had spent time contemplating his requirements, but now he could seriously think about accumulating the items he would need to rebuild this farm. The next necessity would be a good tractor with a three-point-linkage blade, a carry-all, and maybe a post-hole digger. Then there were all the tools he would need. The list was endless. Firstly, however, was the requirement of shelter. It was only mid-autumn but already the air had a decided nip in it, especially in the mornings. He was used to the cold of winters in the central west but this was going to be a different story here on the Monaro. The Southern Tablelands were notorious for long, frosty winters, even with occasional snow. He planned to go back to the shed people and arrange for the big shed he had already picked out. He had allowed himself the luxury of determining the best location of any possible buildings during the time he was deciding on this place. He carefully noted the sunrise and, with a compass, had also determined the summer and winter risings as well. The positioning of the shed would be very important, especially during the bitter winter months when every bit of morning sun would be valuable.

Frank, the erstwhile owner and next-door neighbour, still had a lot of his cattle on the eastern side of John's new property as it was not fenced there. The nearest fence was located several hundred yards inside the actual boundary. John was keen to erect a new boundary fence in order to begin the task of regenerating the grasses that Frank had overgrazed during the last few years, and also to prevent any of his stock from wandering onto John's place.

John was amazed that a farmer could enter a long winter with no groundcover in the form of grazing, as it would likely mean he would be beginning the notoriously hot and dry summer with limited grass available for stock, not to mention the possibility of erosion.

John spent the next couple of days confirming in his mind the internal layout of a shed and its location. He then went back into Cooma to the engineering firm to try to get a shed delivered and erected. He sought out the owner – a cheerful sort of bloke whom John thought had a touch of European blood but was very amiable and helpful. His name was Elliott and his small company seemed very busy. John approached him when he saw him in the yard.

'G'day Mr Elliott. Do you remember me from a few weeks ago? I came and enquired about a shed.'

'Yeah, I remember. You ready to order?'

'Yes, if that's at all possible.'

'We're pretty busy right now. How soon do you want it?'

John feared he may have to wait awhile. 'As soon as you can do it.'

'Show me your specs again and I'll see how we go.'

John explained that he wanted a very large shed and said he would pay in cash. When Mr Elliott discovered that John actually wanted to live in one end of it and had nothing at the moment in which to shelter, he said, 'If you give me a twenty per cent deposit, I'll start fabricating it immediately.'

John was delighted. He explained that he would be happy just to have the sides and a roof up this late in the season. It was all arranged. John paid the deposit and gave Elliott the rough plans he had drawn up and his address. Elliott was also able to pass on the name of a reliable backhoe operator who lived out John's way to prepare the footings and install a concrete septic.

After loading up his trailer with fencing wire and droppers, John headed back out to his property. He called into the address that Elliott had given him of the backhoe operator, who was at home doing maintenance on his machine. During the conversation, John hinted that as well as a septic he may be interested in a cellar being constructed at the same time.

'Would that be possible, Vince?'

Vince was a swarthy ex-digger with massive tanned arms and wearing stained overalls. He explained that he had constructed several cellars in the district and would construct one for John.

John was pleased. 'Would you stretch to a walk-in trench inside the shed to allow access to service vehicles – a sort of service pit?'

'Yes, that may also be possible if the soil is suitable.'

John explained that the shed was being delivered and erected within a fortnight, and asked Vince to commence as soon as he was able. As it turned out, that could be in three days, after he finished the current job, as the next one he had lined up was right over the other side of Cooma, a good day's travel time for Vince. 'That one can wait, especially as you're paying cash!'

Things were looking up. The shed was on order; the footings and concrete works were almost under way, now all he had to do was to arrange the concreting of the floor. Mr Elliott said he would tie that in with the shed if John wished, but demand was furious for concreting supplies with all the construction work in Cooma and the Snowy Mountain Scheme.

On the appointed morning, Vince arrived as scheduled and they surveyed the shed layout. After agreeing on the requirements, Vince commenced preparing all the work for the septic, the cellar and the vehicle service pit. The digging was quite easy as the soil depth was deep, confirming in John's mind that this was indeed fine country with good soil.

Each night, Vince would leave his backhoe at John's and drive the truck back to his place. On the third day, a small convoy of heavily laden trucks wound its way through the timber and into the open paddock to commence work on the actual shed. It took most of that day to unload the iron and sheeting, and for the engineer to lay out the shed dimensions on the ground, with John's critical oversighting of every mark.

Next morning, with the cellar finished and concealed from

view, Vince commenced work on the footings. The septic could wait. The cellar turned out to be a master stroke, according to Vince. It was fairly small, only about ten feet square, but cunningly concealed from view under the living quarters of the new shed. Access was to be from a concealed door constructed off the yet-to-be-made vehicle inspection pit – *very clever*, thought Vince. This afforded security in the event of bushfires as well as a secret place to store valuables – 'Such as wine!' suggested Vince excitedly.

John agreed, but he had much more important things to store in there – *such as money!* John did not drink alcohol and, unusually, he did not smoke either as he found cigarette smoke most irritating. He was prepared to wear the title of wowser in defence of his morals and his pocket.

John was especially pleased with the cellar as it was large enough to accommodate some small pieces of furniture that he was hastily able to acquire and place in there before the room was fully enclosed at the top. Vince was most obliging in its construction, even assisting in designing the access doorway cut from the yet-to-be-constructed vehicle inspection pit.

This was a busy period for John. The shed was taking up a lot of his time in ensuring it was sited correctly and that the important concreting work was done properly. As well as this, there were all the items he needed to buy for the property. Then there were the internal living requirements for the shed; such as a slow combustion stove to keep him warm and heat his water, and all the internal lining material for the shed. He also was keen to commence on the non-existent western boundary fence between his place and the remainder of Frank's property in order to remove Frank's wandering stock.

When he could spare any time, John commenced work on the fence. This involved locating suitable timber from the rear of the block and dropping it. He then had to cut it into six feet six inch billets and split it with wedges and drag it to a central area, then transport it to the site where it was to be erected. He was able to choose the largest trees to be cut into billets and then those of a suitable size to be used as strainers and stays. He had managed to blade the corner clear of weeds and debris, and installed the important corner assembly by the fourth week of moving onto the property.

Frank Dougherty, from whom John had purchased the property, owned the adjoining land, which totalled over eight thousand acres. It followed the road past John's place for about another four or five miles before the road disappeared off over the mountains and eventually petering out to become a fire trail in the distant bush. Frank also owned the fifteen hundred acres opposite and this was where his house was located. The house was about half a mile off the road, lower down in the valley that contained rich alluvial soils and another small creek. There was a thin, leaning power pole not far from Frank's entrance gate that carried the two dangling wires of power from the substation all the way out past this point to the end of the road. John was at least grateful that the poles were on the other side of the road, as that gave him more freedom to blade the fence lines.

On the third morning of preparing the area to work on the strainer assembly and straining up the existing wires, John heard the sound of a motor coming from the paddock where Frank lived. John grew nervous at the prospect of meeting Frank. He knew from Tom that Frank was a strange bloke who lived a solitary hard life and that he had a few money worries. John was also not sure how Frank would respond to him after he had driven such a hard bargain to buy the place.

John was finally able to see the vehicle that was slowly grinding up out of the gentle valley. It was an early model, short-wheel-base Land Rover utility, still in the original green but with no tonneau cover on the back. There were two tan-coloured dogs jumping about in the confined rear. It still had the old metal frames for the long-missing canvas cover and a few boxes and drums tied down in the back. The vehicle slowly manoeuvred over the rough gravel road and thumped noisily across the dilapidated iron grid at his entrance.

John stood up from tying wires as the Rover approached and tentatively sauntered over to the edge of the road where his tractor was, hoping to be able to stop Frank and introduce himself. As the utility approached, John walked over to the driver's side and said, 'Morning. Are you Frank?'

'Yeah,' said Frank.

'I'm John Summers, Frank. Pleased to meet you,' said John, shoving out his right arm to shake. Frank responded in kind. From what he could see of Frank in the car, he appeared to be a small, thin man with strong tanned arms and rough bush hands. He had the remains of a roll-your-own hanging on his bottom lip that jiggled about when he spoke. He was grossly unshaven and was wearing old clothes that needed a wash. John judged him to be in his mid-sixties, but could not really tell whether Frank's appearance reflected his age or his hard outdoor work or whether it was the result of neglect; or maybe all three. The old Land Rover had seen better days too. One light was damaged and there were large chips out of the mud guards where they had met with paddock hazards.

John said, 'I'm just putting up our boundary fence along here, hope you don't mind?'

'No,' replied Frank guardedly, a coolness John did not miss. 'I'll give you a hand if you like.'

'No. Thanks all the same. It's my present to you. I want to install this fence. I knew when I bought it there was no fence here so I've factored that in.'

At that, Frank uncranked the objecting door handle and opened a creaking door to step out. He was quite a wiry man, and short, but he looked very strong. Frank walked over to inspect the work so far.

'You sure you don't want a hand?' he asked with more energy while sauntering over to inspect the new fence post leaning in its hole.

'No, I'm sure. I will eventually replace some of this front fence of yours that I have cut into. One thing I would like to ask you, Frank. Would you mind if I put in a gate here at the boundary? Just in case.'

'No, fine,' replied Frank. 'You do what you like.'

'I might put one in the middle somewhere too, just in case.'

The two men stood there for about ten minutes chatting about nothing in particular. John felt a twinge of compassion for Frank and empathy for his plight. *In a few short years this could be me – living alone way out in the bush with no one to worry about me.*

Finally, Frank continued on to town to buy supplies. John thought he smelt alcohol on his breath, but was not sure, what with all the other odours old men seem to acquire when they live alone.

John pondered the vagaries of life and how old Frank was probably the last of a family that once so eagerly settled and established a home way out here in the bush. He wondered what those early folk would think of his coming in and taking bits from their place. He went contentedly back to his task of straining the wires to his new corner assembly.

John arranged for the installation of rainwater tanks in order to have water at the shed. He organised for the delivery of a couple of truckloads of Besser blocks to place around the massive slow combustion stove as insulation and to protect the metal of the shed. He also decided that when he had more time, he would Besser block the outside of the habitable part of the shed to insulate it from the cold of winter, the heat of summer, and to keep in the heat of his fire.

His next priority after the shed was to erect the common non-existent western boundary fence to begin the process of rehabilitating the degraded land by excluding the roaming cattle. This would take time as it was a long boundary of over three miles and had to be built from scratch. In his wanderings over the property, John had noticed the abundance of rabbit warrens. He also purchased a deep ripper so he could begin to attack the rabbit problem by destroying their warrens as he found them along the fence line.

John gained enormous pleasure from being able to wander over the property and explore the different parts of it. He worked long hours but did not regard it as a grind as he thoroughly enjoyed his life. He would hear the different sounds occurring on his place and carefully listen to the sources. The sound of the young galahs and gang-gangs feeding high up in the gums reminded him of the balmy summer days ahead.

All too quickly, Christmas rolled around. John's first Christmas alone came to him with mixed feelings. Christmas to his nan had always been a sacred time when one took stock of the past year and planned for the year ahead on a personal level – a time of reflection and assessment. He had strong memories of the huge Merritt family gatherings that were all part of their normal Christmas. It was the one time of the year he felt that he was totally included in their affairs. He missed the interactions with all the strangers that ended up at the Merritt's for Christmas and the seemingly endless supply of food and drinks.

On the other hand, his first Christmas all alone in his own house and on his own property gave him an exhilarating and deeply empowering sense of personal success and wellbeing that he never thought he would ever experience. On balance, he definitely preferred this latter feeling at Christmas and hoped that there would be even better ones and many more. As a vestige of the memory of Vera and in respect for her, he allocated time to contemplate the year just passing and map out his hopes for the next. Over the coming years he hoped to turn his property into a working farm and then as a place of recluse and readiness. As a place of defence or observation, he thought he would never move beyond his station; at least he hoped that was the future.

One of John's routines was to continually check the boundary fencing about once a week, but at least monthly. This usually entailed either walking or riding around the entire length on one of the two horses he acquired from the sales, especially the newly constructed fences that he had erected. This way he could clear storm and wind damage from the fence wires and secure any damaged posts.

It was now five months since he had first met Frank. John could just make out the fading name of 'Templemore' on the gate and wondered about its origins. He noticed that Frank's letterbox had mail sticking out of it, which he thought was there the other day. This was unusual, as Frank checked that several times a week. Also, it was unusual for the postman to keep putting mail into an obviously unemptied box. He continued walking along the fence and made a note to check it in the morning on his way into Cooma.

Next morning, as John exited his property onto the road, he shut the gate and turned the Rover towards Frank's place; only about two miles up the road. He stopped at the box and retrieved all the mail, which, by his reckoning must be about two weeks' worth. He suddenly thought that something might not be right with Frank. He followed the track down the gentle slope and followed the curve that took the car down to the heavily timbered confines of Frank's house. John had not been in there before, so was not too sure what to expect. He was mildly surprised at the state of the compound that comprised Frank's house, which was just a shack surrounded by dilapidated sheds and neglected trees and shrubs.

The two tan dogs barked a noisy welcome and greeted him lavishly; they obviously did not see many visitors. John headed for what he supposed was the door and called out if anyone was there. Frank answered from inside and requested he come in. *So far so good – at least he was still alive.* The shack was dingy and dark and had a neglected smell about it. There was the familiar country aroma of decades of combustion stove usage, which could not completely disguise the smell of bachelor squalor.

'You okay Frank? It's John from opposite here.'

'Yeah, I'm okay. Come on in. I'm in here.' John manoeuvred through the small entrance room into a plain heavily bricked old kitchen strewn with cooking implements and a profusion of mess; mostly tins, bottles, newspapers and, John noticed, more than a few hard liquor bottles, probably whiskey. *'Just like a Pakapoo ticket' as Nan would say.*

Frank was sitting at the painted wooden table with the remains of a tinned meal he had finished surrounded by cutlery and papers.

'You all right?' John asked again.

'Sort of,' answered Frank. 'I've cut me foot an' can't drive at present but I'm gettin' better.'

'I brought in all your mail. I saw the box was getting a bit full.'

'Yeah, thanks John. That's very kind of you. Would you like a cuppa?'

John asked Frank to show him his sore foot. He had cut it with a mattock chipping bushes around one of the sheds. It was pretty bad but at least it was now mending and, provided he could keep off it a while longer would probably mend pretty well. John asked him if he could do anything for him but he seemed to require little that John could provide. John boiled the electric jug and made them both a cup of tea. At least that way John could sterilise the cup for himself. He sat down at the table and cleared a small space for himself, spreading the mail about him. He noticed that there were a couple of bills that were final notices. John presumptuously opened a couple of the bills and told Frank that he would take them with him into town and pay them for him, as he was unable to do that himself.

Frank reluctantly agreed, 'Given the current circumstances, you understand.' John was pleased to be of use to his neighbour, thinking back to their initial meeting when the pangs of sympathy were first aroused in John for Frank's perceived plight. He spent about an hour talking to Frank before deciding he needed to leave. He got a small list of stores Frank said he would like from town and went back out to the Land Rover.

On the way into town, John contemplated the last hour or so. He had discovered quite a bit about Frank's background during this conversation. Firstly, his family had originally owned a fair slab of this valley, right up to the end of the cleared part before the Great War. Successive droughts and family break-ups had reduced his holdings to their present smaller size and the way Frank was going, would further reduce it. Secondly, and sadly, Frank had no close family, only some cousins living somewhere up north of Newcastle. He rarely ever heard from them and he did not particularly like them anyway. He had been the only son and after his parents both died he had remained there as the last of his line.

Frank had served in the army in the Second World War in New Guinea and spoke fondly about the blokes he had served with. Frank's family had originally come out from Ireland, his grandmother originating from near a small town called Templemore. That solved that riddle.

Frank's story made John feel melancholic and temporarily thoughtful about his own future. He made his way into town and paid the outstanding bills that Frank had neglected. He discovered that some of these bills were up to eight months overdue. It was no hardship for John to pay these small amounts for his neighbour, maybe even his friend, as he had barely dented the wad of cash that he had access to – let alone the stuffed suitcase hidden in his new cellar. John completed his own purchases and visited the saleyards before heading back out to Frank's.

The rear of John's property was heavily timbered with a

mixture of hardwood eucalyptus trees such as iron bark as well as the softer scribbly and snow gums. All the old trees carried the blackened evidence of previous battles with fierce summer bushfires that seem to rage through the countryside and timbered areas every now and then, usually fanned by the searing westerly winds straight out of the desert. Running a fence through this type of country was both a challenge and a risk as tree-fall and wind as well as fire could damage a fence anytime. John wanted his place to be securely enclosed to keep out strays and to keep his future stock in. He would clear a thin line of trees away from the actual fence and blade a small track along it to assist with inspections, which would need to be regularly performed to maintain the fence.

John did not know the neighbour who owned the property that adjoined his back boundary, but he knew a little about him from Tom. David Quiggin had a bit of a reputation for being 'up himself' as John would put it. He was about thirty-five or so and had been to a private school and was always trying to big-note himself. He owned a vast amount of good country once out of the timber into the cleared paddocks. Tom thought Quiggin was a bit of a snob and only mixed with the better types, not the hoi-polloi. His homestead, though not very old, was supposedly quite grand, and his wife was a very attractive social-climber from the North Shore of Sydney. To John, he sounded just like the types he had detested so much from his former days with the Merritt children and their pampered cohorts who incessantly turned up at their property.

John had erected about a third of the back fence and put in most of the posts along the boundary when another significant event occurred. There was a fire track running right through his place up in the timber that eventually joined up with the Cooma Road some miles further down the valley. John used this fire track to gain quick access to his fence line and drag posts and material conveniently close to the fence. In places the fence was several hundred yards over the crest from the track. It was normally quiet and peaceful working way up in the timber a couple of miles from any roads or homesteads, and sound travelled a long way in the still bush air.

He was pacing out distances between posts and digging post holes late one morning when he heard the distinct sound of a couple of approaching horses bashing and stumbling through the rough undergrowth and fallen timber. It was close by and coming from the direction of the neighbouring property. He hoped they would go away as he was not in the mood to spoil a peaceful day by having to meet the neighbour from the back. The neighbour was probably alerted by the sound of John's chainsaw, so he had half expected someone to eventually investigate – after all he certainly would.

Eventually, with a little annoyance, he leaned on a half-tamped post and awaited the arrival of whoever was approaching. Finally, he could make out the awkward figures of two men in rough farm gear carefully picking their way through the branches and heading for him. They approached without a word, though John had previously heard them occasionally conversing with each other over their horses snorting and the cracking of branches and twigs. They pulled up close by him and one of them dismounted, both of them lighting up a smoke as the one came closer. Both were short and wiry, about five-foot-five with heavy riding boots, grubby moleskins and dark-coloured flannelette shirts. They looked rough with wide hats and a day or so's growth on their chins.

As he got to John he said gruffly, 'What yer doing mate?' He spoke in a rough drawl that echoed hard drinking and many cigarettes. He stood on the down-slope side of John, a position that only emphasised the difference in their statue and build.

'I'm putting up this fence,' replied John in a rather terse manner, staring down at him from under his low-set hat. The first bloke then said as he surveyed John's handywork so far by looking slowly along the fence line, 'Well the boss ain't planned no fencin' along 'ere and ain't interested in puttin' one up.' His cigarette changed nervously from side to side in his mouth. He again turned away to survey the fence work so far.

After a long pause, John answered slowly, 'That's fine. I want a fence along here and I'm putting one in.' The words had a commanding tone about them, unsettling the other man.

'The boss won't be payin' nothin',' he said, trying to appear more menacing by peering from beneath his brim.

'What's your name, mate?' John was looking him straight in the eyes, while at the same time spearing the heavy crowbar deeply into the shaly soil with one mighty plunge from his powerful right arm. This sudden movement made both the horses lift their heads and turn in his direction, causing the other man to gather their reins slightly. John's left hand remained unmoved, covering the top of the half-tamped post. He hoped this manoeuvre sent the appropriate signal to both of them.

'Ray,' he replied.

John detected a slight change in demeanour; *he did not seem quite so cocky now.*

'Well, Ray,' said John slowly and deliberately, lowering his voice to an even more authoritative pitch, 'you tell your boss that if I wanted him to pay his share, he'd get a demand from me accompanied by a solicitor's note.'

Ray decided that this bloke was not to be stirred up and might be a bit too much for him to handle at this point so he turned to go, muttering under his breath and shaking his head. As he got to his horse John said, 'And you tell your *boss* that he knows where I live and not to send his boys to deal with me again.' He paused, and then imperiously continued, 'Is that clear?'

Ray just nodded and reined his horse with a jerk to head in the direction from where they had come. John could hear them chatting as they receded into the distance.

John was annoyed that he had to deal with such obviously unimportant farm hands and that Mr Up-himself would refuse to contribute to their common boundary. He was almost embarrassed that he could feel superior to someone. He was surprised at how rude and brusque he was to fellow workers and how he had tried to intimidate them. He spent quite a while going over the event and wondering if he could have handled it better. The trouble was that he was predisposed to be confrontational and belligerent because of his pre-existing dislike for individuals of the ilk of Dave Quiggin. Nevertheless, he was annoyed with himself that he had reacted so disdainfully to poor Ray. After all, it was not he that was at fault. He slowly calmed down inside and, on reflection, he put it down to his idyll being interrupted and that someone, anyone, would dare to direct him as to his actions.

He hoped it was not going to become a manifestation of his new station in life. He would have to watch this in future.

This incident had two sequels. A few weeks later, while John was walking up the back of his property near the tree line he had seen a large dark car approach his shed and someone alight. This person was obviously looking for him but departed after about five minutes when it was clear that no one was at home. John did not think too much about it again as he figured that if it was important he would return.

Again, a few weeks after the incident, on a warm still day while John was working on repairing damage to a three-point-linkage pin, a large dark American car drove up his gravel road and approached the shed. He assumed this was the same car he had seen from the back of his place a few weeks earlier.

As it approached he could see that there were two people in the front seat, a man and a woman. John let the car pull up outside the open shed door and the man alight before attempting to go out to see them. He appraised the man as he made his way to the shed door. He was about medium height but well-built. As he got to the door, the stranger called, 'Is anybody there? Hello!'

John emerged from beside the tractor and walked over to the man.

'Yes. What can I do for you?'

'My name's Mr Quiggin.' John looked him up and down. He had a feeling that he was not going to like this bloke but thought he should be civil, at least in the beginning.

'G'day Dave,' said John coldly, deliberately deleting the courtesy appellation of Mister as he stretched out his slightly greasy hand. He grasped Quiggin's equally powerful hand with an extra strong grip as if to reinforce that this was his territory.

John deliberately remained standing on the concrete floor while Quiggin stood on the ground outside the shed, emphasising the difference in the height. John was impressed with Quiggin's physique and surmised he possibly played Rugby for his old school and maintained a high level of fitness. His face and demeanour gave the impression of a man who was in charge and used to getting his own way without questions.

'My boys said you put up a pretty good fence.'

'Thanks,' said John.

'You might have asked me first,' said Quiggin, staring directly into John's eyes.

'I'm not asking you to pay,' said John roughly.

'Good. 'Cause I don't do business that way.'

John pursed his lips and looked at Dave in an 'I couldn't care less' attitude. Quiggin changed the subject and began to ask John what he was doing and what his plans were for this place. John suspected that some of his neighbours were a little annoyed with him as they would know what he would have paid for the property as opposed to its real value. The rumour from Tom was that Quiggin had his eye on the place if the price came down low enough and he could snap it up for a steal. John was polite but tried to keep his private business to himself. He was prepared to discuss developmental matters and some of his hopes for the place into the future, but that was all. He also was keen to know what Quiggin was planning at the back.

After about fifteen minutes, Quiggin said that he must be going. John accompanied him to the car, not only out of politeness, but to get a look at his wife, who had remained in the car. She was supposedly an attractive woman with an air of class and John did not see many of those out here in the sticks. He was not disappointed. She was indeed an attractive lady and greeted him pleasantly enough when he said hello. As Quiggin was about to put his hand on the door handle, he turned to John and said, 'Nice to meet you John. Let me know how much the fence costs.' John was taken aback by this. He remained silent for a few seconds and then replied, 'The fence line is just over two miles long. You know the cost of wire and droppers. I've provided all the timber and the labour. If you want to contribute, you know the amount.'

Quiggin smiled wryly and gave a slight chuckle; he glanced at his wife in the front seat, opened the door and got in. He started the car, looked at John with a wave and drove off.

John thought no more about it except to revise his opinion

slightly of Dave Quiggin. A few weeks later, however, John was coming out of the stock agent in Cooma with an armful of gear when Dave Quiggin was entering with one of the men that had first come up to him on horseback, the one who had remained on the horse. John politely nodded good morning and Quiggin stopped to say hello. They chatted briefly and then Quiggin said, 'Where's your truck?'

'There,' John said, nodding his head in the direction of the Land Rover outside the building.

'I'll come with you,' he said. John walked over to the Rover and carefully placed the items into the rear compartment.

'Will fifty quid cover it?'

'What?' asked John.

'The fence. Will fifty pounds cover my share?'

John was astounded. 'Yeah, sure,' he blurted out. Quiggin produced a cheque book from his back pocket and wrote out a cheque.

'Cash or to you?'

'Whatever. To me will do,' stuttered John.

He finished writing out the cheque, signed it with an exaggerated flourish and handed it over to John.

'Thank you very much, Dave. You know I did not ask you to pay?'

'Sure. No worries. See you later then.'

This was a strange turn of events and John had no idea why or how this had happened. It confirmed that he was not a very good judge of people. He tended to categorise people on meeting them, or worse, even before so, and often proved later to be wrong. This was probably the result of a lonely upbringing and that he was happier away from people. That was why he loved his life as it was. He went straight to the bank and deposited the cheque into his account.

The second result of that horseback encounter happened a few weeks later. John was at the saleyards when he identified Ray. As Ray approached, John greeted him with a firm nod and a smiling 'good morning'. Ray stopped and returned the greeting and even allowed a reticent grin. He looked admiringly at John, which pleased him.

By early spring John decided to allow himself two indulgences. One was the purchase of a dozen one-day-old unsexed chickens. To house them he had to quickly build a small shed and erect a very secure wire run to keep them in and to keep out the foxes and eagles. To warm them during the colder nights he brought them into the shed near the fire in a box.

The other indulgence was to buy himself a good stock horse. He was a competent rider and enjoyed being able to ride around the property surveying all its assets and exploring every aspect of the terrain. He already had two nags but now that he was more established, a really good horse would be better.

Then all too quickly yet another Christmas was approaching – this was John's second away from the Merritts. This year he was considering trying to at least see Frank or possibly spend a little of the day with him, as Frank was alone and lonely, and had been for many years – to the point that Christmas to him was just another day alone.

CHAPTER 4

ohn was paying the farm off by depositing between one hundred and one hundred and twenty pounds each month into the loan account. He could afford much more but did not want to arouse any suspicion. He wanted the locals to think he was struggling just as everyone else was. However, Mr Petty retired about nine months after John had bought the property and he felt able to pay it off much quicker. So twelve months after the purchase he was able to pay the final amount and retrieve the deeds, securing them in his cellar safe.

He did not think much more about property in general until about a year or so later when one day he was talking to Tom Grady outside his office. John made a habit of talking to Tom whenever he came into town if Tom was available for a chat. Tom was a good source of information and very knowledgeable about local happenings. On this day, they were talking generally when John, who was casually gazing in the shopfront window, noticed an advertisement. He said rather suddenly, 'What is this here?' pointing at the glass.

Tom replied that it was a flat in a small building around the corner.

'But it's only two thousand pounds. Is that the full price?' John was thinking that he practically carried that amount around with him in his pocket. He asked Tom if he could see it. Tom went in and retrieved the key and they walked around to the parallel street and up to a block that consisted of six flats. The flat for sale was on the top floor up a flight of stairs. John was staggered that this lovely two-bedroom flat was, to him, quite cheap.

After a thorough inspection, they walked back to the office. John asked why the flat was on the market and was told that it belonged to a man working for the Snowy Scheme who had moved to Sydney. John told Tom that if he could arrange all the necessary paperwork, he would buy it using the same solicitor he had used for the farm. John opened his wallet and gave Tom one hundred pounds on the spot for a deposit. He would go to the bank and withdraw the rest of the deposit now, if Tom was agreeable. Tom was bemused by all this but said that he would arrange it all immediately.

'Why would you want to buy this?' Tom asked.

'It will give me a base in town and the price seems very low.'

'Okay,' he said. 'I'll fix it all up for you now.'

John was very pleased with this small purchase. And since Mr Petty had retired, he felt more able to deposit and withdraw large amounts of money into the bank without raising too much suspicion. He could pay for this and hold the deeds himself out at 'Bridgehead'.

John began to realise that he was not making any dent at all into the suitcase full of money. He attended all the clearing sales within about two or three hour's drive and purchased great quantities of valuable items. However, all the antiques and equipment he bought was not going to reduce the stash of money quickly enough. His mind began to think of ways to reduce it and yet not cause suspicion among the locals. Then the thought occurred to him to buy something further afield.

He decided not to buy another farming property as he could not handle any further workload. He thought of buying something on the coast further north, or even down on the South Coast. Then it hit him. *Yes, I'll buy something back in Harbord.* No one knew him there and he could pay cash for a house in an area that was out of the way and not too popular with anyone. It was a long drive to Manly but that would also give him a short holiday as well.

He made plans to go to Manly for about a week and then prepared the vehicle. Harbord was a quiet, secluded working-class area where there was still a lot of vacant land and plenty of building activity to accommodate the housing shortage that remained after the war. The small shopping village of Harbord, or Freshwater as many of the locals called it, contained a few shops, a bank, a post office, a fire station and a real estate office. The office was run by a woman, which

John thought was unusual, but she was very helpful. Her name was Mrs Roberts.

Mrs Roberts arranged to show John a couple of double-brick houses and also knew the history of the suburb. After seeing a few places, he decided to buy one in Wyndora Street. She recommended a local solicitor and John was able to organise the details so he could return in about four weeks to finalise the sale and pay over the full amount in cash.

Before returning to the flat he was renting in Manly, he opened an account in the local branch of the Bank of New South Wales in Harbord and deposited some cash. He then decided to also open an account in Manly. It had occurred to him that this would be another way of reducing the horde of cash and getting it into circulation again. He could deposit money each time he came up.

John returned to Manly in four weeks. Mrs Roberts had all the paperwork arranged and the solicitor was waiting for him. He then left the property in her hands to arrange for it to be rented out. There was a shortage of places in the whole of Sydney to both buy and rent as the population was growing quickly. She assured him he would have no trouble renting it out.

On his return to his property outside Cooma, John began to realise that his financial affairs were becoming complicated and his tax was now a worry. He approached a local accountant and arranged for his affairs to be handled by him in the future. He was able to glean from this accountant that he would be better off forming a company if his affairs became too complex. This way he could separate his private property from any others that he could now afford to lose if something went wrong. This gave him considerable food for thought.

He began to formulate a plan whereby he could form a company in Harbord and buy another house. He could also form one in Cooma to account for anything he bought there. This had all arisen when Tom Grady mentioned, half in jest, that there was a small industrial estate being built on Polo Flat and it would be a good investment for someone who had a bit of spare cash. So, John created a company in Cooma called Polo Investments and acquired the industrial estate, which was now also returning him income.

The purchase of the house in Harbord had proceeded very smoothly considering the long distance involved. He was so pleased with the transaction that six months later he decided to put his plan into action by repeating the process. He ventured back to Manly and visited Mrs Roberts again, this time to buy another house but in a company name. He created a new company for his Harbord purchases and located the office in the Cooma flat. He kept the first house in his own name and used the local solicitor and accountant to keep his businesses separate.

Shortly after this transaction in Harbord, on one of his visits into town, Tom mentioned that three of the flats in the block where his first flat was located were for sale. They were owned by a company involved with the Snowy Scheme and they no longer needed them. John arranged for an inspection with Tom and decided to buy them immediately. He could place them in the company he had formed for investments in Cooma.

John now owned four of the six flats in the block. The top left one was in his own name and he always stopped by every time he came into town and could even stay overnight if he wished. The other three were rented out through his company, Polo Investments.

The other top floor flat, opposite his, was owned and occupied by a feisty retired nursing matron from the Cooma hospital. Her name was Mary Crowther. She had never married and had been matron of Goulburn, Yass, and latterly, Cooma hospitals. She was a plump old woman who smoked heavily and probably drank a bit too much. Her false teeth rattled and clacked in her mouth as she clenched her teeth regularly and spoke in a brusque, bossy manner. She possessed an irritating emphysemic laugh, no doubt caused by a lifetime of constant smoking. Mary was not averse to complaining to Tom's agency whenever she was displeased about anything pertaining to the running and maintenance of the block of flats or of those that were rented out.

John requested that his new acquisition be confidential as he did not want anyone knowing what he was doing. He did, however find Miss Crowther's busy-bodying rather useful as any comments she made were passed on to him by Tom as the managing agent. He did not see much of Mary Crowther, but cultivated her acquaintance for the benefits it bestowed on the monitoring of his assets. John had covetous eyes on her flat as, if he could obtain it, he could close off the two top floor flats and make quite reasonable private and secure quarters. If the other bottom one ever became available, he would snap that up too.

Late in the morning on one of his weekly visits into town, John received some startling news. He was talking to Tom outside the agency shop when Tom said to him, 'Did you hear the news from Canberra that the government now wants to go decimal?'

'What do you mean?' asked John.

'Well,' replied Tom, 'they now want to do away with sterling and replace it with decimal currency.'

'What the hell does that mean? Won't we be able to use our old money anymore? And when does this happen?' he asked, half panicky. He was thinking of that suitcase still nearly full of old notes that suddenly he could see becoming useless.

'Well it's only talk, and early days yet. I think they are talking years ahead in the future.'

'How many years?'

'I think at least five or six, some time in about 1966.'

John was dumbfounded. He excused himself from Tom with a request to keep him informed if he heard more. Suddenly the thought of all that unspent money lying under his floor now becoming useless was enough to give him quite a turn. He sat on one of the street benches and thought about it carefully for some time. He thought his best plan would be to try and spend as much if not all of it as soon as he could: *but how to do it without raising eyebrows?* He considered his best plan would be to unload it into property in Sydney: *that would be best.* He devised a scheme whereby he could get rid of it all over the next few years. The first thing to do would be to determine exactly how much there was.

He went straight home with his mind racing and a sinking feeling in his stomach. He would have to calm down. After all, it had cost him nothing; if he lost it all he would be no worse off. He ventured down into the maintenance pit and opened the disguised door that led into his cellar. There he removed the suitcase from the shelf and placed it on the table. He opened the case and tipped all the contents onto the table. He sorted out the remaining bundles into denominations and began to count the money in each bundle. As he counted each heap he wrote down the amount and then replaced it neatly back into the suitcase. After several hours he had finished and was astonished to reveal the final amount, which was over two hundred thousand pounds. He concluded that he would have to spend up big to unload this sum.

During the course of counting, he came across a neatly written note stuck in the middle of one of the bundles. It was slightly faded and difficult to read so he put it aside to examine later. John sat in the dull light of the naked electric globe in the dank, grave-like silence of the concrete cellar. He was deep in thought about how to convert this large cache before it became useless. It was quite a worry to him. He picked up the note but found it too difficult to read in the poor light so he put it in his pocket and walked outside.

John removed the stiff piece of paper from his shirt pocket and began to read. The faded pencil writing was small and neat, and the piece of paper was an aged dull-yellow colour. He determined that it must have been there for years. It began, 'To-day discovered H secret. Money belongs John. There is C £120 grand in folding 4 AJC Already spent lot put this away for J. WTS died no will car to pars H nicked dosh.' It went on in similar code most of which meant nothing to John. He was, however, struck by the notation referring to 'John' and 'J'. He thought it may have been Vera's writing but it was so old he could not be sure.

This again roused memories of the sly asides he encountered from Henry and Vera, and from June occasionally, in the dim past when he was a child that seemed to involve him. *Was there some foul deed perpetrated by them at the death of my parents? Anyway, that is now all in the past. At hand were much more important needs.*

He took the note into his study and placed it in the top drawer along with his valued old travel notes he had written while travelling around looking for a place to buy.

After much thought, he resolved to attempt to spend the money as fast as he could on properties in Sydney. He would start almost immediately by going up there in a couple of days. He would drive the old Rover up to Manly on a Sunday so he could have the full week of business hours to begin his activities. His first stop on the Monday morning would be to see Mrs Roberts in Harbord. He would buy another house or two in Harbord. This would be a slow way of unloading so much money and what he really needed was a decent outlay to soak up large amounts. He approached one of the better agencies in Manly and enquired whether it was possible to buy a block of flats. He posed as a rich grazier from the Central West with a tax problem.

It so happened that there were several blocks of flats for sale in the immediate vicinity close to the beach and ferry. In a narrow street close to the beach full of Victorian and Federation buildings was a slender block of six flats with a narrow lane down one side leading to a small rear yard suitable for parking. The price was fifteen thousand pounds. *That was more like it. That would make a real hole in the stash.*

John loved the old block of flats. He could already see himself maintaining the top one for himself and keeping the others tenanted. It also had the rare attraction of an off-street park for his vehicle so he could unload it in peace. He arranged to see a solicitor and a local accountant and created another company, which he called Wyndora Incorporated Limited after his first purchase in Harbord. The settlement was in a couple of months so this gave him time to transport the cash up to Manly in several trips and deposit it in three different bank accounts that he had opened.

This system was working well for him, and he settled into a steady routine of driving up to Manly every six months or so and purchasing a quality double-brick house. They had to be freehold and have at least three bedrooms. Harbord in the early sixties was a quiet backwater of a suburb that still had vestiges of its rural past, such as old dairies and market garden plots. These were slowly disappearing due to development and more people moving into the area as Sydney grew during the boom years after the war. John bought another three houses over the next two years, all in the company name of Wyndora Incorporated. That made four in the company title and one in his own name. He paid as much as he could up front then paid them off almost immediately once he was free of the office people.

Living life in the style of the early settlers with wood stoves and no telephone was beginning to lose its attraction for John, especially when returning to the farm in mid-winter. He decided to connect the power to the property, at least in order to have an electric hot water system. This way he could boil the jug instantly without waiting for the stove to heat up. He also finally arranged for the telephone to be connected as his growing business interests required that he be contactable more readily.

The management of the properties was held in two systems. The houses were managed by the Harbord agency from whom he had purchased them and this was run by Mrs Roberts. The Manly building was managed by an agency located on the Corso. Neither knew of the other's existence, as not only were the management rights separated, but the accounting and solicitors as well. There were the usual property problems such as tenant damage and non-letting periods, but as he did not really need the income, it was not a major annoyance to him. There was, however, one major disturbance at the Manly flats that did affect him.

John had insisted on the insertion of three clauses in the leasing contracts for the flats in the Manly building. One stipulated no pets; another was the 'noisy party' clause; and the third was one of his own design. It stipulated that the rear parking space of the building adjacent to the north wall was reserved for him, and he had a sign erected saying 'Do not park here'. The reason for this was, whenever he drove to Manly, he usually arrived late at night after a long trip up from Cooma, and without notice. He also often towed a trailer heavily laden with items for the flat, including antique furniture.

On one occasion, John arrived in the early hours of the morning and found all three of these clauses in breach. He allowed full vent of his anger. What followed involved physically removing tenants and their belongings, and confronting the managing agency next morning. John was, in retrospect, disturbed by his overt reaction. This was a side of his character he was unaware existed until provoked by such an event. He again reminded himself that he must be mindful of this flaw in his character.

Unfortunately for John, his buying spree was still not reducing his stash of sterling currency quickly enough. He decided to buy a building in Sydney. On his many trips to the city, he enjoyed the ferry rides across the harbour and the excitement of the Quay area and the central city area. He had noticed that there were a lot of quaint old buildings all over the older parts of the city centre, and occasionally he had noticed one or two on the market but had thought them out of his league. That was now changing.

The houses in Harbord were only costing around eight thousand pounds, not enough to reduce his cache quickly enough. A city building would set him back around twenty-five thousand pounds. A couple of those would just about eliminate his money by the end of 1965. He travelled up to Manly in the Rover on the old road from Cooma to Sydney that wound all the way through Camden via Razorback Mountain. This time, purchasing a city building was a little more complicated, so John employed the services of a reputable city real estate agent and a local solicitor. He also visited a top accounting firm in the city. They set up a new city company called Bridge Loftus Investments and advised John to also set up a holding company and make the other three companies subsidiaries. The holding company was registered to the small vacant office presently unoccupied in the newly purchased seven-storey city office block just up from the Quay about two blocks from the wharf. It was close to Macquarie Street and could be reached from out of town by arriving at Central Station, then catching a tram down. It was also convenient to the major retailing and commercial area of the city. The compact building contained professional offices on the upper floors and street access through a decorative, wooden double door. It was mostly constructed of sandstone and brick. On the top floor was an unoccupied office with a small entrance foyer and one larger room for the office. Here, John was able to set up his head office and organise a name plate and letterbox as required by company law. He called the holding company JW Summers and Company.

John now had a major tax problem and his accountants were advising him to incur some debt to offset it. He was also now officially listed as a company director, but regarded himself as a small-time grazier, a battling cocky, and was rather melancholy when he thought about this turn of events. His business interests had moved him way beyond his old sheep station, which was now only a depot for his manifold and diverse sources of income.

After the dust settled on the city building, John was contemplating buying another to finally unload the last of his pounds. He really enjoyed the visits to the city and spending time in his office in the building. He furnished it out nicely with some antique office furniture and made it very presentable.

In late 1964 John made one more sortie into the commercial city heart and repeated the process by buying another similar building. This one was nine storeys, again sandstone and brick, but this time it was fully tenanted and a little further into the city. The building cost him twenty-seven thousand pounds.

John's business affairs were taking up most of his time, especially with the travel involved. But finally, the suitcase that was once bulging with cash was almost empty. The income from the bank accounts alone was now substantial, let alone the revenue from all the properties his company owned. John, on advice from the chartered accountant in the city, arranged for the Cooma and Harbord accountants to only prepare, but not submit, his tax returns, and forward them to him. He then submitted them all together to the chartered accountant in the city, who prepared the full accounts for his tax returns.

On a cold June day, John drove the cattle truck into Frank's place to pick him up for the run into town. Frank was a while coming out to the truck and John noticed he was hobbling worse than usual.

Along the way, John said, 'You okay? You seem pretty crook today.'

'I'm surviving,' replied Frank.

One thing about old Frank, he was not a whinger.

'Listen Frank, I'm thinking of going to Sydney again. I've got some money I need to invest,' John said to him, half-joking.

Frank shot back, 'Gees cobber, you must be in the note.'

'Not really Frank. I just put a bit aside for old age. You know.' This was John's way of explaining all his trips to Sydney.

Frank thought for a minute then said, 'I've been wonderin' if you'd be interested in buyin' my place.'

'Hell Frank!' he blurted out. 'You sure you know what you're saying?'

'Well,' said Frank, 'you can see I'm not copin' as well as I use ter.'

That's a bit of an understatement, John thought. *Frank's place has gone to the dogs lately, especially as his health's deteriorated.*

'Frank,' said John, 'if it's a matter of getting some assistance in mustering, you know I'll help you.'

'Sure,' said Frank. 'But it's time I thought of unloadin' the place. I don't have any relatives I want to have it. Them as I do have, never visit. And if you bought it, it would stop that Quiggin feller from gettin' at it again.'

'What do you mean?' asked John.

'Well, old Quiggin badly wanted this place and wasn't half mad when you bought it from under his nose,' Frank said.

'But I thought it was on the market for years when I came along.'

'It was,' said Frank, 'but I held out. He thought he'd get it for a song.'

'I got it pretty cheap, Frank.'

'Yeah, but I'd rather have you here than them. Besides he'd kill for this place. He wants this one even more than your place.'

'Bloody hell Frank, you trying to turn me into a fair dinkum farmer now?'

'What do yer mean?' asked Frank. 'I thought you were fair dinkum now.'

'Frank, I'm just playing at farming on this block. It's almost a hobby. Anyway, what do you want for it?' asked John.

'Thirty-five thousand quid,' said Frank matter-of-factly.

'Crickey! You giving it away? It's worth more than that Frank.'

'Maybe. But you've been very good to me and I'd like you to have first crack. I'm not gettin' any younger, you know. That includes all the stock too, you know.'

'Aw Frank, that's a terrible good offer,' stammered John.

'You interested?' demanded Frank.

'Yeah, sure. As long as you're sure about this. Could I ride around the place a bit and check it out. I might also arrange for a survey if you don't mind. Could I let you know in a day or so, Frank?'

'Sure,' said Frank. 'You don't think you'll ever get married?'

'Doubt it, Frank. Not going to meet any nice girls out here. Besides, I'm not much of a catch,' replied John.

'What about Quiggin's girls?' Frank asked, sniggering.

'Not my type Frank. A bit—' John couldn't finish the sentence. Frank understood.

'Frank,' said John tentatively, 'that reminds me for some reason. Have you ever heard of an Albert who lives around here?'

'Can't say as I 'ave,' replied Frank. 'Why do you ask?'

'Well, a few years ago now I was down by the creek when a bloke appeared with a lad by his side. He said his name was Albert.'

Frank thought a while then said, 'Were this down by the far fence in a small clearing?'

'Yes.'

'That's funny. Many years ago there was an old timber-getter killed there by a fallin' branch. He were buried there and fer a long time his grave were marked be one o' them wooden crosses. It were lost in the last big fires, years ago.'

'Did you know him, Frank?'

'Hell no! It were before my time. But Dad knew him quite well apparently. He was a nice bloke Dad always said.' Frank paused then asked, 'You mean to say you saw a dead man talkin' to you?'

John grinned and let the subject drop. He had other things on his mind. *Wasn't it ironic?* he thought. *I spent seven years desperately trying to unload a pile of money on things I don't*

*really need and just when it's all gone, I get a chance to buy
something I really would like to buy: the next door farm. Still, the
accountant was always at me to incur some debt to offset my tax,
maybe this is a way to do it. Frank's place sure is in need of a lot
of work though. It would keep me very busy and no more tripping
up to Manly for little holidays when I felt like it.*

The more he thought about it, the more he wanted to buy
it; *that would really make me a farmer again.* When John was
in town next, he approached Tom Grady and explained the
situation. The agent told John, with a hint of pretence in his
voice, that now he could really expand beyond his station. By
purchasing this run John could seriously move into sheep.

CHAPTER 5

t was just after eleven o'clock on the Saturday morning of the Cooma show. John was idly sitting on a street benchseat reading the paper and contemplating the mysteries of life. He had left Kelly as usual, sitting under the Land Rover back at the flat where he had just come from. He had bumped into Mary Crowther again. The sign on her door, 'Miss Crowther', always gave him a poignant feeling as he thought of what sadness or lost opportunities had led to her being so alone. He would then often think of poor Frank wasting away all alone out in the bush – *a similar type of story no doubt.* These two more than any others always made him feel he would be the same one day – all alone and no one to care. *Still, that was my choice and, hopefully well off into the future.*

It was already quite hot, but at least there was no wind.

He was half turning the pages while he glanced up and down the street spying on the folks that walked by, eyeing some of the ladies. There were plenty of unpolished country girls in town but he preferred the classier types that rarely were seen in Cooma – much like the types that used to visit the Merritts from the private schools and look down their noses at him as a boy.

As he glanced up the street, he noticed a young woman aimlessly browsing in the windows, her two hands clasped together behind her back. John was a keen observer of the ladies and this one was slightly different and almost out of place.

What a nice sheila, he thought to himself.

She was wearing a pale-coloured skirt and lightweight shoes. As she came closer, he thought he recognised her from somewhere, as she had an understated elegance about her that he vaguely remembered encountering elsewhere. Suddenly, he realised that this was the girl from the real estate office in Harbord that dealt with his properties there. He thought quickly, trying to remember her name, *it was something like Linda or Lucinda.* He had noticed her in the office but did not think a lot about her as she was just another nice city girl, and there were plenty of those about in the city. Then he thought he remembered, *it could be that her name is Livinia ... yes, that's it.* It was a slightly unusual name, that is why he recalled it. She ambled up towards his seat and when she was adjacent, he stood up from the bench and as their eyes met, he said to her, 'Hello. Livinia isn't it? From Harbord?'

She had to raise her eyes to see his face as he was much

taller. She looked slightly startled, then there was the hint of a smile.

'Yes … and yes.'

'What are you doing so far from home?'

'I've had car trouble,' she replied, looking at him quizzically.

'It's John Summers, Livinia,' said John. 'I bought a place in Harbord a few years ago and you manage it for me.'

'Ah, yes,' she said. 'Now I remember. Fancy running into you here.'

'What's wrong with your car?'

'I'm not sure, I'm sorry. Don't know much about cars. It just stopped down the road yesterday. I got it towed in this morning. It's at the garage just down there,' she said, pointing behind her towards the petrol station at the far end of the street. They spoke for a short time then John asked if they could both go back to the garage and he would try to find out what was wrong and see if anything could be done.

At the garage, Livinia pointed to a cream-coloured Morris Minor sitting along the fence with the hood up. John knew the mechanics and asked the young apprentice, Terry, if the boss, Wayne, was around. Terry pointed into the workshop. John entered the workshop and saw Wayne working on an old Holden utility. After a few minutes, John and Wayne walked over to Livinia's car to inspect it again. She joined them as they discussed her car.

'That's the problem piece,' said Wayne. 'The trouble is, we can't get one locally. Jeannette is ringing around but no luck

91

yet. We can get one from Larke Hoskins in Canberra, but it won't be here till Monday.'

Livinia was in a slight daze, worried about getting back to Sydney for work on Monday; worried about the car; worried about the expense, and worried about where she could stay in a strange country town miles from anywhere. She was only half listening now as the technical terms were being bandied about and negotiations continued without her input. After a few more minutes it seemed that something had been agreed to. The men called Terry over and more negotiations occurred. John turned to Livinia and reported that it had all been arranged. Terry would be going to Bombala shortly to deliver a truck part and could pick up the required parts there for the Morris. He was also prepared to work the next day, Sunday, to repair the Morris if John would pay the overtime.

'The car should be ready by Monday morning,' said John.

'Really? Would that all be all right?' she muttered meekly. 'Yes.'

'Good,' said John. 'Would you like to come up to my place around the corner and clean up a bit? We can have a cuppa while we decide what to do next.'

She nodded. John grabbed her suitcase from the back seat and asked her to follow him. On the way back to the flat, John pointed out that the Cooma Show was on and asked Livinia if she would like to go for the afternoon as he never missed a show.

Livinia smiled and nodded again as she followed John into

the front entrance of the block of flats where it was noticeably cooler. They walked up a flight of concrete stairs to the third level. At the top, he turned to the left door that was set back a few feet from the stairwell and put down the case. He retrieved a small set of keys from his left front pocket and inserted one into the lock.

The room was clean and reasonably bright considering the small amount of light the diminutive window allowed in. There were lace curtains across the window and on either side an elegantly tasselled, voluminous, deep-green curtain, evocative of the Victorian age. The carpet was cream-coloured and luxurious. The walls were painted a lighter colour than the carpet. There was an antique roll-top desk with papers neatly arranged in little heaps. On top were a couple of large and ornate bronze statues.

Shelves of a large, ornate antique bookcase were filled with folders and small boxes neatly labelled. An antique office chair matched two leather lounge chairs strategically placed within the room. Along the short wall that half hid the kitchen was a beautiful chaiselounge. Next to it was a long-case clock with a glass-fronted door revealing the slowly swinging pendulum and the massive silver-coloured weights. Its slow tick could be heard clearly once the door was closed. The whole atmosphere was one of undisturbed serenity rather than one of being lived in. There were no knick-knacks or vases of flowers.

John beckoned Livinia to follow him up the hall. As they went, he pointed out the toilet and bathroom. There were two bedrooms at the end. John led her into the second one and placed the case carefully on a small antique low table. Livinia was struck at the elegance and plushness of the room with its tasteful bedroom suite.

'Please make yourself at home,' said John. 'I'll make you a cuppa if you like. Please have a shower if you want to.'

Half an hour later, Livinia was sitting at the dining table eating sandwiches and drinking tea served in fine china. It was now early afternoon and getting noticeably warm outside. John suggested that they spend the rest of the day at the show if she would like to go.

'Why are you travelling through Cooma?' John asked.

'I was visiting an old friend of my mother's in Merimbula,' she replied. 'My mother died a few months ago and she was very friendly with Molly, and when she invited me down I decided to go. It's been a bit lonely and traumatic for me, these last few weeks.'

'I am sorry to hear that, Livinia. It is hard when your parents pass on.'

She detected a slight note of sadness in his comments that seemed to be genuinely felt.

'Are you sure you want to go to the show?' he asked again.

'I love country shows,' she said. 'My mother and I always used to go to the Easter Show, every year.'

'Well, this is no Easter Show, but it's great fun and goes into the evening.'

About three o'clock, after John had cleaned up the lunch things, they departed the flat. Miss Crowther's heavy wooden door creaked open slightly and she peered at them disapprovingly.

'Is everything all right?' she asked.

'Yes thank you, Miss Crowther,' John replied.

Miss Crowther eyed Livinia up and down with her characteristic scowl.

'Sorry about that, Livinia,' he said as they descended the stairs and emerged out into the bright sunlight.

Kelly was still asleep in the shade of the Land Rover, but she woke at the sound of his approaching voice. Livinia was amused when she read the hand-written notice nailed to the fence. He saw her amusement and said wryly, 'It keeps the riff raff out of my parking spot.'

The rest of the day was spent in a pleasant drift of sheep, cattle and horses, sideshows and amusements that all too quickly passed. John bought them ice-cream, chips and hamburgers, and they spent a happy time together. She noticed that John knew a lot of people, chatting to some about farming, the weather, prices and stock.

After the evening entertainment, they drove the short distance back to his flat.

'Would you like to go for a short drive tomorrow once we get the repairs under way?'

'If that's convenient. I don't want to impose on you any more than I already have,' she replied. 'Besides, don't you have to work tomorrow?'

'My job is pretty flexible at the moment. As long as I'm back in a day or so it'll be all right.'

'Where do you work?' she asked tentatively, hoping that was not a rude question.

'I work for a pastoral company an hour or so out of town,' he replied. This was not a complete lie as he did technically work for the company. He just neglected to tell her that he actually also owned the company.

'If you're sure, that would be nice. My mother and I used to travel a lot about the countryside as we both liked it. And as I have never been here before it would be lovely.'

'I might take you out Numeralla way. It's beautiful out there and not very far, though the road's a bit rough.'

Livinia spent sleepless hours contemplating this unusual arrangement. She thought about this man she barely knew. He was a huge man obviously used to constant heavy work, yet he spoke beautifully in a deep but soft, cultured voice. She thought about his chiselled features and piercing strong eyes that could deliver a withering stare if provoked. He was slow to anger but was resolute if so aroused, even mildly as she had already witnessed several times at the garage and the show. He had a shock of thick, brown, unkempt hair that she surmised with some reserve that he possibly cut himself, but not often. He was clean-shaven. To her, he seemed less concerned about his appearance than how he interacted with others.

The next morning, John was up early as usual but did not disturb Livinia. When she arose, he had some breakfast prepared for her. He told her that as soon as she was ready, they could walk up to the garage and see what was happening.

They walked through fairly empty streets, being a Sunday. Terry was already there and working on the Morris. He said he would be about another two hours or so if they wanted to do something. They walked back to the flat. John prepared a flask and some other items and together they drove out to Numeralla. It was a fine hot day and all the windows on the Land Rover were left open. It was a pleasant few hours in idyllic country conditions of quiet and peace.

John pulled the Land Rover into the garage just after three in the afternoon. Terry was in the workshop fiddling with an old Vauxhall. He reported that the Morris was now mobile and should get her back to Sydney. Livinia expressed her gratitude for everyone's kindness.

Before she drove out, John requested that the Morris be filled at the bowser for the trip to Sydney and added the cost to the bill that he insisted on paying Wayne the next day.

John suggested she stay another night and leave early in the morning. She agreed, and that evening, John prepared another dinner and set up the table formally. Livinia was pensive. *How strange*, she thought, *that we should meet this way so soon after Mother's death. The inside of this flat was so incongruous to its surroundings and John seems to be such a gentleman considering the rough country types that were typical of the rest of the locals.* She liked him a lot. She hoped he liked her a bit.

Livinia was an independent woman and she insisted on paying for the repairs. John could see that she was serious and nominated a paltry amount that barely covered the cost of some of the parts, let alone the labour. He hoped she would have no idea of the real costs and let him pay the rest.

Next morning, John prepared some items for Livinia to take with her. Before getting into her car, she pecked him on the cheek and grabbed his arm above the elbow.

'Thank you so much for everything.'

'Can I ring you tonight to see that you get home okay?'

'Yes. I'll write my number down for you on some paper. Thank you, John.'

He watched as she drove up the street and turned to head towards the highway. He felt sad as she disappeared around the corner. At least he knew where she could be found next time he was in Sydney.

February was the planned date of the introduction of decimal currency. John had completely unloaded all the sterling notes before Christmas. This he had managed to do by buying up the two Sydney city commercial properties and banking most of the remaining notes in Sydney. When Frank offered him his adjoining eight thousand acres, he had almost no money left, and ironically had to borrow most of it from the bank. Frank's asking price included all the stock, which he had calculated at about nine hundred head of cattle. John's plan was to truck stock to every sale and market until he had reduced the numbers down to about one hundred. It had taken many months to achieve this, but only then could he tackle the dilapidated fencing and rehabilitation of the pastures.

Frank could not even guess the number of cattle he had on the property. It transpired that there were over eleven hundred.

It was no surprise that the pasture was being ruined. John felt a surge of excitement at the prospect of being a real farmer again. It was strange that this opportunity arose at the time that he was psychologically ready to expand his working horizon.

His time was now fully occupied in attending to the grazing property and managing his small portfolio of commercial investments. He was so busy that he barely had time to spare. He bought an old Holden utility to make the trips into town a bit quicker and the trips to Sydney much more comfortable than in the old Land Rover.

His trips to Sydney were ostensibly to inspect his properties, but increasingly it was also to try and see Livinia. John found himself thinking of her often, but he felt that the price he must pay for stealing the money was not to include anyone else in his life – especially someone so innocent and honest.

Despite these reservations, John decided to risk trying to see Livinia on his next visit to Manly. He really knew very little about her. *She did not mention if she had a boyfriend but that did not mean she did not have one. After all,* John thought, *she was a particularly attractive and classy young woman and surely would have many suitors.*

John made sure all was well around the farms and that he could be away for up to a week, then packed a few items into the Holden and he and Kelly set off on the long trip to his flat in Manly. He chose the long weekend in June in the hope she might be free for a full day if he managed to arrange a meeting. He arrived late in the evening after the usual tiring journey.

About 9.30 am John wandered up the incline that led to

the real estate office where Livinia worked. He confidently strode into the office and up to the front counter to speak to the receptionist while all the time looking anxiously into the depths of the room to see if Livinia were present.

He spied Livinia typing at a rear desk. She looked up at the sound of his voice and, on recognising him, rose from her chair and approached the front counter. She beamed a most welcoming and pleasant smile at him and asked after his health.

John knew the office was a busy one so, after cursorily checking on a couple of items regarding his properties, he asked Livinia if she would be able to see him in her lunch hour. This she willingly agreed to do. John was hopeful that they might at least have a pleasant time together for a day or so.

On one of these lunch-hour ambles, John and Livinia were returning to her office when a well-dressed young man with a briefcase approached them from the other direction. He effusively greeted Livinia and commenced to chat to her. She halted his chatter to introduce him to John. John could see that this young man was keen on Livinia and was sizing him up. He could also see that he would be a good suitor for Livinia, probably heading for considerable success in his chosen field and also possibly a much more suitable match for her than a rough-living farm boy from the back-blocks. When he departed, they continued their walk back up the slope to her office. John was uncharacteristically quiet.

'You must know a lot of boys from around here?'

'Yes,' she replied with a tone of indifference.

'You don't have a boyfriend then?'

'No, not really.'

'But a lady-like girl like you must be busy keeping the boys at bay,' he stated with as much jocularity as he could muster.

They were approaching the door to her office. She could sense that John was fishing for more than just small talk. She stopped in the street and looked seriously at him, trying to think how best to say what was on her mind.

'The young men I meet in my work are planning their futures with success on their minds. Poor girls with no background or position behind them are all right for a bit of fun but don't figure in their future plans.'

John said nothing for a minute or two, then thought that he would risk an invitation for her to spend the Monday Queen's Birthday holiday with him exploring the Northern Beaches.

'Would you be interested in spending tomorrow with me going up to Palm Beach?' he finally asked, a little tentatively.

'I'd love to John,' she said firmly and without hesitation. He was a little relieved and also a little apprehensive. After all, he had never actually asked a lady out before. The Cooma Show did not count, as that was pre-arranged by fate, but this was all his own effort.

'Where shall I pick you up?'

She gave him her address and agreed to meet about eight o'clock in the morning. Then she turned and headed to the office and bade him good afternoon. He thanked her for her time and wandered off down the gentle slope towards the car, eagerly awaiting Monday.

They spent a pleasant day together. She was amazed at how much he seemed to know about the Northern Beaches. They visited many attractive sites scattered around the peninsula and enjoyed their time at Palm Beach, even though it was quite cold. In the evening, she invited him for dinner in her warm house until about ten o'clock. He went back to his flat in Manly with a feeling of serenity after so much time in her company. Before leaving, he tentatively arranged to repeat the process on the long weekend in October.

It was late in the afternoon on the last day of John's short visit. They were strolling along the path that led to Shelly Beach from the Manly beachfront.

'Livinia,' John finally said. 'I was wondering if I might ask you if you'd like to spend Christmas with me.' She was about to reply when he put up his hand and continued, 'Before you answer, I need to tell you a bit more about where I live. I have not told you the full story.'

She felt a slight shudder. He was staring at the footpath in front of them.

Do I want to know this, she thought. *This has been a lovely time for me, surely it's not to be spoiled by something nasty.*

'I don't live in Cooma in the flat. I actually live on a property out of town. In a shed.'

She sighed a silent sigh of relief.

I can cope with that, she thought. *I feared something much worse. So he lives in a shed. On a property. How bad can that be?*

'I'm sorry that I didn't mention it earlier, but I thought it just might never need to arise. But I like you a lot, Livinia.'

He had turned to look at her face and peered into her pale-brown eyes. 'I wasn't sure how far we might go together. I'd love you to come and spend Christmas with me and see where I live and work.'

At last some hint at what he does. I'm dying of curiosity about his life and haven't been game to ask him.

'Tell me more,' she said.

'I live on a small place about an hour out of Cooma. It's not very big and there is a lot of bush. But I work for a company that owns a big place next door. It also owns the flat here in Manly. That's how I can manage to come up here so much.'

'I'd love to come,' she replied. 'But it may depend on whether I can get time off work over that period.'

'Well, if you can make it, I'd like to come and pick you up and take you back down in my car. It's a long drive for you on your own and the train is rather awkward from here.'

'That'd be lovely, John. I will really look forward to it. I hope I can get some time off.'

He reminded her that she would be staying in a shed. He also reminded her that it would be very hot at that time of year down there, even in the mountains. He also pointed out that it was rather isolated – no corner shops nearby. She nodded. She also realised that they were appraising each other as friends – *indeed, maybe more than friends.*

John was totally confused and apprehensive about this development. On the one hand, he was racked with a latent, ever-present guilt about the intrinsically evil deed he had performed that allowed him to be in this position of

103

independence and, on the other hand, the desire to be with Livinia – the sort of woman he thought he could once only have admired from a distance.

On the journey home, John had plenty of time to think about his life and the things that were happening in it right now. He sat at the farm gate examining the scene. He gazed at the neat but ordinary construction that acted as his mailbox. It was quite unimposing, the only embellishment a roughly painted sign that read "Bridgehead" – a name he had decided on after acquiring his first properties away from the farm. Underneath were the obligatory letters RMB and the number 139. John purposefully reused the old, dilapidated gate that was originally there in order to create an air of benign abandonment or desertion so passers-by would overlook the entrance or regard it as uninviting. He wistfully opened the car door and strode over to open the free-swinging gate and enter his property.

John ran a critical eye over the bucolic vista that he called home as he slowly drove along the bumpy, rough gravel meandering through the paddocks and up to the shed. It suddenly took on a different perspective now that he had actually invited someone here. *How would she react to all this?*

He paused just as he emerged from the trees and into the open paddocks. He gazed critically at the panorama laid out before him. In the near distance stood his most valued possession: his home, comprised principally of the massive iron shed. The left quarter was bricked in with grey Besser blocks.

There was no garden at all. This he had done for two

reasons: one to prevent, or at least reduce, the possibility of bushfire damage, and the other because he could not be bothered with the trouble. He had over many years slowly laid out a thin avenue of gums and wattles that followed the meandering track that was the road into the shed. These had grown significantly over time.

The compound surrounding the shed had been filled in over the years with additional buildings, stockyards and animal shelters; chickens, lambs, horses and bull yards. The country was browning off now as summer advanced, but that appealed to him. *Would it appeal to a city girl?*

Next to the Land Rover was an old but immaculate ex-army 6x6 Studebaker still in its original army colour, now faded, but quite serviceable. He had acquired this from a clearing sale over near Tumut about six years ago and used it constantly to cart logs down from the hills when building yards. There was a small fire truck that he kept at the ready at all times, a couple of tractors, an antique car or two, trailers, and the two stock trucks he used constantly to transport his sheep and cattle to and from markets. These were the vehicles he had been using to transport Frank's excess cattle to the saleyards, mostly in Cooma. As he surveyed the scene he cherished so much, he suddenly wondered if his life's little collection of treasures would hold the same appeal to a stranger.

Livinia's boss, Mrs Roberts, was sympathetic to her position, seeing that her mother had so recently died. When she asked for the days between Christmas and New Year to travel south, Mrs Roberts agreed to accommodate her. Livinia was a private and discreet person. She gave no details to either her boss or her colleagues.

She wrote John a letter telling him the news. He responded, telling her that he would come up a day or so before and see her then.

They left Livinia's at about six o'clock Christmas Eve morning. It was a long trip, through the Razorback, down the Hume past Lake George, Canberra and into Cooma. John pulled into the parking spot at the flats and said he would check the mail and collect a few things from the flat.

After leaving the flat they headed back in a north-westerly direction out of the flat treeless plains into the more scenic hill country. A short way out, John turned off the highway onto a dirt road that wound its way through brown, dry grazing country mixed with untouched Australian bush. There was a strong smell of eucalyptus in the air and cicadas were droning loudly in the still, hot late-afternoon sun. The road wound its way on for some time, John occasionally pointing out something of interest. Finally, John said, pointing at thick bush that ran for some way beside the road, 'That post is my boundary. My place starts there and continues along for about two miles.'

'Goodness,' she said, 'it's lovely bush, John.'

He agreed but pointed out that his stock could not find much to eat in there. A short distance further along, he slowed down and pulled into the old gate at the property entrance. She glanced around in the late-afternoon dappled light to identify landmarks and familiarise herself with her surroundings.

Once inside, John drove along the track through heavy timber and tall pale gums covered in hanging ribbons of dull bark until he came to a fork. As the track emerged from the timbered country and hit the sunlit grazing paddocks, he stopped the car and said, 'There, what do you think?'

She opened the car door and stood peering towards the sun which was just above the hilly horizon. Before them was the vista of extensive brown paddocks stretching away into the distant wooded hills. In the foreground was a patch of green surrounding the metal shed. A few animals were keeping out of the heat of the sun under the trees.

He pointed at the shed, telling her, 'That'll be home for the next week or so.'

'It's a huge shed, John. Do you really live in that? I had imagined a tiny little place leaning over in the wind the way you had described it. It's all so neat and tidy.'

'I hope you at least find it pleasant.'

'I think it's very beautiful.'

'Well this is real character country,' he mused.

'What do you mean by that?' she asked.

'It will sort out your disposition and temperament quick-smart and if you're not suited, it wins. You won't survive here without the right make-up.'

That was a strange thing to say, she thought. *But he's probably right.*

John unlocked the first roller door and ushered Livinia into the garage past the Land Rover up to the heavy door that led to the living quarters. There was dim light in the shed as all the other doors were still closed, so Livinia could not make out all the detail. She did notice that the shed was full of trucks, tractors, and assorted farming equipment.

He informed her that the heavy hardwood shutters were put on to protect the windows from debris and wind in the event of bushfires. He followed her in with her luggage. Livinia could detect the familiar aroma that resulted from years of using a wood-burning stove. John opened the nearest shutters over the sink in the kitchen section of the room and then proceeded to open the others.

As the darkness retreated from the advancing light, Livinia began to make out the configuration of the interior. The floor was covered in linoleum in the huge open kitchen and dining area. There was a huge, bricked-in, slow-combustion stove with pipes coming and going in both directions from its sides, and an all-pervasive aroma of the unmistakable country kitchen. But the most striking feature was the profusion of heavy ornate antique furniture.

John led Livinia towards the front of the building into a carpeted area where there were two or three rooms. She was led along a short hallway and shown into a neat, small bedroom with more heavy antique furniture and a well-made single bed. He dropped her luggage and told her he would show her around when she had settled in a bit.

They walked around the front of the quarters and down to the chook run and the small orchard area. John kept referring to 'the compound' which included all the living area, some yards, sheds and other items. This covered an area of about ten acres and was heavily fenced. She agreed to a walk across the paddock to the top of the small rise that separated the compound from the road and kept it from view. Up there he was able to point out the extent of the property that was visible. He could see all of his first purchase and some of the second.

They spent a pleasant, uneventful evening chatting about their likes and dislikes over a rather sumptuous dinner that John had obviously spent a lot of time preparing. Late in the evening, he bade her goodnight and asked her to be sure and tell him if she needed anything during the night.

Her mind was wandering over the other boys and men she had dated briefly over the last few years. The solicitors that admired her but really found her lack of substantial background inadequate for their prospective careers in the law. There were a couple of medical trainees but she was constrained by the responsibility of caring for her ailing mother. There were a few young men interested in her from around Harbord but she never really found them sufficiently attractive. *So why am I now here in this isolated bush setting with this strong personality that led so different a life from anything I knew?*

She slid off the bed and carefully retrieved a small package from her bag neatly wrapped in soft cloth. She carefully unwrapped it and gently fondled a small, folding, silver-covered picture frame that contained a small photograph of her late mother on one side and a cardboard picture of a religious figure with clasped hands looking pensively upwards on the other side. She looked at the pictures for many minutes and tears welled in her eyes as she contemplated her life. Eventually she placed the closed frame on the bedside drawers facing the bed and reached for the other item contained in the wrapping cloth. This was a small black leather Bible that she randomly opened, but tears prevented her from reading.

The curtains were open on the window. She got up to close them but realised that there was no one for miles to bother her. She closed them anyway. She returned to the bed and sat again. She could hear strange noises outside in the darkness. These turned out to be the cattle ruminating close to the shed; the sheep likewise, and the two horses she had earlier seen snorting as they noisily ripped the grass from the ground around the shed. She slept fitfully but sufficiently, and the bed was comfortable.

Next morning, Livinia was awakened by more unfamiliar noises and sounds coming from outside. The room was bright enough for her to see the contents. She peered at herself in the mirror and brushed her hair before getting dressed. It was Christmas Day and she remembered she had a small present for John. She placed it on the dresser and then ventured out into the open space that served as the eating and living area of the shed. John was sitting at the table waiting for her.

John had tried to plan the time to ensure that Livinia would find it interesting, but still do a bit of work while she was there. He still had years of work and repairs to perform on the property that he had purchased from Frank. He hoped Livinia would not mind, on Christmas Day spending the day slowly driving around the property and having a picnic somewhere in the bush, probably by the creek or at the timber yard site he used to mill the trees.

She would have to meet Frank on Christmas morning as the two men had always exchanged greetings and maybe a small gift for many years now. In fact, they had often shared Christmas dinner together at John's, as Frank would otherwise be alone. John had warned Frank that this year he hoped to spend the day with a friend from Sydney. John also hoped Livinia would find Frank's eccentricities acceptable and would not miss going to church. She had often spoken about church and her strong faith, which she and her mother shared. Boxing Day could be spent doing a bit more fencing and then a day or so on the new yards. There would be timber to drop and collect for the fence and the yards.

These activities would give her a fair idea of what he did. There would only be a couple of days to go to town as most shops would be open only two days of that week.

Livinia thought Frank was an eccentric, strange character. Frank lived in a run-down homestead that was well past its glory. The place was rather a tip and there was a mountain of hard-alcohol bottles piled up out one side. This did not bode well with Livinia. But she noticed that John treated him with great fondness and the two got on well. *Perhaps it is the shared isolation and proximity of living,* she surmised. She was relieved when alone again with John, heading up the road checking the boundary fence and being given a tour of the properties.

This would be the strangest Christmas I've ever spent. Alone in the bush with a man I barely know, but I like him a lot. John certainly knew how to prepare picnics. He had obviously had plenty of practice.

Livinia missed going to church on such an important day in the Christian calendar. John confessed to her that he had not entered a church since leaving home many years ago. They drove along the gravel road and he pointed out the yellow plastic signs hanging at regular intervals along the fence. These, he told her, warned that this fence was electrified and any touch would result in a nasty zap. At the large corner assembly, he stopped the Land Rover, opened a cocky-gate and drove the Rover through the fence and into the paddocks. There was a clearly defined track running the full length of the fence, which headed down the gentle slope to the tree-lined creek about a mile in and then back up the opposite slope into the distant tree line.

John drove slowly across the paddock, intently peering at the fence to check it for damage. They chattered all the while about nothing in particular. In time, they arrived at the creek where John got out of the car and walked across a timber bridge that spanned the creek at its narrowest part. He checked the bridge very carefully then drove across and parked in the dense shade provided by the creek's trees.

'Time for a cuppa,' he said. Livinia agreed.

They sat in the cool shade of the riparian splendour, a veritable oasis from the oppressive heat out in the open paddocks.

'Do you miss going to church?' he finally asked. John had been raised in a devout Christian family and church attendance had been obligatory. He understood the strong pull of such circumstances and the pain of non-attendance.

'I would like to go, but it's not always possible,' she said with resignation.

'I'm afraid I haven't been for years, not since I've lived here.'

'Do you have any faith, John?' she asked, knowing that was a loaded question.

'Well,' he offered, realising this could be a significant revelation, 'I don't know too much about it, to be frank. Besides, I'm such a sinner that God would not want to know me.'

'You are not,' she reassured him. 'Besides, that's not how it works.'

'I have wondered a lot about it though,' he continued, a little chirpier. 'You see those ants there?' He was pointing at a large nest of big black ants scurrying about randomly over the top of the cleared head of their underground nest. 'Well, you can follow their trail all the way from here down the bank and to the edge of the creek where they collect moisture.'

'Really?'

'Yes. They toil all day and into the night. This is their universe. They know nothing else. They have no concept of ownership or power. I own them. I can destroy them, move them or sell them to a new owner and they'll have no idea. They just keep on doing their thing oblivious to the world. Sometimes I think I am like that to God: incapable of comprehending and He apparently incapable of explanation. But the more I look around, the more it all seems to be ordered and created to work so well.'

'That's a marvellous analogy.'

John, a little pleased with himself at eliciting such a favourable response, ventured on.

'But I find the Bible incomprehensible and extremely difficult to understand.'

'It's quite systematic, you know … if you are guided by the Spirit. If you genuinely seek, God will reveal it to you.'

That sounded a bit deep to John.

'The Bible is only a history of God's chosen people and their interaction with their neighbours. It's not a history of the world,' stated Livinia.

'You mean the Jews?' asked John.

'No,' she said emphatically. 'It's a history of the Israelites, not the Jews. They are only one of the twelve tribes that make up the nation of Israel.'

'So, don't we rate in God's world then? We're not Jews or Israelites, so we don't rate.'

'That's not what I said. The nation of Israel was dispersed hundreds of years before Christ, followed by the nation of Judah a hundred years later. It's where those Israelites went that matters and the promises God made to them that affect us all today.'

'You're losing me a bit,' he said.

'I know it's complex. Shall we just enjoy the blessings of His creation and the miracle of our being here today?'

'Yes, but how come you know so much about it?'

'My friend is a serious student of the Bible and we have many deep discussions about it.'

John began to pack up the tea items, giving the ant nest a long hard stare, and amazed at how surprising life can be. Here was a quiet, working-class girl with an intellect and knowledge of things he knew little about. He could see they might have many lively discussions.

After this enlightening stop, they proceeded again up the rough track and on into the timber. It was a relief to leave behind the dry, brown and hot paddocks for the cooler shade of the tall timbers. The Rover ground its way up into the trees and finally came to a much broader and more substantial track that ran along the top of the ridge. John told her this was the main fire trail that went for miles in both directions. He crossed it and proceeded down the other side of the ridge until he came to the back boundary fence. Here he turned left and followed the fenceline, stopping occasionally to remove branches or untwist wires.

John headed up the slope back to the main fire trail and into a more cleared area where there had obviously been a lot of timber activity; heaps of sawdust and piles of off-cut branches and neat stacks of timber planking. He stopped and announced that he would be preparing lunch.

It took all day for John to complete the inspection of the entire boundary, stopping occasionally to do running repairs. They did not arrive back at the shed until almost dark.

Boxing Day dawned hot and cloudless with a light warm dry breeze from the northwest. By mid-morning, John loaded up the old Rover and announced that they would again head into the timber and prepare some posts and rails for the new yards he was repairing and building on Frank's old place, or the 'company block' as he called it. It was a rough and slow trip along the track that led down to the creek and then back up the slope to the timber yard area where he dressed the wood he had gathered.

The next day, they continued the work together. John observed that Livinia was a good worker, but she needed advising on how to do things correctly or easier rather than jumping straight in. She had brought with her some appropriate clothing, although it was not designed for long-term farm usage. John decided that maybe a day in town acquiring the correct gear would not be a waste of time.

Wednesday dawned, yet again hot, cloudless, and with a drying westerly breeze. Livinia had found the first three days doing all those different jobs on the property most enjoyable and interesting, although she was not sure whether it was the work, or the surroundings, or the company – or maybe all three. She was getting a little stiff from the manual labour, using muscles that she rarely used and welcomed the opportunity to rest by going into Cooma for a few items.

In town, John's first port-of-call was the haberdashery and clothing store. Here he arranged for Livinia to buy two new shirts, one pair of moleskins, socks and a fair-dinkum country hat that would keep the sun off. She protested strongly at the expense, but John insisted that working with him on the properties would require the right clothing and footwear. She could not better that argument and secretly loved all the gear that would make her at least look like a real farmer and country girl. The *pièce de résistance* was the pair of R. M. Williams he bought her to complete the outfit. She had never seen such wonderful footwear and told him that they were far too good to be worn in the scrub.

They spent a pleasant day in town, passing a little time at John's flat while he attended to what she thought was rather a lot of mail for a country farm hand, and window shopping in the main street. Before leaving, they went around to the stock and station agent and bought a few items for the farm, including several pairs of suitably appropriate working gloves for Livinia.

Thursday arrived much as the other days; hot, cloudless, and with the threat of more nor-westerly breezes wafting lazily over the distant ranges, bringing low humidity and making all the stock doleful, reserving all their activity for the cooler night time.

John announced at breakfast that, as she was now fully kitted out, they would attack the only job she had so far not attempted – fencing. So far, John had completed about half the fencing that ran along the length of the road frontage. Frank's former large block was wedge-shaped or triangular; the entire front running along the dirt road that led either back to Cooma or on up into the distant ranges. John had already completed the boundary that they originally shared. He still had to complete the front fence along the road and then the fence that ran along the back through the timbered country until it joined up with his fenceline in the corner. He had been slow in attending to the fencing on this block as his priority was to reduce the number of cattle on the place to relieve the stress on the grazing.

He loaded up the Rover with a heap of fencing gear and asked Livinia if she would like to drive the Rover to the site or the tractor. A look of apprehension came over her but John assured her that she could soon master the Rover. He showed her how to manoeuvre the gears, saying, 'The gears are the same as your Morris Minor as they're both Pommy cars and work the same.'

She did have more trouble reaching the floor in the Rover, but a few adjustments soon fixed that. Then he told her to follow him as he drove the tractor out across the paddocks towards the west.

'If you get into any trouble, put both feet out and stop!'

The next day or so passed in much the same way, with constant paddock driving and erecting endless fencing. On the Friday, John said to Livinia that he would like to visit Frank again as he usually dropped in on him once a week or so, and ran him into town occasionally.

'Will we be long?' she asked.

'No. Just a quick visit to check on him. You don't like him much, do you?'

'I'm sorry, John, he gives me the creeps.'

'We won't be long then.'

They got into the ute and John drove over to Frank's. By now they were enough of a team for John to let Livinia open the gate while he drove the car through. During the course of the conversation, while John was over at the sink, Frank let slip to her that his family once owned all the land that John had bought from him years ago.

That's strange, I thought that John worked for a company that owned all the property he worked on. Something's not quite adding up.

That evening, as they settled into their usual routine, the conversation drifted around to Livinia's mother.

'You are very fond of your mother.'

'Yes. She was all I had. She was quite ill in the end but I was able to care for her at home. That's why I left my job in the city and got a job close by so I could spend a lot more time with her.'

'You worked in the city?' he asked.

'Yes. I had to leave school at fifteen to support my mother and myself and had a good job in a legal office in the city. That's how I managed to get the job with Mrs Roberts, because of my experience working for lawyers. But all the travelling was very tiring and took up so much time.'

'May I ask what happened to your father?'

'He left us when I was five. I never saw him again,' she said tersely.

'I am sorry,' was all he could say.

A slightly unpleasant quietness descended on the room. In the mildly embarrassing stillness, the rhythmic ticking of the long-case clock loudly pervaded the atmosphere. In the deathly stillness of the dark night, the eerie call of a spur-winged plover was heard. John thought, *It probably had young* ones, *though it was late in the season for that, and was being disturbed by a fox or other animal.*

Livinia was staring at the table and fidgeting with a cup.

'What about you?' she finally shot at him still looking at the cup. Then, turning her face to his, she continued, 'Do you have any family?'

'My parents were killed when I was a few months old,' he said coolly. 'I never knew them. I was brought up by my uncle and auntie.'

'I'm sorry for you, John,' she said, her mood softening as she placed her right hand on his muscular left arm.

'Unfortunately, like you, I had to leave school young to work on the property.'

'How long have you lived here, John?' she asked tentatively.

'Since about 1958.'

She could sense she may be venturing into delicate waters so she wrinkled her face in acknowledgment and said no more.

'Would you like another cuppa?' he asked by way of abandoning that subject for both of them. It had been a moment of mild discomfort and sadness for both but at least it filled in a few blanks for them. She nodded her agreement and he shuffled over to the bench. The disturbance with the plovers subsided, but the ticking of the grandfather clock continued to pervade the room.

After retiring to her room, she sat again on the bed in contemplation, reviewing the events of the evening; the day and the week. She hoped she had not been too gruff on the subject of her father. She detested him immensely for what he had done to her and to her mother's dream life. Despite this, her mother had carried a flame for her long-gone husband all the rest of her days; something Livinia could not understand.

She contemplated how John's house had the air of gentle antiquity. Yet the antique contents were enveloped within a massive galvanised iron shed. She started to think, *If, as he had stated, he left school so young, how had he managed to accumulate so much valuable furniture?*

More intriguing to her, however, was Frank's comment that his family had once owned all the land here. This made her think about what had happened to that ownership. When she came to think about it, John never seemed to be under any direction, but certainly was always busy. He spent some time in the third room, the one she had not yet been into, doing a lot of bookwork. He seemed to get a lot of mail. The other interesting thing was that both the flat in Cooma and the one in Manly were furnished in a similar manner.

The daily pattern became familiar and comfortable to them both. In the evenings, either John or Livinia would prepare the dinner. Livinia found the heat a bit enervating and the evenings would not cool down until quite late. The clarity and brightness of the stars at night were a revelation to her. With no city lights to interfere, the stars were like sparkling jewels in an ocean of velvet. The days sped by until finally the time came for John to return Livinia to Harbord. They agreed to leave on the Sunday so she could have the extra day to recover before returning to work in the new year.

CHAPTER 6

John spent three days in the Manly flat, spending time with Livinia each evening. However, he was now getting impatient to get back to the never-ending work at his property. He bade farewell to Livinia with some melancholy, but also with eagerness to be home.

The next time he saw Livinia was at the Sydney Royal Easter Show. They spent time together and wandered around the beach at Manly. Sitting on the wall at the beach the day before he was to return to Cooma, John looked at her and asked,

'Would you like to come down again?'

'Yes, I think so,' she replied. 'I think I would really like that.'

'You're not put off by the primitive life in the bush?'

'No,' she responded. 'I told you I had a wonderful time. I loved every minute of it all.'

'Well, you have to come down and see what the winter is

like before we go any further.' He realised as he said it, what he had said, but it was too late, it had already come out. He could see the semi-startled look on her face as she too realised what he had said.

'I'm sorry,' he said, a little embarrassed. 'What I meant to say is that I'd like you to come and see what it is like in the mountains in the winter. But you need to understand that it can be very cold.'

'I'd love to come down again. When were you thinking?'

'If you could get a week in July, that's the worst month.'

'I'll see what I can do. Is that an invitation then?'

'Yes. I guess so. If you like.'

John arranged to pick her up again as he did at Christmas time. All that remained was that she could get some time off, preferably in July. He returned to Bridgehead after this short visit and tried not to think too much about Livinia. He busied himself with the last of the cattle removal, re-doing all Frank's old fences and breeding up the few cattle that he had chosen to keep.

July was a quiet month in the beach suburbs as the weather was not conducive to real estate sales, and Livinia was able to arrange for a week off work. It was bitter weather in the high country and it usually snowed. The scenery in the dark gave no clue to Livinia where she was or when they might be getting close to John's property. Finally, John slowed down and turned the nose of the ute into the familiar gateway. She saw the lights progressively coming on in the building. He told her to unpack a few things and place them in her room while he attended to the fire. She returned as the orange flickering glow of the fire took hold in the fire box.

'It won't be long now.'

'I can feel it getting warmer already,' she said through chattering teeth.

They spent a long time huddling around the black stove. It would sustain them through the short days and into the long nights ahead. Eventually the heat was sufficient to encourage short sorties to the car to retrieve items or to venture beyond the open area to the other rooms.

The bitter cold pervading the shed would not retreat without a serious struggle and, John warned, it would be a day or two, accompanied by constant vigilance, before any semblance of comfortable warmness would return to the rooms. He did apologise a couple of times about the situation, acknowledging that she had experienced the searing oppression of summer's sun and now would experience the antithesis in winter's sharp prod. The only consolation he could offer was to assure her that spring and particularly autumn were usually extremely pleasant and just rewards for enduring the relevant precursor.

The days were filled in with the usual tasks with which Livinia was now becoming familiar, only now there was much less daylight to accomplish them. This meant that less was achieved and a lot more time was available to attend to evening chores such as mending tools and equipment and maybe sharpening up cooking skills. It was now that sheep and cattle sales were usually in full swing so there tended to be more trips in the old International tray-top with loads of animals to be taken to the sales.

Each time they went into town, Livinia cast an interested eye over an old wooden church that was located about fifteen minutes from John's place. She was Church of England, but the fact that this one was Methodist would not deter her from attending.

On one of the trips into town as they lumbered past, she broached the topic of the small church. John knew very little about it other than to say he had seen people there on the rare Sunday. He thought it held services about once a month, but was not sure. She asked if he would mind stopping there on the way home. The subject reminded him of the wrong he had committed to even be in this position. Doubts about getting involved with such upright people as Livinia were surfacing again.

A week flew by and it was already time for John to drive her back to Harbord.

Livinia managed to get another week off work in October and they did the usual jobs about the property, although each visit Livinia learned new skills such as learning to ride one of the quieter horses. John had appeared a little pre-occupied to Livinia this visit, but nothing she could put her finger on.

Then on the Thursday evening after a tiring day, but while the evening was still young, he said to her, 'Livinia, do you like it here?'

She looked at him quizzically, replying, 'Yes, John, I love

coming here. It's so much fun being with you in all these strange surroundings. Why do you ask? Are you getting sick of me?' she asked with a hint of humour in her voice.

'No. No,' he stammered. 'I was wondering if you could ever consider living here always. Maybe. Sometime in the future.' His voice trailed off a little with a hint of embarrassment and trepidation.

She turned and looked seriously at him. 'What are you saying?'

There was silence. Only the grandfather clock and the cracking sound emanating from the massive stove broke the silence. He could delay no longer.

'Would you consider marrying me Livinia, and living here with me? You don't have to answer right now. I know it's a big move.'

She was astonished. There was instant conflict within her. She had to temper the desire to accept eagerly with the reality of living an isolated existence.

'I don't know what to say, John,' was all she could muster.

'I know it's a lot to ask. It's not a life for the fainthearted. It's really Sydney or the bush, in a fashion. The big smoke or the backblocks.' He was trying to make light of the situation as she struggled with a suitable answer.

'You mean character country,' she said, amused at her retort. 'May I think about it?'

'That's not a definite 'no' then?' he asked flippantly.

'John,' she blurted, 'I'm terribly flattered. But it's totally unexpected. Just let me think about it for a while.'

It was getting late and John said he would go out and check on the chooks as there had been some noises over the last few nights. Livinia nodded, and when he left, she meandered slowly towards the bedrooms. She had never been in his bedroom or the other room that he called his office.

She lingered outside the office for a few minutes thinking about the night's events. Finally, her curiosity overcame her guilt as she slowly eased open the door to John's office. She desperately hoped he would not return at this exact moment as she gazed into the room from the threshold, leaning inwards in an attempt to see as much as possible but leaving open her rapid retreat if needed. She tried to savour the atmosphere of the room in which John seemed to spend so much time. Here also was more massive ornate antique English furniture; bookcases, bureaux, a huge roll-top desk and the usual bronze statuettes, some quite large and ornate. The bookcases were all extremely neat. There were stationery boxes neatly arranged and labelled filling the shelves, and the desk had papers set along the rear.

She glanced around for as long as she dared, then slowly closed the door. She quickly crept up the hall to his bedroom and repeated the exercise. There was more heavy matching furniture. She had never seen so much opulence and in such an incongruous setting.

She scurried back to the table and sat down to think. An image of her late mother came to her briefly and, with a small shudder, wondered if she would have approved at all. She said a silent prayer to herself.

John was gone for quite some time, but eventually returned. He wandered over to her and placed his left hand on her shoulder and asked if she were alright. His voice and demeanour carried a sense of deep concern for her and she was touched by his disquiet.

Next morning, Livinia was later than normal getting up. John put it down to the stress of his proposal and did not mention anything about it when she finally emerged from the bedroom. She ate in calm silence while he attended to some activities in the outer part of the shed before returning to the living area.

About mid-morning, he asked if she would like to walk up to the top of the rise that led to the front of the property from where the whole vista of his working life lay before them. They strolled up the gentle ridge and turned to stare at the rolling valley scene set out before them. Behind over the low ridge ran the gravel road that led to town. This was the exact same spot to which he had brought her when she first arrived at the property to survey his holding, well over a year ago.

Livinia was slowly drinking in the scenery and deep in thought. Spring was a lovely season in the high country, and on the Monaro, the days were warmer and the pasture was greening up. She was transferred back from the silent spell and magic softness of the moment by the intrusion of John's voice.

'Have you given any thought to my offer?'

She hesitated then replied seriously, 'Yes. I have wrestled

with the prospect you offered and given it a lot of thought. I prayed very hard about it long into the night.'

John could see it had troubled her and continued, 'I don't mean for it to be such a burden that it makes you upset.'

'No,' she assured him, 'I was going to ask you for some more time but I think that would be unfair on you. I would be happy to accept your proposal if you think I'm adequate to cope with life here together.'

John felt a shudder of exaltation pass through his being but outwardly showed little sign. He took her hand in his and leaned over to gently kiss her on the cheek. She squeezed his hand and they stood there for ages holding hands, surveying the landscape.

'I hope I'm allowed a garden?' she announced with a smile.

'Why, of course,' he agreed. 'But, understand it must be all your responsibility as I don't have time to waste on unproductive pursuits. Besides, you need to be aware of fire danger here, especially in the summer.'

His comment reawakened in her the sadness of realising that her dream was transitionary and this idyll would pass.

'Yes, I understand. But surely a small garden to pretty up the starkness would be all right? And maybe move the clothesline.'

'As long as you look after it and don't let it get out of hand.'

'Deal!' she agreed. She could already see in her mind's eye the garden taking shape and all the lovely things she could grow there, even in this climate. 'I think I do love you John, even though we haven't known each other all that long. I think it started way back the first time you helped me with the car. Do you love me a lot?'

'What is love?' he asked, staring out over the paddocks. 'I know I love being around you and having you near. Is that love though? I certainly like you a lot, Livinia. I like you enough to let you go though, if you decided against our being together, for whatever reason.'

She thought that was a strange reply yet it held within it all she found attractive about this extraordinary man and his life that was so different.

There was a lot to arrange but that could be sorted out over the next months. They tentatively set a date in March 1968. Her visit was approaching its end and arrangements needed to be made for her to return to Harbord. They began now to be more at ease with each other and held hands in public but had not told anyone about their decision.

One point that certainly surprised John was the location of the wedding. John had assumed that she would prefer to have the wedding in Manly where her friends and some of her mother's life-long acquaintances lived. But unusually, Livinia told John that as she was marrying him and coming to live on his farm they should be married in the small church that she had so often driven past on the road into town. She asked John if he would mind driving to the church to look at it together.

It was late in the afternoon when they pulled up outside the church enclosed by an old, four-strand plain wire fence. They read the sign that adorned the front of the white-painted timber walls: *St Stephen's Methodist Church, Reverend Robert*

Meagher. There was a telephone number located in Cooma. Livinia wrote it all down and began to walk right around the site.

John returned with Livinia to Sydney and he spent time making plans for their wedding and the overall picture was becoming more certain. The date was finally set for Saturday 9 March the following year, 1968.

The wedding of John Wesley Summers to Livinia Audrey Avery was a composed and serene event with only a small number of attendees as neither of them had many relatives. John told Livinia that he had completely lost touch with the few he had known. Livinia invited some distant cousins and a few of her mother's old friends, but most were unable to attend. John did invite his only true friend, Frank Dougherty, but no other neighbours. There was a small reception back at the farm shed but by late evening all had departed for Cooma or elsewhere. So the deed was done.

Livinia had resigned from Mrs Roberts' real estate office amid much fanfare. One thing that John had insisted on, despite her protests, was that she, at least for the present, keep her weatherboard house in Harbord in her own name and rent it out through Mrs Roberts. This he had done for two reasons; one, it gave her a small income, but more importantly, in his mind, it gave her a retreat if she found the rigours of the Monaro beyond her. He did not couch it in those terms to her and she protested strongly that a good wife should always pass all her possessions to her husband, especially as the bank owned everything he owned, or that's what he was always telling her.

They spent a short honeymoon on the NSW south coast at Narooma, travelling about the secluded beaches together and enjoying themselves in the balmy weather of early autumn. Livinia was not quite sure that she approved of Kelly accompanying them everywhere, but she acknowledged that she had been his sole companion all those years he had spent alone and that she was more than just a working dog.

John found it difficult to be away from his interests so they returned after about a week. He had by now removed all the excess stock from Frank's place and was continuing on with replacing all the fencing. He was also repairing all the old sheep yards and building new cattle yards. The property had a dilapidated shearing shed and he was slowly getting it rebuilt. There was also a derelict windmill by an old dam but he decided against repairing it as there were plenty of dams on the place plus a good creek through the centre of the valley. The windmill still had most of the superstructure intact but did not rotate or turn the blades. John thought he would have to dismantle it at some future date, before it became a hazard.

They were home only a week or so when John decided it was time to try and tell Livinia about his finances. He was not looking forward to that exercise. In the end, as he needed to go to Sydney, he decided it might be easier to tell her there. They arranged to travel to Manly the following week.

It was the first time that the Summers had stayed at John's Manly flat as a couple. Livinia realised that she probably would be unable to decorate the Manly flat as she understood it to belong to the company that John worked for. John was a meticulous person and always travelled to Sydney with several briefcases. Livinia did wonder why he needed so many different cases when he travelled, but put it down to his finicky nature. It turned out that there was a case for each of his companies; she just did not know that yet.

The first morning, John grabbed the case that related to Bridge Loftus Investments and advised Livinia that he had an appointment in the city. They caught the ferry to Circular Quay terminus and walked up to the city centre. After a short walk, John stopped and pointed to his building that comprised nine storeys, tightly sandwiched between taller, but also ornamentally facaded office buildings.

'You see that light-brown stone building over there?' he said to her as she tried to locate it through the melee of pedestrians and road traffic.

'Yes,' she replied quizzically.

'Well remember that building, and I'll talk about it again later.'

Then he grabbed her hand as before and strode off up the street for about two blocks. They came to another building and they entered through ornate, sandstone entrance doors, which John had to hold open for Livinia to enter. Once inside, it had the atmosphere of old-world charm with polished stone floors and a timber-lined foyer. They entered the lift and John pushed the button for floor seven. Livinia assumed this was where John's appointment was, but she thought it was at

1.30 pm, and as it was now only eleven, she wondered why they were so early. The lift was quite noisy and stopped with a shudder at the top floor. John walked towards the back of the floor with Livinia still being led by the hand. He stopped outside a plain wooden door with an opaque glass centre at about head height and pointed to the signage on the glass: *JW Summers and Company*. Livinia looked at it in a baffled and bemused manner while John unlocked the door. They entered a small waiting room that was plainly and sparsely furnished, with an air of austerity about it. There was a second room more in keeping with John's other possessions in that it again had the antique furnishings. John neatly placed his briefcase on top of the desk and proceeded to open it while Livinia shuffled into a chair.

'Where to start,' he finally said. 'I'm afraid my life is a bit more complicated than I led you to believe. You see …' He paused while he exhaled in exasperation. 'Remember that other building I asked you to remember?' he asked.

She nodded.

'Well, that building and this building are both owned by a company called Bridge Loftus Investments. BLI is in turn wholly owned by JW Summers. As you know, I am JW Summers.'

'Let me see,' she replied. 'A company called JW Summers owns this building, and also the other one you showed me?'

'That's right, so far.'

'I don't understand,' she muttered.

John tried to explain his complex business arrangements to

his confused wife. It was proving more difficult than he had hoped and she seemed to be having trouble comprehending exactly what he was saying.

'Why didn't you tell me all this before?' she said, a little annoyed.

'It's complicated,' he answered. 'Besides, that's only half the story. You see, JW Summers is a holding company and wholly owns two other companies that I am also the director of.'

'There's more?' she stammered. 'Should I be writing all this down?'

'Yes, there's more, but you don't need to write it all down as you will soon master it all. One of those companies owns rental property in Harbord … you know, houses, and a block of flats, or units they are being called now, in Manly.'

'You don't mean your flat?'

'Yes,' he answered. 'That flat in Manly is actually owned by my company as well as the whole building.'

Livinia was speechless.

He continued, 'Another company owns the block of flats in Cooma and an industrial complex on Polo Flat. And that one owns the grazing property out of Cooma.'

'Where we live?' she asked with concern.

'No,' he said emphatically. 'I own Bridgehead in my name, the top floor flat in Cooma and one house in Harbord. But the company, of which I am the sole director, owns everything else. It was the accountant's idea. He tried to reduce my tax and also protect a couple of assets for me in case anything goes wrong with it all.'

'I see – I think,' she said. 'Does that mean – I don't know what that means, really,' she said with confusion.

'Look, what it all means is that we, you and I, own a lot of property that I have accumulated over a number of years. I own it all outright so there's nothing to worry about. We are better off than you probably imagined before we married, that's all. Would you like a cuppa?'

'Yes, please.'

Livinia was trying to take all this in. Suddenly things started to make a bit more sense. Now she could understand how all the places had the sameness about them; all the antiques and atmosphere; *John owned the lot*. Now she began to see why he was able to be so free and easy with his time when it came to seeing her. Yet he always seemed to be so busy and occupied with work. It was all so very strange. *Well that was John all over*, she thought.

'Come with me and I'll show you around.' John led her back out into the hall and down to the end of the floor. There was a kitchenette and a toilet adjacent.

'All this is yours?' she asked.

'Ours,' he stressed.

'But how?'

The question he dreaded. He had given this dilemma considerable thought. He decided the best ploy would be to cover the subject with a nebulous answer that disguised as much as possible and gave little detail. In the end, he just answered with comments about hard work, good luck and better management, vaguely dismissing the whole thing as if it had been pre-ordained. She did not pursue it any further, so he felt satisfied that might be the end of that, at least for now.

They spent an hour or so there, eating some lunch John had bought from one of the many food kiosks scattered about the city and going over the papers that he had in the case. Livinia was mostly quiet during this time as she tried to digest all that information and also leave him to attend to some paperwork. When she asked why he had an office here, he explained that he needed a head office for all the companies, and his city accountant had recommended this arrangement. As his requirements were small he only needed a small office. This was one of the smallest in this building, leaving all the rest of the space to be let out.

The afternoon meeting was with John's accountant a few buildings down the street. Livinia saw a whole new side to John that she never suspected was there. She was impressed with John's meticulous presentation to the accountant. After the meeting, they returned to Manly by ferry and spent a quiet evening going over the day's events.

Next morning, John took Livinia on a short tour of the back streets of Harbord showing her the rental properties he had acquired over the years. They drove past her old home that she still owned. It was a contrast, being weatherboard and with a tin roof, to the five he owned, which were all double brick with tiled rooves. Even when she worked in the rental area of the real estate office of Mrs Roberts, she never suspected that it was John who owned so many houses.

CHAPTER 7

On their return to the farm at Cooma, life settled into a steady pattern of farm work, saleyards, and attending to John's administration of his property portfolio. Livinia began to adjust, but often found it solitary and slightly lonely. She did not fit in entirely with the other women, who were all mostly born and bred to the conditions of rural life. They attended the church where they were married once a month when services were held. She rather liked the reverend as he had come to the calling later in his life, giving up a good job to become ordained, and was genuinely sympathetic to the needs of his flock.

Livinia grew more deeply in love with her husband as time passed. She was a spiritual person and firmly believed she would spend eternity in the warm glow of God's Heaven with her soul mate. This to John was an admirable expectation, but not one he necessarily shared. He feared that the gate to eternal life was probably closed to him when the Reaper's blade was finally bared.

The wheel of life was slowly and irrevocably turning for the young couple, and with the passage of time, Livinia announced that she was expecting a child. John was a little concerned at this news. He had not allowed for children in his building and planning exercises.

Early the following year, John was presented with a daughter in the Cooma Hospital. Livinia's pregnancy went well, so John was able to move her into the flat in Cooma about a week before the birth. Miss Crowther, who lived in the flat opposite, was quite helpful, being a former sister at several country hospitals. The child was named Audrey, after Livinia's auntie.

Audrey proved to be quite a disruption to their lives and required considerable attention. This at least occupied Livinia, a task that had mixed blessings, as it also kept her from being with John out and about on the property working. To complicate matters, six months later, Livinia was greeted with the news that she was pregnant again. As her term lengthened and she became less active and less able to do much around the farm, she began to get a little short-tempered with Audrey and John.

One particularly trying day, when she was just over half way through her term and seemed especially cranky, John suggested, 'You know, I've been thinking. Maybe it's about time we thought about building a proper house for our family.'

'Can we afford to do that?' This was an instinctive response on Livinia's behalf. Having left school at fifteen and struggled all her life until now, old habits of frugality were hard to ignore. She, like John, would not, and could not, just waste money.

'Of course we can. You know how we are doing, and it's all right.'

'It would be nice to have a new little house that we built together.' The thought of a new project cheered her considerably.

'Wait a minute,' he countered. 'There are a few rules I want you to consider in the design.' His mind often drifted back to the homestead where he spent his childhood with the Merritts and especially Vera. He had fond memories of the rather old but stately homestead that was built in the mid-1850s.

'Anyway,' he continued, 'I want a solid brick house with at least seven bedrooms, a really big kitchen, three or four bathrooms, a study, a cellar, a wide veranda and a really big entrance foyer. Minimum.'

'You have given this some thought.'

'Yes, I'll draw you a rough plan. Then the rest's up to you.' He began scribbling on the pad a sketch of the plans he had in mind. They spent hours discussing it and refining the drafts. It became a major time-filler for Livinia as she perfected her dreams and accommodated his wants.

On one of the weekly trips into Cooma, John looked up a builder and made some early enquiries. The builder agreed to come out the next week and inspect the site and advise on the prospects for construction. True to his word, the builder arrived at the farm to inspect the area and advise on the building. All seemed in order to him so an architect was employed and plans drawn up. The construction of the homestead was all arranged to commence when Livinia was in the last throws of her pregnancy, so the early stages were a little hectic.

In due course, John was presented with a son whom he named Ethan. John had asked the builders to delay a start on the new house until Livinia was over her pregnancy and she was re-established back at the farm with the two children. Material was constantly being delivered to the site but no actual work begun. One task John did manage to complete was the construction of a much bigger cellar than the one he had hidden under the shed. That one still remained a secret from Livinia, even though there was now no money in it. He hunted up and located the same contractor and, after requesting silence regarding the first cellar, proceeded with the construction of the new one under the new house.

Once John and Livinia had agreed on the final details of the layout, all the management of the building was left to Livinia, a task she relished and managed with authority; in many ways she was more finicky and demanding than John. The building work was anticipated to require about eight to twelve months. This gave them both, but especially Livinia, time to attend to the furnishing of the new house. John essentially gave her an open cheque to purchase what she wanted. His taste ran much more to antiques than hers and he realised that they might not fit into the new home as well as some of the more modern designs available. However, Livinia managed to accommodate some of his antiques with ease.

The new house was built using light-coloured bricks. It had long, wide verandas and a huge portico allowing undercover vehicle access to the house in bad weather. The galvanised iron roof was a light shade of green that blended into the surrounding paddocks better than silver. John was very happy with his new house and praised Livinia's good taste and sense of décor. He was less interested in the detail than in the layout, being delighted with the seven bedrooms and his huge new office. That was the one room he insisted on furnishing himself in due course. He was very sentimental about his old living quarters in the shed and wished to leave it just the way it was. His new life would be reflected in a new office with different furnishings.

Ethan was born in the spring of 1971 and the house was completed before the end of winter 1972. The move to the new house made life much easier for Livinia, and John had no trouble fitting into his new home. The children were easier to manage there and also safer away from the contents of the huge shed.

Coinciding with the happy occasion of their second child and relocating into the new home was the devastating incident that reminded John forever after of the move; that was the sad death of Kelly or Kels as he often called her. Livinia was secretly pleased to be free of the incessant company of his faithful dog but also mindful that John was quite heartbroken.

He carefully buried her behind the big shed near where she often lay in the hot weather. He made a special wooden cross and regularly attended the site, always keeping it tidy.

Trips to Manly were now rarer and more difficult with children in tow, but had to be made occasionally to accommodate John's business requirements. Towards the middle of 1973, their life was further complicated with the arrival of a second son, named Damien. When Livinia fell pregnant again, a decision was made that that would be the end, and four children would be the limit. 'Man proposes, God disposes,' quoted John. That plan was foiled in 1975 when Livinia gave birth to twins, a boy and a girl, being Brendan and Hannah.

Their existence revolved around hectic farm life, trips to Sydney to do John's property portfolio business and the demands and activities of their rural children. This was the aspect for which Livinia was least prepared. From an early age, John encouraged and trained them to ride horses and drive machinery. It seemed to her that as each of them grew in age and size, they drifted more and more to John's life with less dependency on her. This she grudgingly accepted as the price of being a mother and a city girl. When it came to excitement, motherhood and domesticity ran a distant second to mustering, gymkhanas, barrel-races, camp drafting, pony clubs and driving tractors. The eldest was now attending school in Cooma and this was the beginning of another source of difference and potential conflict between John and Livinia; namely, education.

John would not consider boarding school. John still harboured a deep resentment and grievous sense of loss at never knowing his parents, a feeling he realised would never depart. He did hold in high regard the Merritts who raised him, despite their tardy attitude to his circumstances. He often contemplated what the real truth behind those innuendos was in relation to the stash in the Merritts' office safe to which his nan had alluded. He wondered sometimes what became of his cousins who were so disingenuous towards him in his childhood. Then his mind would flash back to the haughty private-school types that frequented the house during school holidays and he would reflect on their less-than-desirable nature.

John had a high regard for education, but tempered that with the certain knowledge that formal schooling could instil only so much in an individual in preparing them for the harsh reality of real life. He had mixed with plenty of self-made men who could be regarded as nothing less than successful despite often attaining quite low levels of education. This often applied in the rural circles in which he moved and not in the city. Nevertheless, that did not alter his opinion. He also knew many people of high intellect who also had limited schooling but their intelligence manifested itself in other ways.

In contrast, Livinia regarded education as critical. Livinia had been dux of her school at fifteen and hoped to go to university. But, owing to her family circumstances, she was required to leave school and began work in order to support herself and in particular her elderly, and slightly infirm, mother. This she reluctantly but loyally did. However, it left her with feelings of remorse and resentment at her lost prospects. Her only consolation was that it provided her and her mother with their only asset in the world – their small timber house in Harbord. She invariably drifted towards positions in the medical and legal professions where she developed an image of class and private schooling. She always spoke impeccably and with a clipped accent that suggested she was born into wealth and high social standing. She was determined her children were going to have the opportunity she had been denied. These matters arose mildly at this early stage in their children's upbringing but were destined to cause serious friction in the future.

John and Livinia's relationship was slightly strained with the advent of the children but, as with most couples, it in no way diminished their desire for each other; it just put it on a different footing. John occasionally found his thoughts drifting back to his halcyon days of bachelorhood when he was younger and the world a wonderful place for a rich young man with no ties doing a job he absolutely loved. He fondly recalled his time living in his shed set up just as he wanted it. He was mature enough to realise that life does not work that way and he was immensely grateful for Livinia and his lovely children.

Livinia, on the other hand, was more ambivalent about her choice. She loved John and admired his ability, but she sometimes felt like an outsider within her family, as if she was the odd one out. While they all thrived on the lifestyle of rural living, she was the least proficient on horseback, she was always scared of the bulls, she was terrified of spiders and most bugs, and she liked to be inside by dark, out of the wilds of the outside world. Life for her was predictable and seemingly headed for its inevitably conventional future.

Then something happened to renew her faith and reinforce her admiration for her husband. It involved the redoubtable Mary Crowther, who by now had been retired for about fifteen years. She had endeared herself to John by reporting any goings-on at the flats to Tom Grady. Miss Crowther was as feisty as ever. She never stopped smoking and her teeth clattered worse than ever when she spoke, something that both fascinated and terrified the children.

Mary and John had an unusual relationship. He rather liked her despite, or maybe because of, her brusque and imperious manner. She and Livinia had become good friends, especially as each of the children came along, and they had shared a lot of cuppas together. She also kept an eye on Livinia during the late stages of each pregnancy.

One evening, John received a telephone call from Tom Grady, who rang to say that Miss Crowther had spoken to him on his last visit to the building as he did his inspection. She enquired of him his opinion of the value of her unit if she decided to sell. She said the stairs were becoming a problem for her in her old age. Tom knew that John desperately wanted that flat to augment his own and close off the whole top floor.

Early next morning, John drove into Cooma and straight to his flat. He made sure Mary's car was in its parking bay and then proceeded to his unit. He made a lot of noise to ensure she knew he was there and then waited a short while. Mid-morning he walked over to her door and knocked.

After a slight delay the door opened and there appeared a slightly dishevelled apparition that John knew to be Miss Crowther.

'Good morning Miss Crowther. I hope you are keeping well?' he asked.

'Yes thank you. I'm fine. How's the family?'

'Fine, fine. All are well. I wonder, Miss Crowther, if I might come in for a minute or so and have a quick talk.'

'Yes, of course. Come in. I'm afraid I'm in a bit of a mess as my nieces are coming down in a few days.'

'That'll be nice for you, Miss Crowther.'

'Oh, it's not that exciting, you know. They only come down when I have something to offer. I'm cleaning up my stuff and I hope to be able to unload some of the family heirlooms.'

'Why?' he asked, sensing a suitable opportunity to broach the subject that was the purpose of his visit. 'You wouldn't be thinking of moving I hope.'

'Not as such, but I might have to think about it soon as my knees are finding the steps difficult.' John sat down at the small table that was strewn with small artefacts, photographs and papers. Mary sat opposite.

'Have you thought of moving downstairs, Miss Crowther?'

'Don't be silly,' she snapped. 'I can't afford to move.'

'What if it could be arranged for you to sell your flat and you moved to number one on the ground floor. That way you could stay in the flats for longer. Otherwise, where will you go?'

'I have enquired of the old people's place further up the hill already, you know.'

'Can you still keep your car?'

'Yes, while I can drive. It's just the steps. Anyway, who would buy this flat and give me enough to afford to move?'

'If you're interested I'll make some enquiries if you like. No pressure. You can think about it and I'll get back to you in time.'

She shrugged a non-committal motion and pursed her lips. John left the subject there but at least the seeds had been sown. He chattered a little longer then made his excuses and left her to her sorting. He made straight for Tom at the agency. John asked Tom to determine when the lease expired on flat number one or two. Both were new and not due for twelve months, but number four was up in two months and Tom suspected that one would not be renewed.

'That's no good,' John stated. 'It needs to be on the ground floor.'

'What if number one moves into number four, freeing up number one?' suggested Tom.

'That might work,' said John.

John asked Tom to sound out the young couple who both worked for the council if they would consider a move to number four above with some inducements such as an extended lease and no increases in rent for eighteen months. John insisted no one was to know that he was personally involved. Tom was to say that the company that already owned four of the flats wanted to buy Mary's and would agree to the proposed moves.

About a week later, it was all arranged. Miss Crowther agreed to sell her flat to John and in return John agreed to move her to the ground floor and lease her that flat for no rent until she was no longer able to care for herself. He got the deeds to the top floor flat and she was able to remain out of the old people's home. The young couple were also pleased to be offered the second floor flat at an extended lease with no rental increases until termination of the lease. It was at this point that Mary Crowther discovered after all these years that it was John who actually owned the entire building.

John was now able to engage a builder to renovate the flat and make the entire top floor available to his family only. This was possible because of the layout of the building. The building was entered by a front door that was centrally located. There was a stairway immediately to the right as the building was entered and the ground floor units were beyond that. There was a common laundry towards the back of the building that led out to a small grassed area where a hills hoist was located. The stairway continued from the second floor up to the third but it was at this point a metal grill could be attached to prevent entry from there on.

John did not have any particular décor in mind and, as his halcyon days of antique purchasing were long gone – he was satisfied to leave this task to an eager Livinia. The flat required a total overhaul, as Miss Crowther's distasteful habit of smoking had left the rooms with a stale smell and much discolouration. The main object was to end up with a comfortable habitation that could accommodate his now large family any time they were in Cooma overnight.

It was tricky for Livinia to complete the task as she still had the demands of five young children, a farm, and a husband who had grown used to an attentive wife. John needed to buy a more suitable vehicle to transport his brood, plus a car that Livinia could cope with if she needed to go to town with the children without him. Her old Morris Minor was not coping very well with all the bush roads anymore. She nevertheless relished the prospect of redecorating the adjoining flat and devoted as much time as was available to the job. John was pleased with the result when it was finally completed. It had also given Livinia a different slant on John's character and she told him often how much she admired him for the way he had arranged things for Miss Crowther.

The next few years were relatively uneventful. Livinia's resentment at being the odd one out diminished gradually as the children grew but never entirely dissipated.

The Cross family owned a small farm on the other side of Frank's. They lived opposite John's place but further along the road. It was only one thousand acres, but John had often admired the property because it had extensive creek flats on which Ron Cross half-heartedly grew irrigated lucerne. The property was well fenced and had plenty of water from several dams and the creek that ran through the middle. It was the same creek that ran through Frank's property and possessed extensive deep alluvial creek flats. The flats were better on Frank's but, as that property would possibly never become available, John often admired Ron's property, and being smaller, he hoped it might one day come on the market. John knew this because Ron and Dell Cross were friends, with whom they also attended the local church when the monthly service was conducted.

It was during the course of this long involvement that John had learnt that Ron's son was not interested in continuing on the property and that they would probably have to move on as they were finding things a bit difficult. One thousand acres was once more than sufficient to support a family, especially through the fifties when wool prices were so high. Nowadays, however, it was becoming more difficult to earn a living from wool alone and Ron had diversified into lucerne for hay on his creek flats. Towards the end of the 1970s Ron found age was also a disadvantage, and John sensed the opportunity to purchase.

John noticed the 'for sale' sign one morning as he was checking his fences. He went over to inspect the sign and note the agency. It was not Tom Grady but another of the many agencies that existed in Cooma. John decided to drive into the Cross's place and have a talk to them about it. It transpired that they were reluctantly selling up for financial reasons and regrettably would have to move away somewhere. John had a critical look about while they were talking outside the neat and well-maintained homestead.

Then he said to them both unexpectedly, 'Would you

consider staying on as the manager of the place if I bought it to grow lucerne on?'

They were speechless.

'You don't have to answer now. Think about it. I would love to get hold of those flats down there but probably couldn't manage to maintain it myself, not just yet anyway.'

John was thinking ahead to the time his boys would be old enough to work irrigated lucerne. This would give him a solid backup during drought times, which were common on the Monaro.

He added, 'I could sure use your expertise in irrigation to at least get me started.'

After a few more pleasantries, John departed, leaving the Crosses with a lot of thinking to do. They had reluctantly arrived at this position, but now their decision to sell up was being overturned by a most unexpected offer. John drove home and went into his office to do some calculating. Livinia noticed that he seemed preoccupied but said nothing.

She discovered his plans belatedly a few days later, and a mild resentment overtook her. It seemed he was at it again, making monumental decisions without consulting her. It was moments such as these that she felt completely left out of his business life.

It took the Crosses a few weeks to come to a decision. Finally, they came to see John and Livinia one afternoon to let them know they would be delighted to remain on as managers and teach the finer points of lucerne irrigation to John. John agreed to purchase the property and to pay a wage to Ron as manager. Livinia was amazed at how grateful they seemed to be and basked in a shared glow of their gratitude, although she knew she had no part in the affair.

Things always seem to happen in threes. The third major event shaping the lives of the Summers occurred in 1982. This was the death of Frank.

Frank had gradually been sinking into ill health from the time John met him. By 1982 he was declining steadily. John's children objected strongly to having to attend Frank, but John saw it as a good civil exercise for his children to at least see that not everybody had their idyllic family life and all their blessings. By this time, Audrey was thirteen and John sent her most mornings to check on Frank.

It was on one of these morning visits that she found him lying on his kitchen floor immobilised but still weakly breathing. She 'phoned John and he drove straight over. John carefully lifted Frank into the car and drove him into Cooma Hospital.

Frank was diagnosed as possibly having had a mild stroke but he was very weak and the doctors predicted his life would be short from here. John was visibly upset by this turn and spent a few days in at the Cooma flat visiting Frank every day. When he passed away three days later, John shed a tear or two, the only time he had ever done so for another human being. John wanted to arrange the funeral and also to inter Frank in the local church that they attended. Livinia pointed out that this was probably not appropriate, as Frank was a Catholic, and it was up to his relatives to make the arrangements. In the end, as no relatives could be contacted at such short notice, John agreed to Frank's burial occurring at the Cooma cemetery.

It was all very distressing for John, and Livinia was worried at how distraught John seemed. Worse was to come, however, when a few days after the funeral and hospital affairs were completed, John received a letter from a firm of solicitors in Cooma. The note was brief and terse, informing him that Frank had left his entire estate to John and made him the sole beneficiary. John was most annoyed at this turn of events. His first thoughts were to wonder what the neighbours would think about it all, and that was important in a close-knit country district.

John never recalled Frank ever mentioning this topic and he was unaware that Frank had even made a will. Frank often accompanied John into town in the cattle truck, especially as his heath dwindled. He never once hinted that he was thinking of doing such a thing. Although, on reflection, John recalled Frank asking about a solicitor about three years ago, but at the time John thought nothing of it. John became melancholy at the thought that he would never again see his old mate.

John realised that, in spite of whatever the outcome of probate and finding Frank's relatives, the animals would need attending to. He was finally able to bring himself to visit the place and at least inspect the stock. Frank was down to one poor old dog, which John thought should be put down. Frank had long ago dispensed with his chooks, which left the cattle and a few horses that Frank had not ridden for years.

John sat at Frank's kitchen table where they had both often sat and talked. He looked about the shabby, dishevelled room thinking of Frank. He scrutinised the dross of one man's brief sojourn through the struggle of living and wondered why one person is so blessed and another so denied. *What would Frank's entry in the great ledger of life read? A one-liner that stated: fought for his country; died alone; without issue, as they say.*

Already, John thought he would have a longer entry, beginning with his sinful act, his offspring and acquisition of many assets – *or maybe that did not count. In the scheme of things, Frank may be better off than I am going to be.*

For some reason, John always compared Frank's miserable outcome with that of Miss Crowther's in Cooma. The very epithet 'Miss' always aroused in him deep feelings of pity. He was reminded of his own life and its multitude of blessings. *Why was this so?* He consoled himself that he still had a way to go before being confronted with the answer. *Besides, many much smarter men had asked that question, all apparently to no avail.*

At John's request, the solicitor attempted to locate Frank's relatives but none could be found. John did not relish the task of going through his dead friend's possessions. Frank had apparently never thoroughly gone through his parent's things, and there were a lot of items that appeared to belong to their generation. It all felt so wrong.

The sad mementos that John found most depressing were the few war medals that John suspected were Frank's, but he had never mentioned them to him. He carefully collected them and respectfully placed them in a small wooden box and took them home. *What can I do with all the faded photographs and items of a dead line but burn them?*

John knew he would miss the laconic asides that littered Frank's slow, drawling speech, especially his oft-repeated comment 'my gawd, she's rough' when commenting on any of his own bush carpentry efforts. Frank had had a big influence on John's life, but he little suspected that Frank was to have a strong influence long into the future, and beginning soon.

CHAPTER 8

John gradually began to accept the loss of Frank and devoted all his energy to running his enterprises again. He spent a lot of time initially with Ron Cross, understanding his property and the intricacies of irrigation. The Summers family was growing quickly and the eldest child, Audrey, was approaching fifteen. Livinia never won the battle over boarding school but accepted the inevitability of local state school education. She could, however, ensure that the children applied themselves to their studies and she always expected that they would at least go on to university.

This proved difficult, as the attractions of rural endeavours were often more appealing than bookwork indoors. Luckily, Audrey proved to be quite studious and talented, as did Ethan, their second child. Their third child, Damien, was, however, beginning to prove quite a handful.

The twins, Brendan and Hannah, were still young enough to be normal, boisterous, country kids, much spoilt and loved. However, disaster struck the Summers family in 1984. It began on a late summer afternoon, after the worst heat of the day had passed and the cooler outside paddocks beckoned. It was early in the new school year and Livinia had tried to encourage a study regime that was proving difficult to enforce so shortly after the long summer holidays. When Brendan objected, John took his side. Despite Livinia's objections, Brendan and his twin sister were allowed to hunt yabbies in the slowly drying creek while the long days lasted. This was an activity they had enjoyed many times before.

Towards evening, Hannah suggested that they return to the house, but Brendan insisted on just a little longer. Hannah went home, and when he had not returned by dark, Livinia was getting annoyed and asked Hannah to go and get him. She returned shortly afterwards without him, stating she could not find him anywhere. John began to get concerned at this point as it was unlike his children to be so inconsiderate. John grabbed the large torch that lived near the back door and began to search where he was last seen. It was quite dark now and some of the nocturnal bush activities were beginning. John flashed the light around on the ground and called his name. With a rising sense of anxiety, he was beginning to walk faster now. He waded into the creek where he knew Brendan favoured chasing yabbies, and shone the light around on the dark almost silent stream of shallow water.

In the pitch blackness, the creek took on a brooding and

threatening atmosphere as a mounting unease rose in him. He tried to stay calm and hopeful that there was a simple explanation. He began to retrace his steps and search more thoroughly this time. He could hear the faint calling of his family in the distant paddocks and creekline further along. Then there was a shimmer in the pale beam of the fading torch light. John raced over in the direction of the shimmer. His heart was thumping in his shaking body. He shone the light onto the water surface and it confirmed his sense of dread. There in the darkness was the inert body of his youngest son lying almost entirely submerged, face up with lifeless staring eyes peering heavenward, the black locks of his fine wavy hair slowly oscillating gently in the meanderings of the passing water.

John was numb-struck. All he could do was stare at the apparition that was once a vibrant living person. A huge welling of emotion cascaded within him and he knelt down slowly in the cool, calf-deep water onto the rock-strewn creek bed. He gently placed his large calloused hands under his dead son's fully clothed body, sobbing uncontrollably. He gently caressed Brendan's cold forehead and face, and began to softly whisper his name over and over again, 'Brendan. Brendan. No. Brendan'. He remained there for several minutes with the cold water seeping into his clothing, but he felt nothing. Gently he lifted Brendan's body out of the dark water and carefully waded through the water, stumbling over the boulders in complete darkness, cradling the dripping, motionless body of his son.

Once on the bank, John placed his son on the grass and cradled him so tightly he could hear his joints crack. All he wanted to do was hug the body of his dead son forever. He was completely oblivious to the bush sounds around him as he softly murmured in whispering tones the name of his son repeatedly, gently sobbing tears of sorrow.

He was so immersed in his moment of grief that he did not hear the approaching nervous chatter of his other children. They were throwing beams of light about the deep darkness of the cooling night when they spotted him in the close distance. They stopped abruptly and silence fell over the tragedy. There was a short shriek from Hannah and a gasp from Audrey as they comprehended the scene. Together they bombarded John with rapid-fire questions to which he did not reply. Audrey quickly grasped the situation and shone her torch on her brother's face. She could see the large lesion on his temple and that he was not breathing. She tried to console her father and her now-distraught sister.

Audrey began calling for her two other brothers. She could hear them through the undergrowth that boarded the creek banks. They arrived shortly after and all together they arranged for their father to carry their brother back up to the house where they knew their worried mother was going to be inconsolable. Hannah ran ahead to warn her mother what was to come. Livinia came bounding out of the house to inspect her son, amid much wailing.

The night passed in much of a haze for John. He could not recall telephoning the ambulance or the police. He held Livinia's hand as they sat in frozen silence. John began violently shaking, both from the night's immersion in the creek and from shock setting in. An ambulance arrived about midnight and removed the boy, and spent some time attending to the living, especially John. The medics pronounced Brendan dead and removed him to Cooma. During the next morning a police car arrived and the police were shown the scene and given details. They suggested that a report would probably be prepared for the coroner.

It was the most momentous event ever to occur to the family. John blamed himself for the accident and Livinia reinforced that prognosis with bitter recriminations about allowing Brendan to skip school work and indulge in farm activities despite her objections. In fact, John was stunned by Livinia's harsh assessment and acidic criticisms of him, and in a moment of pent-up anger and reflection she bombarded him with her discontent about his life, his disagreeing with her over their education and the total loss of each of her children in turn as the siren attractions of rural living stole them from her one by one, finally even to the point of death.

Through bitter vengeful tears, she rained a torrent of abuse upon him that wounded him deeply and astounded him with her apparent distaste for all he thought they held dear. He had no inkling she hated her life here so much and seemingly detested every aspect of their time together. He was so stunned he could not respond. This was quickly turning into a double tragedy for John. The children were also grief-stricken, but doubly so to see their mother so abusive and argumentative.

The next few days were a blur. Livinia calmed down and ceased from her antipathy towards them all, trying to restore some normality to her shattered family. John tried to comfort his crushed wife with constant hugs, but just below the surface was the ringing of those hurtful remarks she had uttered on that night. The coroner's hearing, when it eventually occurred, returned a verdict of death by misadventure, concluding that Brendan had slipped on the unstable creek bed and hit his head on a rock, probably causing unconsciousness leading to drowning.

The day of the funeral, which was held at the church where they were married and all the children were christened, evoked huge sadness and resurrected a long-forgotten episode in John's distant past. Brendan was prepared in Cooma to be transported back to the church. When the family arrived at the parlour, preparatory to commencing the journey back, John was shocked when he looked for the last time at his dead child. Livinia had brought in some suitable clothes to adorn Brendan, who appeared calm and peaceful, a state for which John was immensely grateful. At least he appeared to be at peace and that was all that mattered to the family.

However, Brendan's body was wearing a distinctive, deep-maroon leather belt with an ornate, oversized silver buckle. John's look of surprise and puzzlement was met with a terse comment from Livinia that it was what Brendan had chosen for his tenth birthday, which was in a few weeks.

John cast his eyes over his departed son and stole another glance at the belt around the slim waist. He felt an unpleasant cold shiver shudder through his whole body and a momentary unsteadiness in his knees. In fact, he was so distraught that he briefly needed to sit in an adjacent chair. Those around assumed it was the emotions of the moment. Only John knew it was something else.

His mind was suddenly cast back more than twenty years, in the weeks before he purchased his farm from Frank. It all came rushing back in a torrent of emotion and fear. That spot where he found his son's body was the exact same spot where he had seen the apparition that called itself Albert. It had not come to his mind until he saw the distinctive purple belt and its oversized silver buckle. Albert had his hand on the head of a child the age of Brendan, but more significantly, the child was wearing the same belt with a silver buckle, one of the few details that were really clear to John after all these years.

He sat in a daze for many minutes trying desperately to recall that weird afternoon, in particular the brief words that Albert had spoken. He racked his brain trying to recall, but all that came was the vision and the words, something like 'he's happy and waiting for you'. Another involuntary tear welled in John's eyes. *I must not cry. I must be seen not to cry. I must remain strong for the rest of the family, who so far were coping well considering, seemingly better that I am.*

The funeral was conducted by Reverend Robert Meagher, the minister who had married them sixteen years ago. He had also conducted the children's christenings and now to complete the wheel of life, a burial. He was getting quite elderly but still had an active mind. John had a few long discussions with the minister over the years and had grown to respect him enormously.

At the church service the following Sunday, John received another jolt. Discussing bereavement and associated topics, Reverend Meagher, admittedly in a different context, mentioned that the sins of the father were visited on his children to the third and fourth generation. John was stunned by this revelation and eagerly asked the reverend after the service its whereabouts in the Bible. John became impatient to return home, and on arrival removed himself to his office and retrieved from his bookcase a rarely opened Bible to read the cited passage. *Would God indeed punish me through my children for my sinful deed committed all those years ago?* He read it again and pondered in disquiet.

On the following monthly Sunday service, John sought out the reverend on the pretext of socialising. He asked again about the sins of the father and the wrath of God being visited on the children. Thanks to Livinia, he now knew his way a little around the Bible, but was intrigued by this seeming contradiction of the 'loving God'. An enlightening conversation followed that also dredged up another point that had been concerning John for some time: that of forgiveness. Robert Meagher, the ageing believer and confidante to the small flock, was convinced forgiveness was forthcoming to the truly repentant and those who were truly believers in the Grace of God. John was willing to accept that notion more in hope than in belief, but offered to Robert the comment that he would rather be of better character originally than be a flawed one continuously seeking forgiveness; even if that were also continuously forthcoming. It was pointed out to John that temptation was not a sin, but the reaction to it might be. John reiterated his previous comment; that he should be of better character so as not to succumb. The reverend indicated that we were here to be faithful, not successful.

'Well, I'm not looking forward to the Day of Judgement,' said John.

'Who among us shall abide the day of His coming?' answered Robert.

The conversation was discontinued there, but John felt a glimmer of hope for his eternity. This was not so much for himself, as he was already resigned to the prospect of eternal torment, but more for Livinia, who firmly believed they were going to spend eternity in blissful happiness together. If he ever did entertain the thought of Heaven and his angelic wife, he realised that if he did ever get there, it would not be his doing, but hers alone.

A few days later, John and Livinia were at home while the children had been encouraged to return to normality by attending school. John sat listlessly in the shed pottering aimlessly with some tools in the back when he heard the distinct sound of an approaching vehicle wending its way along the rough gravel entrance. It was a large and unfamiliar car; *probably one of Livinia's many local friends*, he surmised. It pulled up at the portico of the homestead and two people alighted. John could faintly hear his name being called.

As John approached the portico under which the visitor

had parked the vehicle, he saw a man and a woman speaking to Livinia, but he did not recognise them. When he finally arrived, he looked at Livinia for introductions, but the man, a solid and slightly overweight man, leapt forward demonstrably with a large outstretched hand, and announced himself as Dave Quiggin.

Though they were neighbours courtesy of the back boundary, they never actually had any discourse and never seemed to meet in town. John was a little surprised at seeing him after all these years. He had not aged well, and John understood from Tom, who was now retired, that he was having financial problems. His handshake was still very firm and seemed sincere. John felt a twinge of remorse at his tardiness in keeping up acquaintances.

Dave expressed heartfelt sorrow at the news of John and Livinia's loss. He introduced his wife, Imogene. John remembered her from all those years ago sitting in the car. She was still an elegant and quite attractive lady, and obviously paid a lot of attention to her appearance. This contrasted with Livinia, who, thankfully in John's eyes, spent little time or money pampering herself. Admittedly, Livinia had aged well and was blessed with a lovely soft complexion.

Livinia had already been conversing with them for some time before John was called and resumed her conversation with Imogene, inviting them in for some tea if they wished. The ladies led the way into the lounge while the men followed.

'Last time I was here John, you lived in a shed,' declared Dave. John nodded silently.

'I see you also fixed up that front gate so you have a nice wide grid.'

'Yes,' agreed John. 'I was persuaded to alter the entrance when my wife needed to get in and out, and the kids got sick of opening the gate all the time.'

'It looks good. So does this house, mate. I say, you've got some nice stock out there too. Things must be all right for you then?'

'Yes, up till now things were pretty good.'

John and Dave chattered at length about the weather, stock prices, wool, sheep and all manner of farming matters. John could not help but notice that Imogene and Livinia seemed to enjoy each other's company. It was a pleasant encounter brought about by unpleasant circumstances. It revived memories of those long-gone days when John had his first altercation with Dave's offsiders up at the back fence. *A lot of water has gone under the bridge since then.*

The unexpected death of Brendan precipitated a pall of melancholy on the Summers family and it affected each of them in a slightly different way. John lost a lot of his enthusiasm and suddenly his life seemed less blessed. Livinia was broken-hearted at the loss of her youngest son. Audrey became more sullen than ever and devoted more time to causes that left her parents in a daze as to where she was getting her ideas. Ethan, on whom John pinned all his hopes of passing on the farm intact, devoted himself more fully than ever to being a rural worker, much to the chagrin of Livinia, who tried to alert him, as indeed she did for all her children, that there was another life away from the farm.

She finally accepted that he was not only well suited to rural life but that he was also determined to better himself in that field. Rather than fighting it, she encouraged him to enrol in tertiary studies at New England University. This he was aiming to do, with the support of John.

Hannah became introspective and unsure of herself, retreating into a more secure relationship with Livinia. She seemed to withdraw from her father's world and became more interested in domestic interests and pursuits of an urban nature. She expressed a keen interest in possibly working in town and maybe even living there eventually.

Damien had always been different from the other children. He was a fitful sleeper, and as he aged, seemed to be always in trouble, exploring places and dismantling things. He was precocious and difficult to manage, especially in the evenings, and John noticed that he seemed to require relatively little sleep. By the time he was a teenager, he was disruptive both at home and at school, where his grades slowly declined.

Damien was twelve when Brendan died. While his brother's death deeply affected each of the family in different ways, Damien's behaviour did not change significantly other than to continually socially deteriorate. It caused consternation and arguments between John and Livinia, and the subject of boarding school re-emerged. She was fixated with the need for high levels of education and the need for the appropriate schooling atmosphere. She used every opportunity to resurrect her argument.

John was unconvinced, but had to acknowledge that in Damien's case it may have been beneficial. John was a light sleeper in his later years and was easily roused by any disturbances that occurred either inside the house or outside. He had noticed on a couple of occasions during late-night excursions about the house that Damien's light was visible under his often-closed door quite late into the night. He was unsure whether he was up or just asleep with the light on.

John did not as a rule invade his children's private quarters to snoop as he fully appreciated the desire for privacy. However, on one school day when the house was completely empty, John decided to go to Damien's room and check that there was nothing untoward. Livinia made the beds most days and ventured into all the children's rooms almost daily so he did not expect to find anything unusual. Damien was a neat and tidy child. His bookcase was as ordered as John's and his possessions were always impeccably arranged. Unusually though, his desk was often quite a mess and this was an enigma to John. He glanced around the room and it all seemed as usual, including the desk appearing unkempt.

John slowly and a little guiltily sauntered over to the book-strewn desk and began to rummage. There were several notepads of notes with esoteric, and in some cases, unfathomable scribblings and jottings. There were several different books, some opened, some closed and some with bookmarks. Damien was clearly doing several projects simultaneously, none apparently related to schoolwork. In fact,

John could find nothing that would remotely be classed as a school book. He glanced at the titles and the subject matter and was amazed at the topics, the weird themes and strange interests of his son.

The subject matter was cryptic and mysterious, ranging from Velikovsky, ancient cults, Stonehenge, pyramids, Atlantis – on and on. These were mostly subjects John had either never heard of or knew nothing about. As he rummaged, he grew more and more unsure of his feelings. Not so much at the topics, strange enough as these were, but at the fact that his son, who was only twelve should be interested in them. John tried to ensure that no appearance of disturbance was apparent and departed his son's room in a mild state of confusion.

Over the following few weeks, John made a concerted effort to pass by Damien's room late at night to confirm that his light was indeed on. On one of these wanderings, he raised the courage to knock on the door and opened it quickly to gauge the reaction. Damien was at his desk and closed books, dropping pencils, generally ill at ease.

'Are you okay?' John asked. 'It's just that I saw your light on and was checking that you're alright.'

'I'm fine thanks Dad.'

'Okay, I'll leave you be then. Good night, son.'

''Night Dad.'

At least it confirmed that his son was actually at his desk so late at night and not just asleep with the light on. John was now becoming concerned about Damien. There had been problems at school with his work ethic and his willingness to fit in there. John was mindful of the fact that Damien was no fool and had repeatedly displayed his superior intellect on many occasions, especially mathematical. John had begun to wonder if Damien was suffering from frustration and boredom. The signs were there, but John was unable to act on his instincts, and on the one occasion he had ventured to raise the issue with Livinia, she resorted to her hobby horse of boarding school and a proper education sorting all that out.

John began to engage Damien in deeper conversations without trying to arouse too much suspicion and without detriment to his other children. He was finding, however, that Damien was getting more intolerant and short-tempered with everyone and everything. Damien seemed to find solace more and more in simply working in the shed on machinery and riding carelessly about the wooded hills up the back of the property. The situation hit boiling point and something had to be done before Damien went off the rails. The catalyst was his school results at the end of the year of his fourteenth birthday. He was heading for complete failure and suggestions of repeating the year brought out Damien's ill-feelings.

There were a few fruitless and disruptive vitriolic exchanges between Damien and his parents that clearly showed considerable disrespect for them, especially his mother. When finally, through bitter acrimony and animosity, Damien was able fully to express his discontent and feelings, the situation became clear to John that something urgent needed to be done.

'What is it that you actually want to do then, son?' he asked as the three of them sat around the table.

'I'm bored stupid at school. I just want to leave,' he said bitterly.

'And what do you plan to do?' asked John.

'I'll get a job. Ron always needs a hand.'

'You can't just up and leave school and expect to get a job.'

'Why not? You did. You left at fourteen. You did alright.'

'Well you're not leaving school. Get that idea out of your head,' said Livinia severely.

'Well, I'm not stayin' there either,' rejoined Damien.

'Let's just all calm down for a minute and talk about this quietly,' implored John.

John suggested they all go away and think about it overnight, and discuss it tomorrow. Damien stormed off to his room, leaving Livinia and himself sitting at the table despondently, contemplating the problem. As Damien was only fourteen it was illegal for him to leave school for at least another year, but as he was obviously bitterly unhappy, something was going to have to be done.

Next time Damien was alone with his father, he made a suggestion that surprised even John. He proposed that he leave school immediately and start working on Frank's house block growing irrigated lucerne. He offered to move out of the house and live in Frank's old place, do it up and grow about five hundred acres of lucerne for hay and for fodder markets. Damien guessed that he could plough and plant that area in twelve months and be earning an income in two years. John said he would think about it. Damien asked that his mother not be informed of his idea yet.

It was not at first glance a practical idea, but John was more than a little impressed with the fact that Damien seemed to have given the scheme a lot of thought. In fact, the more John thought about it the more it began to have possibilities. A germ began to develop in his mind that might offer a solution. The problem would be convincing Livinia.

A day or so later, John asked Damien to prepare a fully-costed proposal for him to look at with all his ideas. He did not expect Damien to be able to come up with anything closely resembling a satisfactory offer, but it would be a starting point from where they could all progress. John informed Livinia with the fully anticipated explosive results and a point-blank refusal by her to even contemplate such a suggestion.

On the appointed evening, the three of them sat down to thrash out the proposal again. To John's complete amazement, Damien presented a thorough and comprehensive proposal that included projections and accounted for most of the necessary items. There was much toing and froing but finally, in an atmosphere of compromise, John suggested that Damien retire and redo the proposal with attention to some of the details, agree to complete next year at school, and he and Livinia would seriously consider the whole idea. Damien agreed, but Livinia objected strongly. John pointed out that it gave them another year to persuade him to change his mind.

During the following year, Damien became more enamoured with the prospect of leaving school and Livinia slowly accepted that she would lose another battle over her children. She was beginning to be very disappointed and despondent at the diminishing prospect of all her children achieving tertiary education. It appeared to her that sadly there would be no doctors or lawyers amongst her brood.

The year progressed to its inevitable close with Damien thoroughly prepared to take on the task of irrigated lucerne and living in Frank's old house. He spent hours with Ron Cross learning all the intricacies of the industry. The only consolation for John and Livinia was that he attended school, albeit unwillingly for the year, and gradually became more human at the prospect of physical occupation.

The troubles associated with Damien occupied the Summers throughout 1987. *Why do things always come in threes?* As difficult as these problems were for John, they paled into insignificance when compared to the difficulties associated with their first child, Audrey. In fact, the seriousness of their problems with Audrey possibly allowed Damien to achieve his goals because of his parents' pre-occupation with his sister.

In 1987 Audrey was eighteen. She was a brilliant student and achieved entry to several universities on completing high school. Her views on life and the world were at considerable odds with Livinia's, and especially John's. They were devastated at her unprincipled attitude and loose moral approach to the opposite sex, which resulted in the huge blow and ignominy of Audrey's pregnancy at eighteen following a short time at The University of Sydney. To compound the humiliation and dishonour, she not only could not identify the father, but denied any importance to the issue and refused to even discuss it with her parents.

John and Livinia were more than mortified and John could not comprehend how this had happened given her upbringing and the attitude of himself and his wife. When he considered how he and Livinia had conducted themselves during their courtship, he was at a complete loss for an explanation. Her trivialising of the situation compounded his grief when he remembered how devastating it was for him to have been without his real parents all his life. He was so distraught at the thought of deliberately giving a child such a difficult beginning that he harboured thoughts of adopting it immediately. Audrey would not have a bar of this suggestion, insisting that a woman was more than capable of raising a child on her own unassisted. *Were the sins of the father revisiting me again?*

The child, a boy she named Thomas, was born towards the end of 1987 in Sydney. Audrey returned with the child to her rented accommodation in Randwick, and she immediately set about continuing her life of study and promoting causes. John and Livinia were horrified but were powerless to intervene and Audrey made it clear that she was quite capable of coping. Audrey had, unbeknown to John or Livinia, been using marijuana occasionally since late high school, but now was smoking weekly. Neither John nor Livinia were savvy to the signs of its use and never suspected that any of their children would contemplate using any drugs. The whole idea was totally foreign to them.

Thomas fared badly as an illegitimate, only-child of a pot-smoking, single mother and student living in rented accommodation. John was horrified at the friends she seemed to encourage and referred to them all as hippies. Her parents visited her a few times in Randwick before they accepted that it was impossible to cope with her lifestyle. John had grave misgivings for the welfare of his first grandchild. He again had fearful and black thoughts about the 'sins of the father being visited on the children unto the third and fourth generation'. *Was all this developing family trauma solely my own doing? The result of that long-past single act. What better way to punish the evil-doer than to punish his children while he could but watch on?*

Audrey rarely visited her family in Cooma and there appeared to be a mutual drifting apart. John began to focus more on his remaining children, the studious Ethan, whom he hoped would go on to university and one day take over the pastoral aspects of the company; the troubled Damien who was now well into planning for the irrigated lucerne project and the still-young Hannah, who was now barely a teenager.

Audrey was amusing herself with all the challenges life was throwing her way. One of those amusements, however, appeared not to be Thomas. She was not about to let a small thing such as a child interfere with her pursuit of causes and attending university or partying. He must fit in with all the other activities she was involved in. John and Livinia grew more and more concerned for the child as he was obviously suffering neglect; at least by their standards. As they all grew further apart and saw less of each other, John was resigned to possibly losing contact with his first grandchild and this saddened him considerably.

To complicate matters, Audrey began taking up with other men, often older, and moving households frequently. She eventually began living with a high-flying law student and had two children by him. This really frustrated both John and Livinia but they were powerless to interfere. When finally they met the man, whose name was Geoffrey Bales, John in particular took an instant dislike to him and his supercilious manner.

Geoffrey Bales was a man with a slightly weedy frame, rounded shoulders and insipid pale skin, and he was quite short. He was opinionated, self-assured and particularly arrogant. In fact, he fully embodied everything John despised about privately educated people and it disturbingly reminded him of the unpleasant encounters of his childhood back at the Merritts'. John was unsure whether Bales was just deficient in personality or suffered from the little-man syndrome, or possibly both.

Geoffrey was heading places, there was no doubt about that, and his two children wanted for nothing. They were totally spoilt and engendered with their parent's self-same arrogance and self-importance. John was stunned at the contrast between how poor Thomas was neglected and mistreated, and the attention doled out to the other two. Audrey seemed oblivious to Thomas's plight and ignored their concerns. John and Livinia began to surmise that Thomas was a hindrance to the smooth operation of her carefree lifestyle. On the very rare visits that they were able to see Thomas, they detected a deterioration in his socialisation. It came as little surprise to them, therefore, when he began to accumulate a string of petty misdemeanours against his name, mostly misbehaving and car stealing for joy rides. By the time Thomas was thirteen, he was set on the path to perdition.

Livinia and John had been present at two of Thomas's brief appearances in court as a juvenile and could see that the prognosis was not good for him. The magistrates had been sympathetic to his plight but there was only so much consideration they could give him if he kept on offending.

It was with heavy hearts and much misgiving that they were alerted to yet another incidence of hot-wiring and police chases that resulted in another appearance before the court. This time, Thomas was warned that no more leniency would be countenanced and they feared the worst. Livinia decided to try another tack.

Thomas was quite a distraction for Livinia and John, but the rest of their children knew little of his misdemeanours other than his unfortunate existence. John began to realise the benefits of education, and that his educated children would far exceed him in their knowledge, even in the rural industry that had given him so much to date.

This became more evident as Ethan attained a wider experience in the field through his higher education, and his knowledge of farming practices increased, especially through the scientific application of technology. John pondered on this. *Gone were the days, apparently, when a young man could simply wander in off the street and buy a small farm and go from there.*

The more Ethan learned, especially at the UNE in Armidale, the more John began to realise that his own input would decrease as he got older. Ethan was enthusiastic to implement some of the admirable techniques he was discovering at university.

Damien, on the other hand, settled smoothly into his chosen occupation of growing lucerne on Frank's old home block. He contented himself with doing the best he could with this enterprise, with occasional forays into Cross's place next door as Ron and Del grew older and less able to carry out the manual work. Damien met a local girl at one of the B&S balls that were regularly held around the district or tablelands. She was admirably suited to farm life and seemed compatible with Damien. She aspired to nothing more than to be married to a farmer and raise lots of kids on the farm.

In due course, Damien's life would follow the predictable outcome and by the time he was twenty-two he was happily married with plans to have a family. He remained a hard worker and made a success of the lucerne business. This gave John, more so than Livinia, cause to be proud of his son and his beneficial enterprise that augmented their winter and drought feeding programmes while also bringing in a handsome income for Damien. He was even able to sell substantial amounts of hay and was running a small trucking sideline to bolster his income.

Hannah changed noticeably with the death of her twin brother, becoming more introspective and shifting her focus from rural pursuits to urban ones. She was an average student and gave no indication of ever excelling academically, so Livinia consoled herself with the fact that Hannah would probably not advance beyond Year Twelve. She showed aptitude for accountancy and bookwork, so Livinia encouraged her to attempt the subject at the TAFE where she eventually gained post-high-school qualifications that enabled her to obtain a reasonable job with the local council in Cooma. In time, John decided to buy her a small house in town to avoid the long trips back and forth to the farm, especially appreciated in the cold winters when daylight ended so early.

John still maintained his extensive portfolio of investment properties in Cooma, Harbord, Manly and the centre of Sydney. These required him to occasionally visit the city for inspections or tax purposes, but it was a facet of his life about which his children knew nothing at all.

However, John finally suggested to Livinia that, despite some foreboding, he would like to introduce their children to the complex business arrangement as each attained legal age. This was for several reasons, he explained to Livinia, but mostly as a way of successfully passing on the inheritance in an equitable and suitable manner so each received a share of the wealth, especially during their own lifetime. It was also essential in John's eyes that the central feature of the business, the farm itself, not be broken up into unviable portions.

To this end, the family understood that Ethan was to inherit the farm intact. This had been made easier when Damien decided to become a lucerne farmer on Frank's place, and the death of Brendan made that issue redundant. Now that Hannah seemed content with town life, the issue was further diluted, and Audrey was ensconced in her hippy-type lifestyle in the eastern suburbs of Sydney. John sometimes wondered if this pre-ordained arrangement ever had any influence on Audrey's approach to life, and the lifestyle decisions she made.

In order to equitably distribute income to his family, John decided to arrange for each to become a shareholder in the unlisted family company. This meant he had to divulge the details to each child at the right time. He was so disappointed with Audrey, doubting her ability to maintain the secrecy he would demand, that he had so far avoided passing on her entitlement to her, even though she was now well past twenty-one. However, as Ethan was now approaching his twenty-first birthday, and exhibited all the qualities that John thought suitable for this exercise, he would begin the process with him.

Ethan turned twenty-one in 1991. There was a small party at the homestead to which quite a few of Ethan's friends were invited. John liked most of them and spent many hours in discussions with young people with rural backgrounds, something he rarely did. These would be the future farmers of the country and he was fascinated to learn their desires, plans and hopes for their chosen industry. Ethan received a gift from his parents, but also an envelope with nothing but a slip of paper inside indicating that he was now a legal shareholder in the family enterprise. He was confused by this as he understood that the family enterprise consisted of the rather extensive, but still small-scale farming property that he also understood he would inherit solely and intact. John just smiled and said they would discuss it later.

The next afternoon, when all the guests had departed and just the family remained, John asked Ethan to join him in the study. Ethan knew this was serious as the children were rarely invited into their father's sacred place of refuge. When Ethan was seated, John began by saying, 'You know your mother and I are very proud of you and your achievements so far, son.'

'Thanks Dad.'

'I s'pose you're wondering what the share in the family business is all about?'

'I am a bit confused as I thought I would be running this place eventually.'

'And so you will. But I need to talk to you about some other matters, Ethan, but first I must ask you to agree to keep it secret from the rest of the kids for the time being.'

'Sure Dad, if you insist.'

'No, Ethan, I mean this. This is complex and serious and I want an assurance that you will maintain our confidences until I tell you otherwise.'

'Yes, of course,' he responded solemnly.

'You are the first of my children to be in this position as I have avoided this with Audrey. I don't think she is capable of handling it, especially the discretionary aspects. They will all get the same treatment when their turn comes. As far as Audrey is concerned, she scorns the gift who values but a part.'

What on earth did that mean? he thought. *Dad did sometimes say the strangest things.*

Ethan began to realise that this might be more than just a father and son talk about the farm. He had never actually seen his father quite so serious, except, of course, after the death of Brendan.

'In front of you there is a folder that I want to go through with you,' began John, pointing at a one-inch-thick, black leather, four-ring binder placed neatly in front of the chair Ethan was occupying.

'I'll start with this place here first,' he said, indicating that Ethan should open the first page of the folder. 'It's all explained there in the papers I've given you and you will need to go away and read them carefully, especially all the financial details. As you know, I want you to run the grazing aspects of the business.'

Ethan nodded knowingly, and with a little impatience.

'Sure, Dad.'

'Well it's much more complex than you could know. I own the property known as Bridgehead in my own name. It's only four thousand acres and a lot of that is still timbered. But next door, what used to be Frank's, part of Templemore is owned by a separate company. I'm the sole director of that company. It also owns property in Cooma, including the block of units off Commissioner Street.'

'You mean we own the whole building?'

'Yes, plus some industrial property in Polo Flat. Damien's place and the Cross's place are also part of the company. It's all in the papers there.'

Ethan began to survey the folder and leaf through the pages as John was talking. After the first half a dozen pages he came to a coloured divider. As he flipped that over, John continued,

'Now this bit,' he said, pointing at the next section, 'belongs to our properties we own in Harbord. I run another company that owns four rental houses in Harbord. They're now actually very valuable but when I bought them they were quite cheap. I own one house in Harbord in my own name and your mother also owns one house in her name. The company also owns the whole block of units in Manly where we stay.'

'You mean we own that building as well? I had no idea,' enthused Ethan.

'Yes. All the details of all that are in that section you're in now. If you turn to the next section, you'll find details on two office buildings I own in another company in the commercial city centre of Sydney.'

Ethan opened the next section, which was accompanied by photographs of buildings.

'That's them there,' said John, pointing to the folder. Ethan slowly turned all the pages until he arrived at the last section.

'In there,' advised John, 'is a summary sheet of the finances.'

Ethan glanced at the neatly typed page that listed all the assets, the gross income and the nett income. 'But you're talking in the millions, Dad,' he said, his eyes widening noticeably as he ran his uncomprehending gaze over the figures.

'Yes, as you can see Ethan, one share entitles you to a substantial annual income. I want you to think about the implications of that on your plans, not to mention your tax. Now all the information about it is in the folder. I will ask you to keep this strictly to yourself, please. Of course your mother knows, but no one else. You understand?'

'Yes, sure Dad. I'm just staggered. You certainly kept all this quiet.'

'There's a good reason for that,' was all John said.

Ethan was still bewilderingly flipping through the contents of the binder when John advised him to take it away, read it thoroughly, and keep it safely somewhere.

Then John said, 'We'll talk about this again when you've had time to go through it all.'

Ethan respectfully gathered up the leather binder and stood up. He was thoroughly confused, but he had much more respect for his father.

'Please close the door on your way out. Thanks,' added John. There was a dull clud as the solid wooden door slowly swung shut and closed behind Ethan.

John sat for a minute strumming the desk with his fingers. He had watched his son carefully as he drifted quietly over to the door, opened it with a click of the brass handle, and gently closed it behind him. The room was totally silent now and only the severest of disturbances could penetrate the sanctuary of this space.

Ethan was a solid lad, but much shorter than John, and not as well built, probably because John had started heavy physical work at fourteen. Still, John was very proud of Ethan and his achievements. He slowly leaned back in his chair accompanied by the creaking of the well-worn leather.

John gazed around the room slowly, drinking in all the familiar detail of his haven. He hoped he had done the right thing commencing this process. But he knew it was better to begin early while he was still in control rather than leave it all to be discovered after his death. He had total confidence in Ethan to be able to absorb the information and keep it to himself for the present. His mind drifted back to the first days of arriving at Bridgehead, which had no name then as it was still part of Templemore, Frank's family's original place. He had named it Bridgehead shortly after he began accumulating the other assets because he thought it was a bit like a bridgehead, a stepping stone to bigger and better things.

He fondly recalled those early days when he lived in his shed and had so much money that it was actually a problem. Life was much simpler then. This always evoked feelings of guilt in him – that he remembered that period with more fondness than his subsequent times with Livinia and his family. He could never decide whether that was because life was so much simpler and he so much younger back then or whether he actively begrudged the worries and responsibilities of family life.

He began to think of each of his children in turn and the angelic, wholesome woman who became his devoted wife. *Thanks to her, I've had the life-experience of being married and raising children; an experience I determined I would be denied; a self-imposed choice predicated on the premise that the serious immoral act of stealing the cache that gave him such material security should preclude such normalities.*

Audrey had often told him that private property is theft. *You know, in some ways she is right.* But he also acknowledged that he would never have worked so hard if the rewards were shared communally by others who may not have applied the same determination. He was sure he had made the right decision to delay offering her a share that was accompanied by a substantial income.

He admired Damien who was now making quite a success of the lucerne business and could see no reason for him not to be offered his share issue in a year or so when he attained age. He had cleaned up Frank's old hovel into quite a decent and clean house. Damien seemed to have no qualms about living in Frank's place despite him leaving several lifetimes of accumulation and possessions behind.

On the desk was a photograph of the only sour note in John's life so far; the loss of Brendan. John looked on his dead son as a 'Summer that never was' – a new form of life, a bit like himself – a new summer different altogether from the departed one. Brendan had died; John had morphed into a new man. It gave him some solace at least. John often reflected on his loss and sometimes it made him most desolate. Suddenly a great up-welling of emotion clouded over him and a single tear trickled down his tanned face. He so missed his son. *How much of his death was attributable to me? If only I had agreed with Livinia ….*

Unexpectedly, a great urge overcame him to free his son. He sat in deep silence except for the slow rhythmic tick of the mantle clock. He had an impulsive urge to release Brendan from the chains of his short existence on Earth. For some reason, it suddenly came to John that Brendan wanted to be free and John needed to let go. Brendan's room had not been touched since his death a few years ago. John occasionally entered to ensure all was tidy, and Livinia went in at least weekly. The other children, while understanding their hurt, often remarked that it was time to admit he had gone and for them to move on. John was the one finding it the hardest.

John was so deep in his broodings that at first he did not hear the gentle knock at the closed door.

'John dear, are you all right?' He finally heard the soft, caring voice of Livinia, which aroused him from his thoughts.

'Yes. Yes, Liv,' he stammered. 'Come in, angel.'

Livinia slowly opened the study door and peered in.

'Just checking you're okay. It's very late, dear. Would you like some lunch?'

John peered at his watch. He was staggered; it was now nearly three o'clock. He had been in the study since before eleven. He got up out of the chair hurriedly and went over to Livinia.

'How did it go?' she asked.

'Pretty well, I think,' he said. 'Did he seem alright to you when you saw him?'

'Yes,' she replied.

They exited the room together, he with his arm over her shoulder. John then announced that he felt like a short walk and would be back shortly. He headed for his old shed living quarters and entered into his erstwhile domicile. He peered around nostalgically and walked up towards the room that was once his study. It had all remained exactly as it had been before the new house was built. In the old study were his roll-top desk and all the antique bookcases. He sat briefly in his old chair and glanced about the room. Fond memories flooded back. He opened the drawer and removed the faded yellow slip of paper that he found hidden in one of the bundles of money when he was counting it years ago. He read it again. The cryptic message was still not fully comprehensible to him, but he felt that within it there was a clue to all his confusion and the deprivation of his childhood.

He stared at it briefly then replaced in the drawer and slid it closed. Then he abruptly arose and departed the building, and headed for the creek and the place where Brendan had died. It was also the same place John had seen the apparition that called itself Albert. He often went there in the hope of its reappearing, but nothing ever did. He sat on the cool bank slowly drinking in the scenery and wondering where Brendan was. The afternoon was now quickly advancing, so he returned to the house and his family.

Ethan was sombre all evening trying to digest the implications of his meeting with his father. John felt surprisingly liberated and unburdened after revealing his secret to his oldest son. He had also come to another decision, this time regarding Brendan. The afternoon's proceedings seemed to act as a catalyst for making monumental family assessments.

Later in the evening, when only he and Livinia were together, he asked, 'How would you feel if we cleaned out Brendan's room?'

Livinia was slightly startled at this unexpected development.

'Well,' she began, 'if you feel it's time, I'm happy to do whatever you like.'

John went to her and sat beside her. He clasped her hands in his and looked into her face.

'I think it's time to let him go,' he said to her in a low voice. 'I feel it's right and that he wants it too.'

'What would you like me to do?'

John expressed a desire to remove all Brendan's things from the room, clean it up, and prepare it to be used again for family or the children's friends if they stayed over.

The introduction of Ethan to the family enterprises and the allocation to him of an income-producing share was a turning point for John. It seemed to lift some of the burden of the illicit actions of his youth. Ethan spent some time studying the paperwork that John had given him and asked a few questions over that time.

Unfortunately for John, divulging this information increased Ethan's management desires as far as the sheep and cattle property was concerned. He began to agitate for a rationalisation of the assets, in particular, removing most of the non-farm possessions. This was an unexpected consequence and one for which John had not prepared. His only defence was to stress the need or preference for as diversified a holding as possible to cover events such as droughts. John also stressed that he would like to see a few more family members involved before he made any commitments.

The exercise of introducing each of the children to knowledge of the company and issuing them with an income-producing share gave them a sense of independence and allowed them to remain in the business from choice rather than by necessity.

The only one denied their right was Audrey. John and Livinia remained desirous of passing to her a share of the wealth, however, the major stumbling block for John was whether she would be discreet. That was paramount to him.

During this period of family consolidation, there occurred the final event in the link of John's original connections: the death of Mary Crowther. Mary had ended up quite an acquaintance of the Summers. She remained a feisty and truculent old lady but did appreciate the kindness of John and his family towards her, particularly towards the end of her life. She died in the flat and was discovered by a neighbour. The nieces arrived from Newcastle and were dismayed to learn that their not-so-close auntie did not even own the unit and left them only a few personal possessions.

John had the flat thoroughly cleaned, and removed any old furniture left behind. It saddened him yet again to be involved with another old and lonely friend whose only legacy to the world seemed to be a few memories left to those remaining. It was a melancholy and depressing affair for him, and again brought into sharp focus the blessings bestowed on his own undeserving existence. The glumness for John was further increased as it was the last of the connections emanating from his beginnings in Cooma.

John and Livinia were now increasingly alone in the evenings as the children were now mostly leading their own lives away from the homestead. On one of these evenings, the cosy tomb-like silence was interrupted by the telephone ringing in the hallway. Livinia always answered it as it was usually for her nowadays. She re-entered the living room to announce to John that it was for him and seemed to be something about a distant cousin. John sat upright and felt a sense of unease. The last thing he needed was contact with the family with whom he had spent an unpleasant childhood.

Livinia tried to listen to the conversation but the telephone was too far away for her to hear properly. John spoke for quite some time then returned with a rather worried look about him.

'Who was that, dear?' she asked.

'That was a ghost from the past,' he replied cryptically. 'Remember I told you about the Merritts, my cousins whom I lived with as a child?'

Livinia nodded.

'Well, that was someone called Meredith Sebastian – what a name, eh? Anyway, she's Eleanor's daughter. Eleanor was the youngest of the three kids I lived with and a proper little *b* she was too. Anyway, they want to call in to meet us in August when they return to Sydney from their skiing holiday in the mountains. What do you think?'

'That would be nice for you, John. You never mention your relatives. I'd like to meet them myself.'

'I'm not so sure you would, you know. I'm not too sure I want to either after all this time. I was never that close to them at all,' he said, thinking back on the things he had missed out on while they experienced it all.

'Is it definite?' asked Livinia.

'They'll ring back and confirm it, but I think so, towards the end of August.'

'How did she track you down?'

'Meredith is into genealogy and has all the family on a tree. I'm not sure I approve of that. She found me through the internet. I told you I don't like all this new stuff.'

'Well, what harm can a visit do?'

John was wondering the same thing, only he had a reason to fear reawakening family connections, given his seedy departure and the heist he inflicted on them as a parting gift.

True to her word, Meredith contacted them again nearer the time when their booking was definite for their chalet. They would go on their skiing trip then on the return, call in to see John. It was arranged for late August. Livinia was excited at the prospect of meeting family and made extravagant preparations well in advance. It was with unrestrained eagerness that she awaited their arrival. Not so for John.

Eleanor Hewitt and her daughter Meredith, who also had a daughter aged thirteen named Chloe, drove slowly along the gravel road looking for the signs they had been told to look for. Eventually they came to a more bushy area and then a large fenced entrance with the cattle grid set back from the fence line. Meredith stopped the car and looked around. There was the letterbox just as John had described with the letters RMB 139. On the solid post near it was the name plate with the word 'Bridgehead' painted in white.

This must be the place, she thought, and turned slowly into the drive and headed up the slight incline into the thick bush. The large trees were slightly swaying in the cold breeze and the road looked foreboding as it entered deeper into the scrub. *John did say he lived in the bush.* Eleanor was a little apprehensive as she was unsure what to expect.

They meandered through the dense trees and shortly after following the main track to the right, came out into the open country John had described. Meredith was a little stunned and pulled up in the middle of the driveway. There in front of them was the vista of expansive paddocks dotted with sheep and cattle with the homestead in the close foreground. The view extended into the distance for what seemed like an eternity to those in the car. The contrast between the foreboding timber country and the pleasant pastoral scene was startling to the weary travellers. Eleanor was amazed. She said to Meredith, 'He must have married well.'

Meredith replied, 'What do you mean, Mum?'

'Well, he left home at seventeen with nothing. This must come from her.'

'Whatever. It's beautiful, if not a bit isolated. Let's go down and meet them.'

Meredith restarted the car and they wound their way slowly along the gravel road towards the house. She drove in under the large porch as John had instructed.

John walked over to the passenger door and helped the elderly lady alight from the car. Eleanor was a slim, petite woman with short, greyish hair and well dressed. *As usual* with most women, John noticed, *she had on far too much make-up.*

He kissed her on the cheek and said, 'Hello, Eleanor. Nice to see you again. You haven't changed that much in all these years. I'd still recognise you as Eleanor.'

'Hello, John. You look very well. Nice to see you again, too. John, this is my daughter, Meredith Sebastian and my granddaughter, Chloe.'

John stretched out his right hand to greet Meredith, but she stopped, with both arms outstretched and said, 'Haven't you got a kiss for your cousin?' and she went forward and embraced him effusively, muttering all the time how wonderful it was to finally meet this long-lost relative. Chloe tentatively extended her hand in contrast. Livinia received the same treatment in turn from each of the visitors, as they all chattered on the porch. Finally, Livinia remarked how cold it was and asked them all to come inside where it was warmer.

Eleanor retrieved some shopping bags from the boot of the car and then led the way through the double wooden doors into a large tiled open foyer where an antique wooden coat rack stood for them to hang their coats and scarfs. The house echoed to the sound of the heavy doors being closed and then there was only the rhythmic ticking of the long-case clock opposite the coat rack. Livinia led the way through the dark hall out to the glassed-in sun room where there was an inviting and welcoming spread laid out on the low-set table.

There was a crocheted lace tablecloth that draped onto the polished wooden floor. Livinia motioned to them all to be seated. Eleanor appreciated that Livinia had gone to a lot of trouble to make them feel welcome. The three visitors each glanced around the room and then out through the windows onto the expanse of scenery that stretched forever into the distance.

'What a lovely room,' Eleanor finally said. Meredith nodded demonstrably in agreement.

'Yes,' replied Livinia, 'we spend a lot of time in here if the weather permits.'

'Funny,' commented Eleanor, 'we all thought you'd gone to Queensland, John. We'd never had thought to look for you in New South Wales, especially in this cold country.'

John thought he detected a hint of condescension in her tone, aloof superiority almost. He was also aware that any conversation was going to be news to Livinia, whom he had no doubt was all ears. After a small pause, he replied softly, 'I did go to Queensland for a while but eventually ended up here. It's a long story but I love living here. I find the heat and humidity a bit hard to take further north.'

'And how long have you lived here?' asked Meredith in a more genuinely interested tone.

'Many years now,' John answered. 'I moved here in about 1958.' He knew that would cause minds to be doing quick calculations.

Livinia sensed John's mild discomfort, so interrupted the conversation to ask who was for tea or coffee. Eleanor reached down to her parcels and presented some cakes and biscuits she had purchased in Jindabyne. She always followed the country custom of never arriving anywhere without some contribution. While Livinia was out of the room, Eleanor asked if the food on the table was homemade. John said that Livinia was very pleased to have visitors and always went to a lot of trouble.

There was a noticeable silence, John wondering what to say next, Eleanor thinking furiously, trying to compute dates and time to calculate how soon after leaving home he had managed to be in this place. She wondered how that could have been. Her thoughts were interrupted for the moment by John asking, 'Do you ski often?' looking at Meredith.

'Mum has a share in a chalet in Smiggin Holes and we come down every season to the fields to ski,' she replied. 'Do you get snow here?'

'Not to ski on, but it does occasionally sleet and snow here briefly. Usually once or twice a year.'

Livinia returned with a tray full of teapots and water and began pouring the tea. They all chattered for an hour or so. Livinia asked to be excused while she went to attend to the lunch. She returned shortly afterwards to ask John to show the guests where the facilities were and then to escort them to the dining room.

The dining room was a large formal room with ornate furnishings and curtained walls. It was elegantly presented with a large dining table with six high-backed chairs along its sides and a carver at each end. It was formally set with silver cutlery and fine china crockery. There was an ornate pottery epergne adorning the centre of the spacious table. The room was cosily warm as the open log fireplace was blazing away in the centre of the far wall. Livinia then wheeled in the serving trolley laden with baked vegetables, sauces and what looked like half a lamb sitting in a large baking dish still sizzling.

'I don't eat meat,' announced Chloe with a haughty air. There was a stunned silence on behalf of John and Livinia, but a knowing nod of acknowledgement from the other two ladies.

'Yes, she's a vegetarian,' offered Meredith by way of casual explanation. John was furious. He could feel his hackles rising already.

'Livinia's been all morning preparing this,' he announced sternly.

'Well that's too bad. I'm not eating any animals,' responded Chloe.

John looked at Eleanor then at Meredith and announced that it was bad manners to refuse hospitality. Chloe defiantly declared that it was evil and cruel to eat animals and we would all pay for it one day. John again looked at the two older ladies, then turning his fearsome countenance towards Chloe, announced in a deep but soft voice, resonant with authority, 'Well, my child, you should be more respectful of the feelings and efforts of others. It is only the labour of others who do all the dirty work that allows you to live the pure life and bask in the safety of such ideology and opinions. If you were closer to the environment and real world that you so fondly advocate, you'd soon see that the heart is very uncaring in nature. There is no sentiment in God's creation.'

John cast a withering stare at Chloe and then turned his

formidable intent to her mother and grandmother. They stared at him. By now Livinia had regained her composure and smoothed the whole thing over, offering Chloe a large plate of vegetables only and apologising for not asking. John was seething. *Not a good start to a family reunion.* He was most mortified at how both Eleanor and Meredith allowed a mere child to rule the situation. *That would never have happened in my day.*

The lunch was now conducted in a sombre note and accompanied by much clanking of cutlery on china, with only a smattering of small talk. While Livinia was clearing away the evidence of the first course, Eleanor finally asked John about his family.

'Do you have any children?' she asked.

'We have four children. Ethan, our eldest boy is finishing his Ag degree at UNE. Audrey, our elder daughter, is studying law in Sydney. Our next son, Damien lives over the road on another property managing that. And our youngest daughter, Hannah works for the council in town and lives there during the week. She usually comes home for the weekend.'

Livinia re-entered the room and sat at the table to allow time between courses. She arrived just in time to hear John saying, 'What about you?' more in deference to his guests rather than any real interest. 'And how's the rest of the family?'

'Well,' Eleanor began, 'there's a lot happened in the years since you left us. When we arrived back home from the show we were greeted by a terrible shemozzle. Nan was furious. She really laid into poor old Dad for treating you so badly and letting you go. I didn't know he hadn't paid you for months. We all knew nothing about that side of things. Then there were all the holidays we were having while the place went to rack and ruin. I can see that now. Nan was beside herself. I was terribly sorry for poor old Dad. You knew William, my older brother, was dead?'

'No!' gasped John in genuine shock. 'What happened?'

'Well he drowned up at the north coast in 1965. We never found his body but I reckon he was on drugs – that's what really killed him.'

'That's sad,' said John, recalling his own family's brush with drugs. 'But he was always wilful and head strong. Not enough discipline at home,' he risked opining.

Eleanor just nodded slowly. 'Anyway,' she continued, 'Dad never really got over that. Nor did Mum. But Dad just went downhill after that. Any interest he had in the property went with him. It just deteriorated into a mess. He finally employed a manager who was a pig of a man. His name was Neville. No one liked him. I reckon he robbed us blind. When Nan died, there was almost no money anywhere to be found. She was supposed to have a bit socked away. I reckon Neville took the lot. I left home after school and went to uni for a while. I finally married a law student. He became a barrister eventually, but we were never really happy together. My only consolation from him is Meredith. My younger brother lives in Brisbane and works for a large merchant bank with offices in Hong Kong and now China. He married a nice Chinese girl. They don't have any children. He travels a lot. When

Dad died we sold the farm and Mum now lives in a retirement home in Bathurst where some of her friends are as well. She's 90 next year.'

'Is she all there?' John asked.

'More or less. She has her moments, but she still knows us all and asks after the kids.'

'Maybe I should go and see her, if she'd still remember me,' John said. 'After all, she gave me a home when no one else did. I don't forget that much.'

'That'd probably be nice of you.'

After a long lunch, Livinia asked them all to sit in the lounge where it was more comfortable. John and Eleanor sat side by side to allow for easier conversing. John requested more information about his nan. Eleanor explained that she suffered badly from ill-health, especially after his departure.

'She was always going on about how useful you had been to her and reliable. She really missed you terribly. She didn't last long after you went. She left you some money in her will you know.'

'No, I didn't know that,' replied John. 'I never heard from anyone.'

'No, we all looked for you in Queensland but the solicitors said they could not locate you. I wondered how hard they really tried, you know. I think there was more in it for them if they didn't find you.'

Eleanor continued, 'After her death there were some papers in the safe.'

'No money you said?' replied John, his fears slightly

dissolving after those references about someone called Neville helping himself.

'Well, there was quite a bit actually but nothing like we expected. But to get back to the papers, what was the AJC?' she asked.

'I've no idea,' replied John. 'What is it?' He suddenly remembered the cryptic note in his old study with those very letters.

'None of us knew, well at the time anyway, but there were some papers there for a Mr Summers to become a member and receipts for all sorts of money. We assumed it was your father. Anyway apparently, according to Dad, your father had been very wealthy but lost it somehow.'

'Did your family get any of it?' he asked, guilty at the thought of having relieved them of most of it himself.

'I've no idea. Mum is still unclear about it but Dad often said John was entitled to a share of the cash. There wasn't enough to go around and by the time we paid off Dad's farm debts at the time, it had all but disappeared.'

The riddle of all those innuendos about John's money cropping up again made him feel uneasy. He did feel a slight relief at no accusations being levelled at him over any money shortages. But again there was the puzzling and bewildering arising of money belonging to John.

The visitors were keen to leave before dark as they had to be back in Sydney by the next day so wished to be underway. It had all been pleasant enough in the end and further meetings were agreed to by all. They retraced their steps along the winding gravel track that was John's entrance and stopped the car just before they entered the timber to have another look back over the property. The old lady appeared quite ill at ease for some time and was also jittery.

'It seems to me,' she finally blurted, 'that he has definitely climbed beyond his station – way beyond.'

'What on earth do you mean, Mum?' asked Meredith.

'Well, you saw that place. It's way beyond his ability to acquire that on his own, lording it over us like Lord Muck.'

'Mum! I do believe you're jealous,' replied Meredith with a grin.

'He was a very nice man, Mum. How could you be so ungrateful?'

'Well, when I think of all the advantages we've had compared to him and look at what he's got now, it seems odd.'

'Well I liked him, even if he was a bit bossy,' said Meredith.

'I didn't like him one bit,' chipped in Chloe, still smarting from the vegetarian quip from John.

'I hope to keep in touch with them. I really like Livinia too,' finished Meredith.

True to her wishes, Meredith did keep in touch. Every year after their stint at the ski lodge she would call in to visit, accompanied by whomever happened to be with her and Eleanor at the lodge. They also often met up when John and Livinia were in Manly staying at the unit. John was ambivalent about rekindling family ties for a number of reasons. One was his latent guilt and remorse at relieving them of quite a sizable stash of their cash. Although he did not dwell on the remorseful side so much when he reminded himself how they had treated him. It was not so much mistreatment; rather total neglect and ostracism at the hands of people who thought of themselves as his betters – probably still did.

Another reason was that he did not like many of the relatives he had met so far. In fact, he did not really like people very much and took to strangers only reluctantly, unlike Livinia, who thrived on people and missed their interactions very much.

It was, therefore, with much misgiving that John received the invitation to one of the Merritts' dowager great aunt's eightieth birthday celebrations to be held in her ancestral mansion on the North Shore. She was, Meredith advised him, a formidable woman, parsimonious, difficult and fearsome, and a lady not to be trifled with under any circumstances. The old lady, who was slightly infirm and mildly deaf, had expressed an interest in meeting this long-lost relative emanating through John's mother. She also used a walking stick, which she wielded with great effect at any unfortunate bystanders who did not obey her commands instantly.

Unfortunately for John however, her crowning cardinal sin was that she was the bearer of one of his most detested pretensions – a hyphenated surname. He was especially aggrieved at the prospect of mingling with a host of his distant relatives in every sense of that word, with whom he knew he would have nothing in common and probably totally abhor.

The party was to be an afternoon affair, continuing on into the evening for those able to remain. Livinia was looking forward to the gathering and the chance to meet quite a number of John's relatives. John was unenthusiastic and showed it by being dour and grim the day before driving to the estate.

As he feared, there were dozens of unlikable people there and endless quantities of strange children running amok about the grounds outside, but definitely not inside where the dowager remained ensconced on her throne being attended by servile relatives whom John thought were more engrossed in ingratiating themselves rather than attending her needs.

Eleanor and Meredith attended along with Arthur Merritt and his young Chinese wife. It was the first time John had met Arthur since leaving the Merritts in 1957. They had little in common then and appeared to have little now. However, as Meredith had hinted that John could be worth considerable money, this at least encouraged Arthur to be civil and reminisce about the early days. John chatted with a few people but found none were to his liking, especially as there was no one else there with any rural background.

Things livened up after dark, and the adults gathered in the large dining-lounge room. John had made himself known to the hostess earlier in the afternoon but spent very little time with her. She was exactly as he had predicted and satisfied himself with avoiding her the rest of the time. This was easy as she was chair-bound, needing her walking stick to manoeuvre about.

He quickly livened up when the old lady prodded Livinia with the stick and referred to her as farm girl. John sauntered over to the old lady and casually said, 'If you poke my wife one more time with that stick I'll break it over your chair.' He was menacingly bent over her face.

'I beg your pardon young man,' she demanded.

'You heard, sweetie,' said John condescendingly, but softly.

'Now listen here, bushy,' she announced, her voice taking on the tone of a wounded party and increasing in volume, 'how dare you speak to me like that. Get out of my sight. Now!' And with that gave him a whack on the leg. Silence descended on the room. Without a word, John grabbed the stick, which was made of lightweight, but strong, aluminium, and in one motion slammed it over the arm of the chair, breaking it in two and discarding the pieces on the floor in front of her. In a much more audible voice, he then announced to her, but for all to hear, 'There, now try to poke my wife with it, you obnoxious old bag.'

'I say, old man,' a voice was heard to say, coming from a man who was approaching John.

'Here, that's my mother,' was heard another.

'Please John, don't cause a scene,' he heard Livinia saying.

By now there was a bevy of concerned relations attending to the widow.

'Don't you know she's quite ill, mate,' one of the men said.

'She's dying,' another said. 'Show some respect.'

John turned to face the gathering throng and clasped Livinia's hand.

'I've never seen so much hypocrisy and disgraceful grovelling in my entire life,' he announced to the stunned audience. 'There's nothing wrong with that old trollop that a good flogging wouldn't cure. As for dying, I can assure you, even God is in no hurry to have her.' With that he headed for the door holding Livinia's hand.

The drive home was in total silence. Livinia was furious with him for causing such a rumpus and for removing her from a gathering where she was enjoying herself.

The next day was initially frigid at the Manly unit. John explained that he would not tolerate his wife being mistreated and Livinia calmed down, especially when she realised that he meant what he said about her defence. However, she regretted that line of possible acquaintances was now probably closed to her for ever.

That afternoon there were two 'phone calls to the flat. One was from the ever-reliable Meredith ringing to discuss the events of the evening and the reception from the others of the outcomes. The other was from another attendee who was shocked that anyone could act so despicably.

The major repercussion, however, came about three weeks later, when John received a telephone call one evening from another attendee. His name was Edison Hargraves. He wanted to tell John how much he admired his courage in confronting the 'old dragon of the family', and the other reason was to ask him some advice.

John was taken aback on both accounts. Apparently, Edison had been in touch with Meredith and discovered that John and Livinia would be in Manly during the next week. John agreed to meet him then, but not without a certain amount of trepidation. He seemed to fare badly whenever he had encounters with any of his family.

John thought little about it except to wonder why any of them would want to see him again, let alone ask advice of him. The small family gathering was arranged for the Saturday of their arrival and he left it at that.

On their arrival in Manly, Livinia went to a lot of trouble as usual whenever guests were invited. Edison, his wife Annabel, and their two young daughters duly arrived about eleven.

Edison began by discussing 'that' night and chuckling about the huge kerfuffle it had caused in the family. He again congratulated John on his bravery in standing up to the dowager. John felt it was a genuine appreciation and wondered why it was so. Edison introduced his wife, a fine young woman with a sculptured face and porcelain-like skin. She had shoulder-length, mousey-brown hair and held herself with dignity and humility. Strangely, John rather liked her.

Edison was about average height but slightly podgy around the middle and greying slightly on top. John judged him to be about thirty-five or so. The two children were reasonably behaved.

After lunch, Livinia cleared away the things into the kitchen and Annabel joined her, partly to leave the men alone and partly to chat with Livinia. John could see that Edison was a little nervous, so he asked the women and children to go and sit on the balcony and enjoy the view.

When finally alone, Edison began by asking, 'John, I was wondering if I might ask you for some advice about farming property?'

'Sure,' answered John. 'If I can be of help.'

'I've been looking at a small farm near Goulburn, but the country is similar to yours I would guess.'

'Yes,' he agreed. 'How big is it? And what are you planning to do on it?'

'Well, I'm not happy at work. There's a chance we'll be taken over and they're offering redundancies. I'm not sure what to do. I always wanted to have a small place.'

'What do you do, Edison?' asked John.

'I'm an accountant specialising in corporate matters and charters, things like that.'

John suddenly felt a tinge of pity for Edison. He hardly knew him, but already he rather liked him and fully understood the possibilities of being unhappy at work, something he had not experienced since purchasing Bridgehead. He also began to realise that Edison might not be the ideal person to be buying a farming property, especially with two small children.

'What's your wife feel about all this?' John asked.

'Well, she's not entirely in favour of it but understands how bad things are at work. I'm only looking at this stage.'

'How big is the place an' what's it run?' John asked again.

'It's only about one thousand acres, running mostly sheep.'

John could feel his heart slide a little. *This is not looking good.*

'Look Edison, I can go over all the details with you, but frankly, I'm not sure I'm your man anymore. My son Ethan is the real expert on the financial stuff. Would you like to come down to our place and we'll spend some time on it there?'

John could see Edison's demeanour visibly change.

'You mean come down to your farm? Could we? I mean, could I?'

'Sure, if that's convenient. I'll just have to ask Liv.'

The two men sat in silence for a brief moment.

'You've got a lovely place here, John,' he said finally.

'Yes, we're happy with it. The view's not that wonderful but it's so central to the beach and shops, and the ferry. Let me just go in and see the ladies for a minute.'

Annabel was a bit staggered with John's invitation, which Livinia wholeheartedly supported. Annabel knew her husband was serious about at least looking at a farm before deciding about his future. She had been grilling Livinia about life on the land and was not all that certain it was for her. They made arrangements to visit John in a few weeks when they knew Ethan would be at the property.

The Hargraves came to Bridgehead on the Saturday and were convinced to stay the night. They spent a torrid afternoon going through the intricacies of property management, covering all the aspects from animal husbandry to the particulars regarding government restrictions and legislation dealing with everything from workers compensation to limits on dam building. John could see that Edison was becoming more depressed with the gradual realisation that what he was planning was probably not viable.

Livinia and Annabel found they were very compatible and John felt saddened to see a man have his dreams so potentially destroyed. After a short discussion with Livinia, he decided to put a proposition to Edison. The two men sat on the veranda together and John began, 'Edison, what is it that you would like to do if the farming angle fails?'

'I'm afraid I'm only suited to accountancy. As I mentioned to you, I'd love to set up my own firm in the city, but don't think I can raise enough capital to establish myself,' he said despondently to John.

'What if I could arrange for you to get about one hundred or so square metres of office space in George Street? No promises, you understand.'

'I don't think I can afford the rent and the set-up costs.'

'What if I offered you access to that floor space rent-free for two years?'

'How can you do that?' he asked, confused. 'Besides, why would you?'

'Are you interested?'

'I might be. If you tell me why.'

John said little, other than to ask Edison to discuss it with his wife and think about it seriously. John would do the rest and all he would ask in return was a signed contract giving John twenty per cent of any nett return over the first two years, with an option for Edison to continue at a more normal commercial arrangement after that.

The upshot of that intriguing weekend was that Edison agreed to jump into the new business agreement with John's company before he was pushed by his employer into redundancy and unemployment. Edison was at a loss to know why John was so supportive of him and his family and how he could manage it, since he was supposed to be this fire-brand farmer from the back-blocks of Cooma.

John's solicitor did all the legal work and Edison was offered a small office on the sixth floor of the building in which he himself had his own registered head office. Edison had managed to bring across with him a few of his own clients so he had a base from which to begin the difficult job of building up his business in the city. Deep down, Edison realised that he probably would not really make a go of something so chancy as farming, with his limited experience.

Livinia was yet again astounded by the enigma that was her husband. He had no sooner torn up any chance of her having some new in-laws to befriend with his antics at the eightieth, when he turns it into a chance to help one of them in a manner that few people either would or could. She was very supportive of his endeavour as she had made a deepening friendship with Annabel.

John and Livinia were coping well with what life was throwing at them as they prepared to settle into the routine of an older couple with diminishing family responsibilities. However, unplanned by them was an event that was to have far-reaching influences not only on them but on the rest of the family and for a long time into the future.

CHAPTER 10

The only thing that prevented Thomas going into juvenile detention resultant from what was to be his final appearance in the Children's Court, was the agreement of his grandparents, John and Livinia, to taking over his supervision at their own home. This had arisen due to Livinia suggesting it to the Court. John had grave reservations but Audrey seemed ambivalent to Thomas's fate and wellbeing. In fact, it was apparent she was grateful to be rid of his presence in her otherwise happy, carefree life.

The Court agreed to an order that removed Thomas from his apparently incompetent parents as far as his welfare was concerned, and his placement with his distraught grandparents at their family property outside Cooma. Contact with his mother and her de facto was to be limited, if not discouraged, and all responsibility placed with the grandparents.

Thomas was released into the care of John and Livinia that afternoon and he was to be removed to Cooma. The trip back from the unit in Manly was a depressing and sullen affair with Thomas sulking in the back and gazing out the window.

It was now late winter and Thomas had few possessions. He had no experience of the bitter Monaro winters. John was not relishing these first few days as Thomas would not fit easily into an ordered family existence. *How could he after the miserable deprivation of existence in Audrey's weird way of life?*

Thomas was shown his room and a few of the facilities of the house, then some rules would be laid down. John looked at his defiant and nervous grandson, who sat derisively at the sparse wooden table in the kitchen. He was thin and weedy, especially for his age, with unkempt ratty dark hair. His pale and puny body suggested enduring neglect. Thomas had intense, defiant eyes that spoke of inner intelligence and cunning. His countenance radiated uncertainty, but reflected latent aptitude.

John surmised that Thomas had gained his sharp mind from his undoubtedly intelligent mother, but probably also from his unknown father, who may have been a charismatic lecturer or young professor from the university who took advantage of Audrey when she was so vulnerable and susceptible to such persuasion. It was of little consequence right now, however, as this young man was in serious trouble, and John and Livinia were his last chance at redemption.

Livinia prepared a wholesome dinner after their disrupted last few days. Thomas immediately began to eat but was halted by a fearsome command from John.

'You wait for your grandmother to be seated before you start.'

Thomas was startled by the order and dropped his cutlery, staring with a puzzled, slightly fearful look at John.

'Then we say grace,' John announced. Thomas looked at his plate and then at Livinia for reassurance.

'We always say grace before every meal,' she said in a soft and comforting voice, trying to smile at him reassuringly. After Livinia was seated and grace was said by John, it was indicated to Thomas that he could begin. Both John and Livinia were struck by Thomas's complete lack of table manners and they stared knowingly at each other. *That lesson would have to wait. Getting him to wait was enough for now.*

The next few days were fully occupied with familiarising Thomas with his new order, where John would be in charge and Livinia next in line. There was nothing for it but to begin his rehabilitation by accompanying John on all his tasks about the property. It would be a difficult responsibility, as Thomas had no knowledge of farm work, let alone having done any of the myriad of activities. Thomas was kitted out with suitable clothing for hard physical work about the farm.

John started off in the new stockyards he was half repairing, half building at the far end of the big property that he had bought from Frank. It was at some considerable distance from the house. Thomas was warned to pay attention and obey all of John's orders as farm work was full of potential hazards, especially for the inexperienced. Thomas started by helping to lift up the logs that were to be used for rails, and holding them in position while John twisted them in place with heavy-gauge tie-wire. It was strenuous work for a young unfit lad working in unfamiliar surroundings. Boredom quickly set in.

After only a short time, and three or four rails, Thomas decided that he had had enough and unwisely, and indelicately, said so. In an instant, John had him by the scruff of the shirt collar with a massive and calloused hand, firmly gripping his throat rendering him unable to speak and only able to breathe with difficulty.

'Don't you ever speak to me like that again,' he bellowed, his iron grip tightening and his huge powerful arm now pinning Thomas to the half-hung rail. Thomas tried to speak but nothing happened.

'You will do exactly as you are told and exactly when I tell you. Always!' With that he hurled Thomas forcefully out into the centre of the yard where he sprawled inelegantly onto the sparsely grassed dirt like a tossed bag of potatoes. He got up defiantly and dusted himself, turning and glaring at John. John could see him weighing up his options just as a cornered calf or sheep did. John could also feel that unsettling anger rising in him that had manifested itself with Quiggin's men on the fence-line just after he had bought the place; the same anger with which he had evicted tenants from the flat in Manly years ago; and the same loss of control he exhibited at the eightieth when Livinia was mistreated. It was a feeling he was uncomfortable with because he sometimes felt he could lose control and do something he might later regret.

While Thomas stood glaring, his nostrils flaring as he

drew quick short breaths, John strode over with a fierce countenance to the lad, who was now rubbing his arm as if hurt. He quickly raised his fists, but John struck him firmly on the face and he crumpled again to the dirt, this time holding the side of his head.

'Come on lad, if you're game?' he fumed. Thomas stood up slowly and began to puff again with short breaths. John stood towering over him menacingly with legs apart and a firm resolve in his face.

'Now, this is your last warning and your last chance, mate. You better decide right here and now what you're gonna do because you only have two choices. One is jail and the other is working your bum off here with me until you're knackered every night. So what's it gonna be?'

Thomas began to shake a little, pulling at his dusty, grass-stained clothes. John could see he was sorting out his options in his mind.

'Well, what's it gonna be?' he asked again.

Thomas had never been treated like this before in his life. He was used to the soft and amenable people associated with his mother and all her cohorts. They were always on about individual rights and doing your own thing, children's rights, and personal freedom. This was a new experience, being severely treated by an authority figure. He stared at John and quickly comprehended that John had the whip hand. He lowered his gaze and sauntered back to the rail without a word.

'Wise move,' stated John.

Together they resumed the steady assembly of the rails to the posts that John had put in over the previous months. John was so heated up that he refused to halt for morning tea and worked at a furious pace, even for him. By lunch time he had calmed down a little and decided to break for a later than normal lunch that Livinia had prepared for them.

In unpleasant silence, they ate the lunch and sat awkwardly together, Thomas sulking slightly from the altercation and the weariness of such unaccustomed hard work, and John from the regrettable incident that he hoped would at least straighten out their relationship from the beginning. There was still a long afternoon ahead with a lot of rails requiring assembly.

The afternoon passed in sullen silence, but Thomas worked steadily and without any more whinging. John detected a mellowing of attitude and a grudging acceptance of the situation on Thomas's part, at least for the time being. During the course of the day John's temper subsided and he regretted slightly his outburst. He tried to balance the eruption, at least in his mind, by arguing that Thomas needed to understand how serious his position was and that someone was at last in control of him.

They laboured well into the evening before John announced that it was time to go. He was slightly dreading returning home in case there were any repercussions about the altercation. Thomas was covered in grass stains and dirt as well as sporting a sizable facial injury that would have to be explained.

John parked the vehicle in the shed and asked Thomas to

go in and prepare for dinner. His entry into the kitchen was greeted with a relieved Livinia followed by an interrogation as to the cause of the injury. Thomas dismissed his appearance as being the result of stockyard labour and a slight trip while moving timber.

It was John's habit of returning from outdoors and having a shower and changing clothes before having dinner. This was a novelty for Thomas, whose personal habits were less than scrupulous.

By the end of the evening, John could see that Thomas was exhausted from unaccustomed hard manual labour, compounded by the confusion of the abrupt change in his young life. John was impressed that Thomas seemed to accept the discipline.

The days slowly drifted into a week as Thomas settled in, and John and Livinia gradually began to fit this huge disruption into their lives. As the time passed, Thomas became accustomed to the constant hard work, the early morning rises and the evening cleanup, all accompanied by Livinia's marvellous cooking, something he had never experienced before. He became less reticent and more agreeable as the rhythm of their lives took on the semblance of permanency and routine.

When the monthly service was due at their local church, Thomas was told that he would accompany them.

'I'm not goin' to that sort of thing,' he defiantly informed them.

'It's non-negotiable, Thomas,' stated John firmly. 'You will be with us at all times. That is the arrangement.'

'You don't really believe in all them fairy tales, do you?' he asked with all the assurance of youth.

'Have you ever actually read the Bible?' asked John.

'Of course not! That's for people with no power in their lives.'

'Is that your opinion Thomas, or that of those you overheard?'

Thomas looked sheepishly at John.

'I thought so,' said John. 'Well don't comment on things you know nothing about. And you better pay attention,' finished John.

It was a mild Sunday and the church had the usual small attendance. John and Livinia spent time after the service chatting with the few attendees that they had come to know very well. They arrived home in time for a late lunch. During the course of the meal, John asked Thomas, 'What did you learn this morning?'

'Nothin',' answered Thomas defiantly.

'You mean you sat there for an hour and came away with nothing?'

'Yeah.'

'How can that be?'

'I told you I don't believe in all them fairy tales. God, and Adam an' Eve, and virgin births and all that stuff.'

'But you've never read the Bible.'

'So?'

'Well how can you comment on something you've never even read? As for virgin births, we've been doing it for years now.'

'What d'yer mean, doin' it for years?'

'Haven't you heard of invitro fertilisation?'

Thomas shrugged.

'What about cloning?'

Thomas nodded.

'Well, it's taken us till now to be able to do that so don't you think God is capable of doing that too and thousands of years ago?'

'That's not the same.'

'Isn't it? Starting today you can begin reading the Bible a bit at a time and we'll discuss what you read. Then we'll see what you can learn.'

'Why would I want to do that? Besides, I'd rather be with the stupid sheep than readin' that.'

'Why are the sheep so stupid?' asked John.

'Well of course they are. Stupid things lettin' us treat 'em like that,' replied Thomas.

'There are one hundred and fifty million sheep in Australia and only fifteen million of us. Who spends all their time looking after whom? Not the sheep. They can't be all that stupid. Alright, here's something else you can read,' said John, getting up from the table and retrieving a large book from the bookcase. He placed it on the table in front of Thomas and opened it up near the front. Then he said, 'You read this bit here on sheep anatomy and reproduction then tell me what you pick up.'

Thomas fingered the large volume and read with disdain the subject headings. 'Alright,' he agreed, 'if I must.'

Thomas removed himself from the table, and clutching the large animal husbandry book, sauntered dejectedly to his room, muttering under his breath. He spent the afternoon alternately gazing out the window and reading passages from the book, aware that John would probably be enquiring what he had learnt. John was able to spend the whole afternoon in his office, a pastime that had diminished considerably with the advent of Thomas's arrival.

When Livinia finally called to them that dinner was ready, Thomas knew that the conversation was going to be renewed from where it had finished earlier. He was right. John began by asking, 'Well, did you learn anything of interest?'

'I must admit I never knew that sheep could be so complicated. All that stuff about adjusting automatically to the climate around them is pretty neat.'

'There's an awful lot you don't know,' said John.

'Yeah, it's pretty complicated about how they breed, an' all that, isn't it?'

'Do you think all that happened by accident, do you?'

'What do you mean?' asked Thomas.

'Well it's so complex, do you think it all came about by chance?'

'What d'yer mean?'

'If it's so complex, wouldn't you think someone designed it all to happen that way?' asked John.

'Yeah, I guess so. I s'pose it's possible.'

'Well, keep an open mind. The more you learn, the more you realise the less you know. Then if it's possible to be all planned out, don't you think there's a place for God in there?'

'I don't know about that,' said Thomas. 'I s'pose so,' he said again.

'Well,' continued John, while Livinia looked on silently, 'I can make you read but I can't make you believe. I can make you read about sheep, but I can't change your mind. That's up to you. If you start to believe or change your opinion, that's a gift from God. You don't earn it, it's a gift. You don't have to do anything else but believe and search,' said John.

Thomas was looking down at the table and fidgeting slightly, but it was the first real talk that they had had since his arrival. John was rather pleased at the attention Thomas had paid to his preachings and the apparent understanding of some of the points he was trying to make. *Getting this streetwise urchin to mend his ways was always going to be difficult but maybe today a few encouraging steps had begun.* John, enthused by how seemingly well it was going, decided to finish on just one final note, 'Just remember, belief is a gift. Your coming here is not our doing. God must see something in you that He wants you to be saved from your previous life.'

After Thomas had departed for his room, Livinia grasped John's hand, leaned over and kissed him gently on the cheek.

'You were wonderful today. I really hope he will turn around a bit.'

'You know, I really didn't know how to get to him, but maybe there is a way. You know what that boy needs is some real responsibility. And you know what? I might just have the thing.'

'What's that?' asked Livinia.

'Well, what we need is either a puppy or maybe a lamb for him to raise for starters.'

'Are there any?' she asked.

'There will be something shortly. I just need to look out for it. In the meantime, if I can just get him to show some interest in things we might get somewhere.'

The next day, John took Thomas over to Damien's farm to help him with moving irrigation pipes and maintenance work on the engines preparatory to the coming summer, when the plant would all be working incessantly. Thomas seemed to have an affinity with engines and mechanical devices. Suddenly, John had a brainwave. *Why not set Thomas the task of repairing Frank's old Land Rover that had sat mostly idle since shortly after his death?*

John was still fond of the memories of Frank and could not bring himself to either remove the vehicle or actually maintain it; he just left it as a reminder. *Maybe it could be put to better use rehabilitating young Thomas.*

Thomas was at first less than enamoured at the suggestion, but he was finally won around when it was pointed out that he could keep it to use if he could repair it properly. Thomas helped Damien move it over to John's place, which involved a bit of problem-solving and learning to co-operate all thrown in together.

It took a few days for Damien to be ready and available to remove the old Rover, and together, with the use of a tractor and a trailer, they were able to bring it over to the main house, where Thomas could start working on it. Thomas was no mechanic, but showed surprising enterprise and learning ability with all things mechanical.

John wanted to find some living responsibility for Thomas, and the opportunity soon arose once lambing commenced. There were inevitably casualties when dealing with livestock and normally not all lambs survived or some of the ewes did not make it. There were two lambs that were motherless and John took this opportunity to pass them onto Thomas to raise. Thomas took to lamb-raising with surprising gusto and proved quite adept at it, once the initial bugs in understanding bottle-feeding lambs were ironed out. Now he had two things to occupy him, Frank's old Land Rover and two lambs to attend to.

One of the issues that created serious concern was Thomas's education. Initially it was not an issue because saving him from detention was the first priority. However, his education would need to be addressed. It was generally agreed that Thomas could not be sent into Cooma to attend school unaccompanied. This created problems, as Thomas was still only fourteen and was legally required to attend school. Livinia spent many hours wrestling with this issue. In the end, she decided it would be best if he could do some sort of technical training, *but what sort?* She had sent off for prospectuses from all sorts of institutions and TAFE colleges and was trying to determine what would best suit him. This was a topic that Thomas was reluctant to address, and Livinia dreaded the arguments she knew she would again have with John over education.

On a couple of occasions she had broached the subject with Thomas but received a cool response. She knew it could not be put off too much longer however. She gathered her literature onto the big dining room table and braced herself for the inevitable showdown with both Thomas and John. She called them in on a quiet Sunday afternoon and asked them to sit with her.

'Thomas,' she started, 'it's time we talked about your going to school.'

'I'm not interested in that at all,' he said matter-of-factly. 'Besides, I'm really happy here doin' farm work.'

'That's all very well but you must get some proper education as well.'

'Why must I?' he asked.

'Your grandmother's right,' said John quietly. Livinia was stunned. *What, no argument?* Emboldened, she continued, 'It's all very well to play with the animals and cars, but part of our arrangement is that you receive adequate schooling.'

'Yes,' agreed John, much to Livinia's amazement. 'Thomas, education is the key to your future. Don't you like working with the animals and all the different engines on the farm?'

'You know I do.'

'Well, you need to learn much more than I can teach you here. It's very important that you get some qualifications.'

Livinia was so grateful that John was in agreement that she smilingly thrust a couple of books in front of Thomas to keep the momentum going. It was finally agreed that Thomas would receive some agricultural training from a technical establishment that specialised in remote education. Livinia would arrange it all. John was a little surprised that Livinia would initiate a schooling programme that centred around rural training.

Ethan completed his tertiary studies at the university with distinction. He was itching to implement a raft of ideas and innovations on the property that he felt was ripe for improvement. He and John had animated discussions about his ideas but John was quite truculent about change. He accommodated those required by law such as electronic tagging of stock and followed restrictions incurred by diseases but was defiant about really modernising his farm. This created a healthy conflict between them, but neither appreciated the stand-point of the other very well. The one subject John refused to ever discuss was selling off the non-farm assets in order to acquire more grazing country. Despite the ever-increasing costs and taxes on investment properties, John regarded them as a solid back-up. Besides he was sentimental about the places he had acquired in his earlier days.

One other thing Ethan had managed to bring back from his time at university was a wife. He had met her at university while they were both students of agriculture. She was regarded as a Northern Tablelands local as she came from a long-established New England family that ran a prize-winning merino sheep stud and commercial and stud beef cattle. Her name was Sophie and she was quite a catch for Ethan as she was a very popular and attractive girl. John and

Livinia were delighted to meet her when she finally came down to visit during his final year at university.

John began to realise that some of Ethan's inspirations may have emanated from her family's direction. The impending marriage of Ethan created a small problem of where they were going to live. John was totally opposed to anyone using his old shed quarters. It was finally decided that initially they would have to be content to live in the main homestead. In time John agreed that a new smaller house could be built close by to accommodate the newly-weds.

It was ironic for John and Livinia, that as their own children required less of their time, Thomas appeared on the scene to occupy more of it. Thomas proved to be better than average as a student of rural subjects and learnt his new trade rapidly. He even adjusted to the requirements of technical study despite a complete lack of any background. Thomas slowly began to fit in with John's life and proved a solid assistant about the property. John taught him to use all the equipment and he became a competent horseman and stockman with both sheep and cattle.

In his final year of technical study, Thomas was required to complete a project to count towards his results. He was at a complete loss what to do when John finally had an inspiration. He could completely repair and rebuild the abandoned windmill located on the large block he had acquired from Frank. John had never thought it necessary to repair it as there was adequate water already on the property. If it were fixed, however, it could be used to pump water from there to the lucerne dam over the road on Damien's place. John was grateful that he had never had the time to dismantle it and now allowed Thomas a free hand as far as money was concerned to repair it, but stipulated that he must do or arrange all the repairs himself, not get in a contractor. In the end, Thomas found the project stimulating, but more importantly, he acquired a thorough knowledge of windmills and became the only one capable of maintaining it.

As time elapsed, John found he could devolve more responsibility to Thomas and he was reliable in return. The first real show of this trust occurred after Thomas had been there for three years. It was late in the bush fire season and inevitably there arose a serious fire sweeping in from the west and threatening their properties. The serious aspect would be if the fire gained a foothold up in the timbered country at the rear of the place. John had two heavy trucks set up as fire fighters and a small four by four used mostly for spot fires. Thomas was asked to take the small truck up to the timber line and try to prevent spot fires starting there while the rest fought the grass. They would join him there shortly. Livinia was filled with trepidation and seriously questioned the wisdom of this. John was adamant.

It was late in the night before the worst had passed but Thomas felt a real sense of achievement and for the first time he felt as if he were approaching adulthood. He asked to be allowed to drive the stock trucks to the sales unaccompanied and to pick up stock from various sales as required. John agreed and he was able to reduce the amount of time he spent hands-on.

In the early days, Livinia tried to encourage Audrey to visit Thomas at the farm, but this soon proved unsuitable. John could see that Audrey and her well-supplied offspring were an annoyance and irritation to Thomas, and John always took him far away when he knew they were coming, purposely so Thomas could avoid seeing his step-family. This irritated Audrey, but John was adamant, and in the end requested that Audrey refrain from visiting altogether, much to her chagrin. Thomas grew further away from his immediate family, as did John and Livinia; there was nothing in common. Thomas was slowly settling into the routine of his new life.

At one of the monthly sheep sales in Cooma, John was there with Thomas, who was unloading the sheep when a man John knew approached him.

'How yer going, John?' the man asked. John turned to see him and recognised him as one of the people who bought a lot of Frank's cattle when John was trying to reduce the numbers.

'Oh, g'day Ted,' he said, thrusting out his hand.

'Nice lot of sheep there, mate.'

'Yes, it's been good so far.'

'Is that your lad there?' asked Ted.

'No. He's my grandson.'

'You don't say,' said Ted, shaking his head. 'You short of labour are yer?'

'No mate. I've got my lads as well. Why do you ask?'

'I got a large run in Queensland and I'm lookin' for a head stockman or a manager. How would you feel if I asked him to think about it. Would you mind?'

John was stunned. He had never thought of Thomas as being sought after.

'No. No,' he said. 'I'm sure he'd give it serious thought and I'd never stand in his way,' replied John.

'I don't s'pose he knows anything 'bout windmills?' asked Ted.

John shook his head and grinned. There was a long silent pause, then John replied, 'Why do you ask?' he said, almost sure he already knew the answer.

'The place is watered by bore an' has a lot of windmills.'

'Funny you should ask that Ted, but as it happens he's quite an expert with windmills.'

'You don't say. How 'bout that, eh? Well, I'm still lookin', but he strikes me as a fine lad for that sort of work. I'll be in touch, maybe. Nice to see you again, John.'

'Yes, Ted. Likewise.'

John was suddenly struck with the reality that Thomas could be striking out on his own anytime, so he better enjoy his company while it lasted. When he thought back to that skinny ruffian who had never even seen a sheep or cow let alone become an expert, John was proud of his grandson. *It was so strange how that windmill came to be involved in all this. Good old Frank.*

That evening, as he sat in the lounge reading and Livinia was doing some needlework, John related the events of the day to her. She was less than enthusiastic at the suggestion, especially so far away in Queensland. John was just proud that someone else could see in Thomas so much as to possibly offer him a job. He would miss Thomas. He had come to look upon Thomas almost as compensation for the dual loss of Brendan and the estrangement of his daughter Audrey.

John did not have to wait long for the sequel. About a week later, Ted rang in the evening to speak to Thomas. John knew what it was about and waited with trepidation for Thomas to return to the room. He was some time on the telephone and then returned with a dazed appearance, announcing that he had been offered a job in Queensland as a head stockman, or probably manager if he wanted it. He had a week to think about it. Suddenly and without any warning, Thomas's life was potentially in turmoil. He was in a complete quandary what to do. John suggested they would all talk about it tomorrow.

It was an unexpected and difficult decision for Thomas. Livinia made it clear that she disapproved of the idea but would not prevent his going. John, on the other hand, left it entirely to Thomas but confided to Livinia that he secretly supported the proposition.

There was a lot to consider if Thomas agreed to depart. John was conscious that Thomas had no suitable transport for a start. He began to develop an idea that if Thomas did decide to go; he would at least be able to supply a new vehicle, probably a new ute or a Land Cruiser.

Thomas rang Ted a couple of times over the next few days and finally came to a decision. He advised his anxious grandparents that he was leaning towards accepting the offer to try his luck. Once this information was public, John began to encourage him openly to go, even though he would miss him enormously. Thomas was probably tipped over the edge by John's offer of a new vehicle. He proudly took delivery of a new Ford ute, which, he was informed, would be suitable for western Queensland as most of the roads were well maintained or even bitumen. It was a poignant moment when the time came for Thomas to drive out of Bridgehead for possibly the last time. Thomas was barely nineteen.

One person who would not miss Thomas entirely was Ethan. They did not always hit it off and Ethan was possibly a little jealous of the effort and respect that Thomas managed to glean from the family. Ethan was also becoming frustrated at the constant baulking by his father at any suggestions about upgrading the management of the grazing concerns. This was becoming evident to Livinia and John. But somehow, John could never bring himself to undertake the effort required to absorb all the learning necessary to master the latest practices. John was settling into a semi-stupor of total contentment and ease, and he had no particular desire to fight it, especially now that Thomas was gone. After all he was now well into his sixties.

This was about to change as circumstances were thrown up that John had not anticipated. Ethan came home one day from town with some startling news. He had seen that the property belonging to David Quiggin at the back of their own property was on the market. It had a common boundary along the back, up in the hilly, tree-covered back country. He gave John a brochure from the agent in town with the details about the sale. John had rarely seen Dave in the intervening years since his first encounters with him over the fences and the odd meeting in town. It gave him quite a start to realise that his long-time neighbour was selling up. He wondered why. John glanced at the spiel and asked if he could study it later as he placed it on the table.

John departed the chatting family and went into his office, where he closed the heavy door and entered into the silent world of his retreat. He sat in his chair for many moments reviewing the connections he and Dave Quiggin had shared. He clearly remembered that first meeting of Dave's offsiders up in the wilds of the timber where he was erecting his boundary fences after he first bought the place.

He recalled the time Dave drove into his shed compound with his attractive and haughty wife with the classy and sophisticated name of Imogene, and the strange turn of events that followed that conversation. John had always thought of Dave as a successful grazier, so it rather shocked him to learn that the property was on the market and in the hands of the mortgagees. That was not indicated in the advertisement but Ethan had gained that much from the agency. The reason for the sale was that the place was so debt-riddled that he would have to sell up. The last few years had been fatal, with continuous bad seasons and a long drought. All the more reason, John thought, for them to hang onto their assets off-farm for income so they did not also suffer the threat of succumbing to drought as well. It was precisely the abundance of diversified income sources that allowed John to manage his grazing enterprises so conservatively. He hoped Ethan would observe that lesson.

What John did not anticipate, however, was that Ethan had been seriously investigating the prospect of purchasing Dave's place and to incorporate its running into that of Bridgehead as a way of intensifying the management programme. When Ethan finally broached the subject, John dismissed the suggestion out of hand. But a few days later, Ethan again raised the topic and this time John could see that he was serious about the matter. John was a little taken aback but said he would think about it.

In fact, John had indeed been thinking about it. He had retreated several times to his office and closed the door to do some serious thinking. John retrieved several of the contour maps he possessed on the local area and perused them thoroughly. He had a rough idea where Dave's place was in relation to his own holdings. He also calculated and recalculated his financial position, and the relative strengths of all his assets in relation to servicing any costs and debts. He began to find the idea of acquiring the neighbouring property more attractive, purely from a business viewpoint. He had no desire to rub Dave's nose in his own success. As much as he hated to admit it, Ethan was possibly right in thinking that it did have potential benefits to his own enterprises. The clincher for John was the shrewd observation of Ethan's that this acquisition would expand the rural holdings enough to accommodate the growing number of third-generation children wanting work in the family business, something impossible on the smaller Bridgehead and Templemore properties. John was impressed with that argument. His old drive and vigour were being rekindled slowly over the following weeks as he considered the proposal.

John made an appointment with his old accountant and raised the issue of finances and debt. His accountant had been almost pleading with him to acquire some debt somewhere in order to reduce the complete, and in some ways, futile loss of revenue caused by the taxes, especially land tax on his city properties. John was convinced by the accountant that he could cope with an acquisition of this nature if he wanted to proceed.

A few weeks after Ethan had first raised the issue, he entered the familiar surrounds of the comforting family kitchen while John and Livinia were still seated at the table finishing lunch. After a few pleasantries, Ethan said, 'I don't s'pose you've thought any more about the Quiggin place have you?'

John looked at him for a moment, but made no reply.

'I thought not,' said Ethan with a resigned air of disappointment. 'You have no ambition at all anymore, do you Dad?'

John kept looking at his son and thinking about all the issues involved with the decision to buy or not to buy this property, or for that matter, any property.

'I'm sorry you won't think about it.'

'Well,' said John, in a low voice, 'you're wrong there, son.' There was another long pause, then he continued, 'I have actually.'

'Have what, actually?' asked Ethan.

'I have actually given it a lot of thought.'

'And?' asked Ethan, knowing full well what the answer was going to be.

'I've decided that you might just have a sound basis for your argument.'

'What?' he demanded, unsure of the meaning. 'What d'you mean?'

'I agree that you may have a sound argument.'

'You mean you will buy it?' he asked excitedly.

'No,' announced John very calmly, 'I mean, if you prepare me a sound and thorough plan to show me your ideas for that place for the next ten to fifteen years, I might then consider it as an option.'

'You serious?' asked Ethan, gaining in enthusiasm.

John looked at Livinia and smiled slightly. Then he continued, 'As I said, I have given this a lot of thought over the last few weeks and I agree with a lot you say. It has a lot of potential to suit our future, but I need a careful analysis of the whole situation. You up to it?'

'Am I what!' announced Ethan. 'Look, I have a few ideas in my head already. Listen to this.'

The next few hours went by in a haze of figures and ideas, mostly from Ethan. John was impressed so far with the thought he had devoted to the idea, but wanted much more before he would commit to it. John finished by asking that the whole thing be kept quiet from everyone until all the facts were laid out.

Ethan spent a lot of time and energy preparing a submission to present to John and Livinia, with hopes of passing it onto a full family meeting the following Sunday.

The family meetings had drifted into merely being an excuse to socialise and indulge in the entertainment expertise of Livinia, who adored having the large family gatherings. She excelled herself with enormous lunches, followed by a contented brood of satiated offspring whiling away the Sunday afternoons chatting about family matters and discussing the business details of their varied enterprises. This Sunday, however, there was an air of expectation as there was a rumour that something more serious was afoot; a rare occurrence nowadays, as everybody knew John was more than happy with everything going along just as it was.

The after-lunch joviality was this time replaced with a more sombre note of sobriety. John asked all to be quiet while he outlined a proposition that had been raised by Ethan. There was a long and animated exchange of opinions that lasted well into the late afternoon as all the pros and cons were raised, noted and discussed. A final decision was postponed until the following Sunday when a vote would be taken, but the general consensus was leaning towards being favourable to Ethan's request to add to their holdings.

In the meantime, John and Ethan had agreed to thoroughly investigate the property by conducting an inspection arranged through the advertising agent. This they did on the Tuesday. John knew a bit about Dave's place before they went there. From the top of the timbered ridge at the back of Bridgehead, John had often stared out through the trees and over the vast expanse of the next valley. It was an enormous valley that stretched many miles across to the next hills, with a sizable and permanent river that ran through the grassy plain to eventually join up with the Murrumbidgee. It was a more settled valley than John's property and was also located much closer to Cooma than his.

He also knew that Dave had accumulated about fifteen thousand acres of fairly prime sheep country and also cropped quite a bit of the flats that bordered the trout-bearing river. On inspection, however, John was shocked to observe that the property was extensively over-grazed and showed all the signs of neglect, or more to the point, abuse. There were considerable areas of weed infestation and much of the pasture was actually damaged. It turned his head to see such disregard. John considered that Dave must have been forced into this position by circumstances, as he considered him a man who would not deliberately or wilfully exploit his environment.

The sad state of the property rather overshadowed John's inspection. He tended to miss some of the other vital features that the property offered. There was a modern, sumptuous, double-brick homestead and many outbuildings and sheds, including two other residences. The property was well watered with many well-fenced paddocks and several yards. There was a large collection of modern machinery and implements, and the stock was of good quality.

Ethan seemed pleased with the prospect of acquiring the property and John wondered what he saw in it compared with what else they might purchase for roughly the same sort of money, even if it were further away or in another region. John was rather disappointed, but was not going to be able to discourage his family from pursuing development or expansion forever.

John went for a long drive up to the back of his property in the old Land Rover and drove slowly along the well-used fire trail that ran along the ridge through the timber country. He stopped regularly to inspect sites that may be suitable for creating an entrance road that would give his family easier access to the back property, if by chance they did buy it, as it was a long way around from the Bridgehead homestead to Dave's place using the public roads. That was because Dave was in another valley altogether, which used a different road to reach it. While he was so occupied in the quiet wilds of the tranquil timber reaches of his beloved property, John did some deep thinking about this proposed enterprise. He decided to ring Thomas that evening to gauge his opinion.

Livinia often rang Thomas in the evenings, sometimes about once a week, but this time John requested to be able to speak to him as well, something he did not always do. Thomas seemed to be happy working in Queensland but John thought he had detected a mild dissatisfaction creeping in over the last year or so as Thomas mastered the conditions and found less stimulation and reduced challenges in his chosen field. He even admitted to John of actually missing sheep work, something he never thought he would hear from Thomas. Then John told Thomas about the chance to buy the adjoining property that backed onto his own and what did Thomas think about that idea.

There was a long pause on the other end of the line and then Thomas answered by asking John what was involved and what condition the place was in.

'Pop, you know that the way of the future is in technology and genetics. Why would you want to buy a rundown place that needs maybe millions spent on it to bring it up to scratch when you can buy one already setup?'

While John was engaged in deep thought, Thomas continued, 'I bet Ethan is behind this.'

'Why would you say that?'

'Well,' continued Thomas, 'it's just the sort of thing Ethan would want to build up to prove he can do it, rather than just buy one ready to go. You know, *I can do what Dad did too* sort of thing.'

John was stunned by these comments. He did not realise just how perceptive and astute Thomas was when it came to business and family matters. It was an insightful observation.

'So you're not in favour then?'

'No, I didn't say that. It all depends on the business aspects of the deal. If it's a good buy then it's probably okay. But if that sort of money will buy a high-tech set-up, why wait years while you build it up? They can be labour-intensive you know.'

John continued to speak with Thomas for over half an hour gleaning from him his understanding about the future of primary production in Australia, given the constraints placed on it by climate, changing demands and environmental considerations. John was again impressed with his grandson, the once wild and recidivistic young man who had entered their tranquil lives so many years ago. John longed to have Thomas return. He wondered how he might manage that.

John spent many days quietly talking to his family, sounding them out about buying Dave's place. All seemed in favour of it, almost as though they had all been infected with the enthusiasm of Ethan for this project.

John had two thoughts about it. He was unsure whether to engage in debt finance in order to ensure that the family would grow to appreciate the necessity of keeping the city buildings as a sure source of secure income. This was to pay back the debt if farming conditions deteriorated to a point where this was impossible. The other point was that they might simply see the city assets as a way to pay off debt by selling them. Either way he was concerned that his beloved investments would be sold off after he was gone. He was unsure how to protect them for the long-term security of the whole set of enterprises.

At the following Sunday family meeting, there was to be a vote on this issue. John heard them pass their opinions about the project. He spoke last and indicated he was not entirely in favour but would be guided by the majority. The majority wished to proceed. It would be left to Ethan to secure the purchase. John passed two stipulations about the deal. Because of the parlous state of the pasture, he insisted that the place be bought bare of stock and he also insisted that the project be run and managed entirely by Ethan with little or no input from John and Livinia in a physical sense. It was agreed.

The price was finally agreed and the place was sold to

the pastoral company that John had set up years ago when Frank's place came on the market. This had the hoped for advantage for John of avoiding Dave from finding out that his backwoods neighbour had managed to buy him out. This was a sentiment that the children found difficult to fathom, but John requested that that information be confidential if at all possible.

Ethan seemed to gain a new lease on life once the purchase was set in motion. He spent most of his time planning and calculating how he would run the new business. The new burden of debt also had the added advantage of pleasing John's accountant; a sentiment with which John failed to concur and he slept a little more uneasily for quite a while thinking about it. John need not have worried about that issue at all. If he had only known what was about to be unleashed on his unsuspecting, burgeoning empire, he would have had total peace.

In the meantime, Ethan went about the business of rehabilitating the rundown property and devising and instigating the management plan that would enable him over the next few years to rebuild the large holding into a modern and successful farm.

CHAPTER 11

The telephone rang in the early evening, but as it was seldom for John, he took little notice of the interruption. Hannah, who was there for the weekend, came into the lounge shortly after and announced to her father that a Mr Holpin would like to speak to him on the telephone. John was puzzled for a minute then got up with a hint of annoyance, mumbling to himself. Livinia could just hear one side of the conversation from the other room.

'Hello?' There was a long pause. 'Yes, that's right, but where did you get my name from?' Another long pause. 'Well mate, that's all very interesting, but I'm sorry I'm not interested in selling it at all.' Another long pause.

'Listen cobber, it's not for sale.'

Livinia could hear that John was getting annoyed. 'No thanks mate, I'm not interested. Thanks for calling. Bye.'

'Who was that, dear?' asked Livinia as John ambled back to his chair.

'Would you believe it? Someone wants to buy George Street. I'm staggered. Anyway, it's not for sale. And don't tell Ethan that someone wants to buy it,' he said wryly.

John thought nothing about it again except to contemplate how, by being able to diversify years ago into some income-producing real estate, he had been able to weather the ups and downs of the wool markets and survive the dry times better, not to mention assist in paying off the loans for buying Dave Quiggin's place.

About ten days later, while they were all in the lounge in the evening, the telephone rang. Livinia answered, expecting it to be for her. However, it was Mr Holpin again asking for John. John was annoyed this time. He strode over to the telephone and brusquely and threateningly said, 'Hello!' There was a short pause. 'Mr Holpin, I thought I made myself quite clear that I am not in the slightest interested in selling that property.' There was an ominous and short pause.

Livinia rolled her eyes in a fearful sideways glance in the direction of the conversation. 'Oh dear.'

'There's no point in meeting, Mr Holpin.' There was a longer pause. 'All right. If it will get rid of you, we can meet in Cooma.' A short pause. 'No that does not suit. Yes that might be okay. Alright, we'll see you then.'

John replaced the receiver and strode back into the room.

'What a damn nuisance. Now he wants to meet me Friday in town. Would you like to come in with me Liv?'

She nodded in agreement and nothing else was said about it that evening, although Livinia could see John was quite irritated and fidgety.

On Friday morning, John and Livinia waited at the park looking for the maroon Jaguar that Mr Holpin described. At precisely 11 am, as agreed, John spotted the Jag slowly cruising the street looking for a parking spot. John watched it circling Centennial Park and finding a parking spot. John and Livinia ambled over in the direction of the parked car. John watched as two well-dressed men in suits and ties got out of the car and peered around looking for him. John grasped Livinia's hand tightly as they made their way over to the two men.

When they were close enough, John called out, 'Holpin?'

The man who had been driving looked at him and replied strongly and deferentially, 'Yes, thank you for coming to see us. I'm Roger Holpin. Is there a café or somewhere we can go for a coffee?'

After introductions, they walked up the main street to a small café where Holpin ordered refreshments for everyone. This was the same café that John had visited many times in his younger days when it was a milk bar. It was still run by a family of 'New Australians' whom John got to know very well. The lady's name was Milcha and she spoke a fractured kind of English. Once seated, she came over and greeted them all effusively.

'Hello John!' she exclaimed. 'How you are?'

'Hi Milcha,' answered John. 'I'm fine, thank you.'

'Same I,' she responded in her quaint way. 'What I get you, eh?'

They ordered some coffee and cakes. Roger Holpin was a well-groomed man about fiftyish, greying and slightly haggard as if from years of high-level stress from working in the city. His companion was much younger but very polite and had the appearance of a university graduate. Holpin made some small talk about the weather and remarks about the country; things he thought might break the ice with his adversary, whom he knew to be very successful in the grazing industry and in business.

'Look Roger, let's not mess about. What is it you want?'

Holpin paused. He was used to dealing with high-powered, aggressive men, and half expected John to be direct and forthright. *At least he was polite, if firm.*

'Alright John. As I said on the 'phone, I work for a corporation that has big plans for the section of the city that includes your building. Plans are not finalised yet but we can't proceed much further without all the titles in our hands. We are prepared to make you a very good offer for that property.'

'It's not for sale.'

'Hear me out,' Holpin said. He realised that when somebody made that remark, they were probably going to be difficult to deal with, but he also knew from long experience that everybody had their price – eventually. He then went on to explain a few more details. John requested to know all about the corporation that he was dealing with and a lot more information about the development. He went on to explain that he had tenants he felt obliged to look out for and other issues.

It was a pleasant enough meeting, but left John perplexed

and confused. The purchase money they were hinting at was more than its real value, but not enough to tempt him.

They spent about an hour talking over the deal and then John said that he wanted time to think about it and read over the proposals.

Back home, John spent time contemplating the events of the day in Cooma. He made arrangements to see his accountant and his solicitor in Cooma over the next few days in an attempt to find out more about the offer, but he was still inclined to have nothing to do with it.

His accountant, when the situation was explained to him, was supportive and had several suggestions. He was still trying to get John to have more debt to reduce his tax, but always had major difficulty trying to convince him. Now that he had taken on the Quiggin place, his taxation problems were of a lesser nature. John's solicitor was also quite supportive, and recommended that, if John agreed, he would attempt to discover more about the offer and would ring him back, hopefully in a few days. John thought that his solicitor, though not revealing much at the time, knew more about the companies involved than he was letting on.

True to his word, four nights later, John's solicitor telephoned him in the evening. It transpired that the solicitor had found out quite a bit and suggested John call in at a suitable time for a meeting. This he arranged for the following Monday morning.

John drove into Cooma on Monday with Livinia to see the solicitor. Miles Selkirk, had been doing John's local legal work since he had bought the practice from the original owner whom John had first used when he arrived in Cooma and needed any legal work done. He was quite young when John first met him – not long out of university. He was quite a cultured man, well-built and athletic. John discovered that he had come from a farming background locally and had been forced by family responsibilities to remain in the neighbourhood rather than pursue a promising career in Sydney. Miles Selkirk had purchased the practice from its owner Paul Ryan, an Irishman whose health had forced him to give up work.

John and Livinia made their way into Miles's office and sat in the two chairs in front of his desk. It was a tidy desk with piles of papers and files neatly set out at various places.

'You remember my wife Livinia, Miles?' John began.

'Yes. Good morning Mrs Summers.' Livinia nodded politely but said nothing.

'What have you got for me Miles?' asked John.

'Well, John. I've managed to find out quite a lot for you about this. A mate of mine I went through uni with works for the corporation involved and gave me as much as he could without breaching confidences. It turns out the developer is actually a subsidiary of PFR – you know, run by Storeman.'

John nodded. Everyone knew of Terry Storeman, the larger-than-life corporate magnate known as 'The Big Fella' because of his height, weight and business acumen – and the power and influence he wielded in the business and political world in Australia.

'A lot of what I'm going to tell you is confidential you

understand, so please keep it to yourselves. It appears that Storeman senior is not very well. It is not generally known because if that got out the share price of his companies would drop enormously. He recently acquired the title to this building here,' he said, pointing to a colour on the plan, 'after many years of negotiations trying to buy it. Now he owns all the buildings in a group along these two streets here.' Miles spread the plan out further and pointed to some more colourings on it. 'As you can see, your building is crucial to the development on this corner. Yours is now the last piece of the puzzle he needs. He is planning to apply for a redevelopment application to build a huge international hotel and casino on this site. It is no certainty he will get it as there will be a lot of opposition from the other casinos in Sydney and Australia, and the local city mayor has already stated that he will oppose any more development in the city. Now this is the interesting bit. Because Storeman senior is not well – I'm talking terminal here – and Storeman junior is much less interested in this project, senior is pushing hard to complete it before fate intervenes.'

'So what's this mean for me do you think?' asked John hesitantly.

'It means for you that you may be able to sell for a very good price. The current market value for that property in that location is about seven to eight million dollars. You might be able to ask twelve to fifteen.'

'And what am I going to do with twelve million? I've got enough tax problems.'

Miles made some positive suggestions about property purchases and farming enterprises, but John felt that he was past all the wheeling and dealing involved in that sort of thing. Miles went on to explain a few more details and gave out more information that his contact had passed on. Before ending the meeting, Miles began to fish around a bit at the bidding of his ex-university friend who was involved with the deal. Unbeknown to John, he had already informed his contact that John was quite a wealthy and successful citizen of the district and was motivated by matters other than money. Miles had told them he considered John would not be assuaged by money alone and that the offer was going to have to be a good one.

'Would you be at all interested in a share offer in PFR? Storeman would be prepared to offer you a considerable number of stocks if that were of interest?'

'No. I have never owned shares and don't like them at all.'

'Okay, just checking,' replied Selkirk a little disappointedly.

John was ambivalent about all this. He was rather fond of the old building and the tenants, including Edison Hargraves. Then there was all the legal messing around with changing the head office location of his companies. All in all, he still was not convinced. John thanked Miles, gathered up all the paperwork and said he would think about it.

Two nights later, Roger Holpin was on the telephone again. He was prepared to make an offer of twenty-five million dollars for the property. John was stunned. Storeman must want this project in a serious way. It was becoming almost impossible to refuse. John thought about it carefully for a few days. It occurred to him that if Storeman got this property but then died or the project stalled for some reason, all the buildings in this group would probably come back on the market – especially if the company was in so much debt as Miles had pointed out. Storeman's serious illness was not common knowledge, but a fact that might be of benefit to John. *Maybe I could arrange to be given first refusal on his building if that ever eventuated. Surely that can be put into a contract,* he thought.

John was mildly disappointed that Holpin had made such an attractive offer. He knew deep down that he could not really refuse to accept twenty-five million dollars for a property that was actually only worth about eight million. All John wanted from life now was to quietly play with his grazing properties and manage his buildings and houses as a sideline to an easy life. If Ethan found out about this, he would almost demand to be allowed to develop the grazing enterprise into the scientific development of fine wool with shedding, nutritional balances, and embryonic advances he was always on about. John wondered if this would lead to him losing control of his happy life.

John again made arrangements to meet with Miles Selkirk in Cooma and finalise his plans for attending to the offer from PFR. After long discussions, a form of contract wording that satisfied him was drawn up and the draft sent off to the legal contacts in Sydney. It was only a few days later that they contacted Miles's office with a reply, which contained some minor amendments but effectively agreeing to the clause giving John first refusal, at market value, in the event of a collapse of the project and the building coming onto the market.

John really had no reason to refuse the deal now. He waited to be summoned to the office of Mr Storeman in Sydney for the final signing. John had asked Miles if he would be able to accompany him to Sydney when the signing was arranged.

Things had developed way out of John's control. He had never mentioned any of this to the family meetings, mainly because he knew how they would react. He hoped it would all just go away before it had advanced too far. This clearly was now not the case. He was getting in too deeply now and may have to discuss it all with the family, something he would rather not do.

There was some more minor toing-and-froing, but a few weeks later, Roger Holpin arranged for John and Miles to be picked up in Storeman's personal helicopter at the Cooma airport and be flown up to Sydney to finalise the deal. It was all a bit surreal for John, but Miles was enjoying the excitement of a big deal, something he had foregone by choosing to live in Cooma where most of his work was conveyancing and estate matters. It was certainly a novel and efficient way to travel to Sydney and they were there in about an hour or so, right at the site where the deal would be fixed. John and Miles had already thoroughly perused a draft of the final documentation so it only needed a final reading through to ensure all was in order.

John had fully expected to be greeted by Storeman

himself, but Roger Holpin was managing the deal. He was accompanied by a team of assistants, one of whom was Miles's erstwhile university colleague who apparently was now regarded as instrumental in getting the deal this far by virtue of his invaluable contact with Miles. Between them, they had, behind the scenes, navigated the nuances of John's objections and reticence in selling.

John carefully read every line and especially checked the price; the method of payment; the extra he had asked for to give to Miles as a fee and payment; and especially the clause that ensured he be given the first offer, and at market value, if the property ever came back on the market. It was all there and all in order as far as he could see. All it needed was Miles's concurrence.

Miles Selkirk read the document with great absorption, relishing this rare instance of power finances and his moment in the spotlight. Eventually he was fully satisfied and recommended to John that he could sign it. With that, John handed the deeds to the property over to Roger Holpin and Roger handed over a cheque for twenty-five million, two hundred and fifty thousand dollars. John looked at it wistfully and thought that this bit of paper represented all the memories and efforts in locating, buying and maintaining a fine old building that he was very sorry to be parting with.

There followed refreshments and Roger offered to arrange for the flight back to Cooma. John asked if he could go to the bank located nearby and deposit the cheque. Once that was done, the flight back to Cooma could be arranged. It was a sombre John who sat contemplatively in the chopper gazing out the window all the way back to Cooma. Somehow the twenty-five million dollars was not the same as a real live building.

John arranged for his solicitor to contact the tenants of his former property to advise them of the sale. His one word of caution to each was that they may not need to hurry out of the building as the proposed plans for redevelopment were not advanced enough to worry about yet. That was all he could say about it. He was unable to mention or even hint that Terry Storeman was involved, let alone his tenuous state of health. In the end, John was resigned to the fact that Storeman rarely, if ever, failed in his enterprises and he had probably lost forever the lovely old building that was once his head office.

Edison Hargraves was a different matter. The next time he and Livinia were in Manly, he arranged to meet Edison and his wife Annabel in his office. Edison had furnished his office in sleek modern furniture that gave the air of efficiency and frugality tinged with a hint of success.

After pleasantries John said, 'Edison, I'm sure you've heard by now the news about the sale of the building.'

'Yes, your solicitor contacted me.'

John felt he owed his cousin a better explanation than just a cold letter from his solicitor.

John spent some time talking to him and advised him that he would try and keep him informed of any known developments. He emphasised that there was no certainty that the plans would proceed so there was probably no hurry to move, but be prepared in the future if it happened. Edison had been grateful to John for the helping hand in the beginning and had wandered around the building to familiarise himself with the other tenants. He was surprised to discover the registered head office of J W Summers & Company on the seventh floor. He tried to find out a bit more about it but information was limited and it was only a holding company anyway. He had even surreptitiously interrogated Livinia when the opportunity arose. On one of the visits to his office he had said to her, 'Has John any interests outside of his place?'

'You mean beyond his station?' Livinia asked, feigning ignorance. 'Well,' she stuttered, knowing he was fishing, 'sure, he has many other interests. It's just that his other interests don't show themselves as much. At heart, John's just a grazier from the country.' She hoped that would satisfy his curiosity. As he asked no more, it seemed to have worked.

John was quite unsettled by this event. He learnt from Edison that the new owners had already increased the rental on all the office space in the building. He spent some days in quiet contemplation, wandering down by the creek where he had first sat thinking about whether to buy this farm all those years ago. It was here that he had seen the apparition that Frank thought might be Albert. He never was able to fully confirm in his own mind the child that Albert was with and whether it was his lost son, drowned at ten. In the calm stillness of the bush, with only the dull murmurings of a myriad of insects and the occasional rustling of the heavy eucalyptus leaves, John sat on the grass and thought about his life. In the distance he could hear the occasional far-off muffled screech of cockatoos and the dull drone of an aeroplane, barely audible.

John asked Livinia to keep this sale a secret for a few months as he was still hopeful, though not confident, that the development might fall through and he could be offered the property back, or at least keep his head office there for a while longer. In the meantime, he would think long and hard about what to do with this amount of money. He and Livinia discussed in detail any number of options, so he had plenty to think about.

Six months after the sale was finalised, John received a telephone call from Miles Selkirk to ask him to come by the office the first chance he had. The next sale day that John was in town, he called into Miles's office.

'John, some news that might interest you. Mr Storeman is going into hospital next week. It's all described as routine but my contact in the firm up there informs me that it's quite serious. This is all hush-hush you understand, but thought you might be interested.'

'Yes, thank you indeed, I certainly will keep an eye on matters for a while. Many thanks for the info.' That set John to thinking how he could get information about developments.

Two months later, Terry Storeman was dead. He had died of a massive heart attack. He had been gravely ill for many months and suffered from bad health for years. This information was kept quiet and the public had no idea how serious it had been. John's only interest was in the possibility of retrieving his beloved asset from the company that may now have different priorities. He could not wait to get home and tell Livinia.

John was very lucky to have Miles Selkirk as his solicitor as Miles had inside information on the company and its business machinations where the George Street building was concerned. To his delight, he was informed that, indeed, Terry's son was not interested in any domestic hotel and casino developments and wished to unload the buildings to reduce debt and free up capital to pursue his interest elsewhere, mostly off-shore. He had already sold a large parcel of the properties to another magnate and would be trying to sell all of them quickly. Miles's mate in the company advised that Roger Holpin might be making contact shortly.

Finally the day came for John that contact was made. To honour the letter of the selling contract, PFR's subsidiary company wished to unload the building in George Street that it had purchased from John Summers' company. Roger Holpin offered the property back to John at the purchase price. John was staggered; and quite annoyed. There was no way he would be paying twenty-five million for a building that was worth about eight at the most. There were some furious negotiations between the parties but ultimately John had sealed up a binding and water-tight clause in the contract that gave him the right to buy back at current market price. John could understand Holpin's trying it on, but he would not budge on the letter of the law on that clause, and he intimated that he was prepared to go to court over it, something that PFR wished to avoid at all costs. John had them over a barrel and they knew it. Admittedly they did not foresee this eventuality ever arising and initially agreed to the insertion of the clause, mostly at the insistence of Terry Storeman, in order to expedite the creation of his final dream before his life may be over.

Roger Holpin finally came up with a compromise suggestion that might suit everyone. As well as John's original building of seven stories, he was prepared to offer the building next to it, a building of eleven storeys, as a job lot. Storeman had purchased that building some time before he got John's, as it was in some disrepair, but very well located. It needed some considerable expenditure to bring it up to standard, but was essentially sound. Holpin would offer both buildings as a lot for twenty-three million dollars. John would accept no more than eighteen million. This valued the eleven-storey building at more than its market value but it afforded PFR an acceptable way out of the binding contract, reducing their potential loss to a minimum, and it got John two buildings where he originally only had one and still gave him a considerably large sum of money in excess as pure profit. Both Miles Selkirk and his contact in PFR held John in high regard and wondered at his luck and business acumen. In fact, all those in PFR involved with this deal admired the small-time grazier that fate had allowed to put one over the great Storeman.

But John had a bigger problem than before. This time he and Livinia would have to discuss this complication over many months. He had no excuse now but to give Ethan some free-reign on the direction of the property's development.

One of the first things John did was to reduce the rental on the premises back to its original level.

Months drifted by and finally a plan began to form in John's mind. There was a highly developed, scientifically-based, fine-wool property rumoured to be coming onto the market in about five months. The owners had spent millions developing the infrastructure and blood-lines but family tragedy might force the selling of this valuable enterprise in the near future. John's plan was far-reaching in its scope. He would call a family shareholders meeting and ask for suggestions of what to do with a spare seven million dollars (plus interest). John hoped that if the family could be persuaded to purchase this place or one like it, it would satisfy the demand for improvements in the blood-line of his own properties but allow him to keep his original Bridgehead intact. It had the added bonus of possibly allowing Thomas to return from north-western Queensland as manager and be close by as John and Livinia grew older.

It was arranged that the family would gather. There was to be a big announcement of great significance to everyone and all were required – including Thomas from Queensland. Rumours abounded. The best guesses included John and Livinia's retirement; their moving to the coast; selling some of the investment properties to reduce the debt; or maybe a wedding.

John had asked if everyone could assemble at the house on the Friday evening this time. It was the first time all the family had been in one place in many years, as the casual

Sunday afternoon get-togethers were very informal affairs and not everyone could always attend. Livinia and the ladies prepared quite a feast for the gathering and all the rooms in the homestead would be occupied.

The few Sundays previous to this meeting, John had finally decided to admit Audrey to the inner family circle of shareholders. She had not particularly changed her ways or opinions, but was nevertheless more circumspect and guarded in her manner, especially as she grew older and her children matured. He had called her into his study just as he had done with the others and explained the position and her obligations, especially discretion away from the family. She referred to some of the aspects of the family fortune as 'obscene' and 'immoral' but agreed to accept the conditions. He agreed to include her if she abided by the rules. She could see no reason for her children to be excluded from the income produced by her family if it were on offer.

John wanted to add Thomas to the inner circle. He asked each in turn their opinion. Audrey was not in a position to comment. Ethan reluctantly agreed, voicing his concern that all the children would want membership. This John dismissed. He also allayed any fears of a reduction in income for those already holding shares. He pointed out that there were only ten shares in total; the only effect of new members was to reduce the amount going to the sinking fund. Damien was all for it and Hannah agreed with him, so the offer was made to Thomas. He had no idea of the significance of this offer, so gladly accepted something he thought entailed little more than a family gathering. He was to learn shortly that it was much more than that – and especially for him.

During the early afternoon, John excused himself from the gathering and went off to prepare the papers for the meeting. He carried a briefcase full of folders into the dining room and shut the door. He gave himself an hour or so to prepare for the meeting. He put the case on the table and opened it, then he slowly removed one folder. He put it on the seat that was for himself. He repeated the procedure and put one down for Livinia. He gathered another out of the case and stood there holding it in a slight dream. This one was for Audrey, newly admitted to the circle. He recalled the afternoon that he summoned her to the study and the latent trepidation he felt about that talk. He wondered how she would react and if indeed she would even accept. He still loved his daughter, his first child and the mother, albeit in terrible circumstances, of his first grandchild, Thomas. He did not like her choice of husband, for by now they had married, as he found Geoffrey Bales the most arrogant man he had met. Still the circle was complete with her on board.

He picked up another folder and proceeded to consign it at the place reserved for Ethan. Ethan was his chosen successor and heir apparent. He was securely married and now lived in the neat cottage that was built about one kilometre from the main homestead, although he was making noises about moving over the hills to live on the developing property that they had purchased from Dave Quiggin. His children, two boys, were lovely children, well behaved and quite an asset about the farm. Their future, John hoped, would be too far distant to be of concern for him with regard to the property assets and inheritance.

John sauntered back to the briefcase and sat down to think about his children and his life. He fumbled in the case to withdraw another folder, this one for Damien. *How different his offspring were from each other*, he thought. *Where Ethan was solid and tall, confident and extroverted, possibly because he was the first-born son and inheritor of the grazing enterprise, Damien was shorter, more wiry and introverted to the point of being apologetic. Damien's wife, Helen, was a simple country girl who seemed to make him happy and they worked together on their irrigation fields all the hours of the day.*

John placed a folder on the seat for Hannah, the least offensive of his children. She was a soft and gentle young woman who now lived permanently in Cooma in a cottage that John had purchased for her when she completed her accountancy studies and began to succeed at her job in the council.

There were two folders left; one was for Thomas, who still had no idea whom his father was and this played on John's mind because he never fully came to terms over the loss of his own parents as a child. John dearly wished he had a folder for his ever-young lost son, the permanently ten-year-old Brendan.

John returned to the chair at the head of the table to contemplate his own life that had started so inauspiciously. He slowly began to count all the blessings that had been bestowed on him and wondered momentarily why and how that had occurred. He was a little melancholy and fearful of the proceedings that were about to occur as he felt this could be a significant fork in the road of the family's future and the outcomes stemming from those choices.

Among much chatter, the family assembled in the large dining room where the neat folders were laid out in front of each chair that was to be occupied. Only immediate family members and shareholders in the family business were to enter the dining room – no spouses or children. Each person found his or her chair and sat down. They were asked not to open any folders.

John commenced by saying, 'Thank you all for coming. Some of you have come a long way to be here. Firstly, welcome formally to Audrey to the meeting of the family and you will soon see how things operate as we go along. Secondly, also welcome to Thomas. I know this will be a little unfamiliar to you but things here will involve you so I want you present. I know you are all intrigued by this gathering but all will shortly be revealed.'

John sat at the head of the table fiddling with the folder in front of him. He displayed a certain amount of nervousness, which was unusual for him.

'Some months ago,' he continued, 'in fact, many months ago now, I was offered a considerable sum of money for the George Street property.'

'Take it,' said Ethan.

'We'll sell,' said Damien, thinking of the improvements he had hinted at for the lucerne production.

Thomas looked blankly at the group, missing the whole point of the conversation so far.

'Steady on,' continued John, followed by a short pause. 'It's not that simple. You all know about the death of Storeman.'

There was a mixture of acknowledgement and perplexed looks.

'You mean the magnate in Sydney?' asked Ethan.

'Yes, that's him,' answered John.

'What's he got to do with us?'

There was a slight murmur around the table.

'Well, before he died, he offered me a lot of money for George Street.' John looked at Thomas and said, 'We own property in the centre of Sydney, too. It will all become clearer to you as we go.' He returned his gaze to the assembly, then continued, 'In fact, he offered an obscene amount. I eventually agreed to sell on one condition – that I be offered first refusal on any resale.'

'You haven't bought it back?' asked the familiar voice of Ethan. 'You haven't even sold it, have you?'

'Worse than that,' said John sheepishly.

'You mean you didn't even sell it in the first place?' repeated Ethan.

'Yes, I did finally sell it. But he died well before his plans could be implemented and when it was offered to me, I bought it back.'

'No! Think what we could've done with the dough.'

'Look,' continued John, 'the gist of it is that I sold it for twenty-five million dollars.'

'That's ridiculous!' said a couple of voices.

'Then I bought it back along with its neighbour of eleven storeys for eighteen million.'

'Fair dinkum?' gasped Ethan.

'I told you he's all arse and no class,' said Damien slyly to Thomas sitting beside him. Thomas managed a half grin at the comment but was lost in the details of all this. The sums of money that were being bandied about were beyond his ken.

'Yes. Now I have two buildings in George Street instead of one AND over seven million dollars to spend,' continued John, pausing to allow that information to sink in. John looked at Thomas and said to him as an aside, 'Sorry Thomas, I know this is all a bit new to you but bear with us. Now I want you all to nominate what you think would be some good suggestions for us to do with this dollars.'

'Say all that again.'

'It's all in the folder. Please now all go away and read them, then we'll all discuss it after dinner. How's that?'

There was a shuffling of folders and a rummaging through of papers as, in silence, they all sat there stunned; mute with the magnitude of affairs and the total unexpectedness of this peculiar turn of events.

'Dad and I will be here if you want to ask us anything,' offered Livinia. No one spoke as they read the contents and tried to assimilate all the information.

'Have you got any preferences?' asked Damien.

'Yes Dad, what would *you* like to do,' chipped in Hannah.

'As a matter of fact, I do have some thoughts, but I'd like

you all to read the folders and look at some of the suggestions, and maybe come up with some of your own first.'

John watched as one by one they slowly pushed back their chairs and prepared to leave. As they proceeded to the door, John said, 'Thomas, I wonder if you'd mind staying back with me for a few minutes?'

Over the next two days, there was much discussion and many questions. John had listed his ideas on one of the sheets and there was gradual agreement for one, which included Thomas returning to manage a close-by property. This idea had generated strong opposition from what John regarded as an unexpected quarter. Ethan seemed vehemently opposed to it for some reason, something to do with the project being his idea all along and why could he not manage it. He said he was much better qualified and more enthusiastic and experienced than Thomas. *Thomas could manage Bridgehead or, even better, take over Dave Quiggin's place while I moved to the new place.*

John stuck to his guns on this issue and would not hear of any changes. John insisted that he wanted Ethan to manage not only Bridgehead and the new Quiggin place but also be the chief executive of the family company that managed all of their other off-farm assets. Thomas, on the other hand, was initially lukewarm. He enjoyed his life on the Barkly in western Queensland and was confident and coping well with the divergent challenges life outback offered, despite the diminishing availability of labour and because of the technical innovation to master.

The weekend finally drew to an end and a tentative plan

was sketched out to which everybody had agreed. Thomas flew back to Mt Isa and resumed his life on the Barkly, while the rest of the family returned to the business of the day back in their own lives.

Four months later, just as John had predicted, the desired property, named Auvergne, came on the market, to be auctioned in six weeks on site or in the Sydney office of the selling agents. John again requested Thomas to return to Bridgehead in order to undertake an inspection accompanied by John and hopefully Ethan and Damien.

On the agreed day, the four of them were driven by John in his now aging Holden WB Brougham sedan to the prospective property to undergo an exhaustive inspection of all the facilities. The property was located nearly two hours from Bridgehead in a renowned part of the shire that possessed unusually good grazing capabilities. They arrived at the site at 10.30 am as arranged and were met by the selling agents and the young representative of the vendors. They were given a brief address by both the agent and the vendor regarding the facilities and the production techniques used in producing the high-quality and highly sought-after very fine wool. Ethan was particularly interested in the science and technology and Damien was interested in the feed production management and facilities. Thomas was interested in how they managed the technical sheep side in combination with the commercial sheep flock in the paddocks while coping with the cattle herd, which was grazed entirely on the open range.

The difficulties that seemed to arise for Thomas related to the intricacy of finding and retaining suitable staff to cope with such a range of qualifications that such a complex animal production system needed in order to be successful. In Queensland, he only needed jackaroos or stockmen who were competent horsemen and bike riders with occasional helicopter assistance, but here there seemed to be a need for that ability, plus almost a scientific capability to work technology.

They were accompanied on the tour by the chief technician, the man responsible for the embryo and genetic side of the enterprise. His name was Warren Costello; he was about thirty-five years old and neatly dressed in clean farming gear, with shining riding boots. This struck Thomas as strange, but then he realised that hygiene was probably paramount in this practice.

Importantly for Thomas, he was very personable and prepared to discuss any aspects of the enterprise in a manner conducive to imparting difficult concepts to those less knowledgeable than he was. While in the artificial breeding complex, Thomas found himself standing beside Warren while the others took in some finer points of the rams located in the stalls.

'What are your plans after the sale, Warren?' asked Thomas.

'Well, all being well, I hope to stay on here if that's at all possible. It may not happen, as one of the prospective buyers is an overseas company and I understand their plan is to bring in their own people.'

'You'd like to stay on though?'

'Yeah.'

'Would you be able to take me over the property if I want to look at paddocks and stock?'

'Yeah. Sure. If the boss agrees, I have no problem.'

They all wandered up and down the shed complex poking and prodding and admiring the animals and their wool and trying to take in the enormity of the entire scene. John was a little perplexed and bemused by it all. It was way out of his realm, but he did not worry about that as it would not be his problem. *If the young blokes wanted to move into this new-fangled animal production it would be their problem* – he had made that clear from the start. The inspection took several hours. Close to the finish, Thomas said to the assembled company, 'Can I arrange to be shown over the property by Warren in a day or two?'

The vendor's representative, a young family member and manager of one of the aspects of the business replied, 'No, Warren will be occupied in the sheds for the next week or two, but I will gladly show you around in the ute.'

'I'd really rather Warren show me if at all possible. Especially as he may be staying on,' said Thomas, in a surprisingly authoritative, imperious tone that surprised John, in particular. John had not seen Thomas in his role as boss cocky, but then thought, *if he can manage a large Queensland station with the wild ringers and jackaroos he must get up there, he should be able to run this little enterprise, even if it is a tad more technical.*

271

John smiled to himself with satisfaction that he had indeed chosen the right man for this new project. There was an awkward silence for a few seconds.

'Fair enough, I suppose. I guess that makes sense.' Turning to Warren, the young bloke said, 'Would that be okay with you, Warren?'

'Sure, boss.'

Turning back to Thomas, he said, 'When would suit?'

'Tomorrow would be good.'

It was arranged. Thomas and John would return in the morning at nine-thirty to be shown around the property by car. The other two showed little interest in that arrangement, which John found moderately disappointing.

The next morning, John drove Thomas back to Auvergne to inspect the whole property by car. Warren had arranged for the four-door ute to be available in order to drive the three of them. As the homestead and animal complexes were located approximately one quarter of the way into the property, Warren chose to commence the inspection by heading west and driving along the long western boundary and into the cattle paddocks.

The general consensus on leaving the property was that they should proceed with the investigations with a view to bidding at the up-coming auction. The intention was hopefully to be successful in submitting a bid for this property. John was satisfied with the visit and the general reaction of the other three. His only stipulation, apart from still insisting that Thomas manage the place, was the bidding limit was to be seven million dollars. The feeling among the agents was that this amount should be sufficient to acquire this property at auction. There was now nothing to do but proceed with searches and legal inquiries and wait for the date to roll around.

The day of the auction, John was accompanied by Livinia, Ethan and wife Sophie, Damien and his wife Helen, and Neil Brody, the leading hand from Quiggin's place. The auction was to be held in a Cooma legal office, as there had been many local parties interested in the valuable property. This was fortuitous, as it was more convenient for the Summers family than if it had been held in Sydney.

Bidding opened strongly at five million and proceeded briskly to six and a half even. At that point it was evident to all present that John was determined to be successful; bidding stopped with John holding the bid. At hammer-fall, it was his. He was roundly congratulated by his family, who were very expectant that this property would fall to them. It remained only to telephone Thomas on the mobile to inform him of their success. This John did while the others were conversing with the agents and vendor about the sale.

Thomas waited for the call at the homestead as he was also anxious to know the outcome, as this would have a huge impact on his future. It was with some trepidation that he awaited the call as he was still uncertain how he would cope with this big move and the expectations his family had of him, especially his grandfather. Thomas received the news of their success with a quiet demeanour and hushed voice, trying to sound happy but not too thrilled. He replaced the receiver and sat back in his chair to contemplate his future.

Thomas had thoroughly enjoyed his time as manager of the Queensland property. He was competent, and fully understood the requirements of western Queensland grazing. He was also very happy, and felt that he was completely appreciated by the owners who lived not far from John's place in the Cooma district. He hoped he knew what he was doing and that he would still be as happy as he had been in Queensland.

There was now a lot to organise before Thomas could arrange to return to Cooma. His top priority was to alert Ted that he had an offer to return to the family farm in Cooma, and that he would need to arrange for a replacement. Thomas made plans to return to Cooma within the next few weeks and organise with Ted to find a replacement.

On his return to the Monaro, Thomas took the opportunity to revisit Auvergne and renew acquaintances with Warren Costello. He spent a full day out at the new station with Warren, being given a full inspection of the holding. This visit reinforced his feelings that finding suitable workers was going to be a major problem. He met two of the local boys who were employed on a casual basis to muster and truck stock when needed, but was totally unimpressed with their character. He was tempted to recruit some of his boys from the Barkly, but respected Ted too much to poach all his other staff.

John spent the first few weeks familiarising himself

with the new property and the facilities but was not really interested in the detailed technical aspects. *That was for Ethan and Damien to master and especially Thomas when he could get away from Queensland.* He was quietly pleased with his purchase because he now believed he could retain Bridgehead in its present form and live out the rest of his days quietly playing with his stock and enjoying time with Livinia. She was beginning to miss the seaside more than ever and John hoped from now on to be able to spend more time alone down on the south coast at some of the more out of the way beaches. He felt it was time to reward his faithful wife for all the sacrifices she had made for him. After all, he always felt she could have and should have married better, and maybe more suitably than an unsophisticated farmer boy from the backblocks of Cooma. He was always conscious of that fact.

John wandered contentedly up to the small ridge from where he could survey most of his domain. It was the same featureless ridge from where he first contemplated where to start his farming projects when he bought the place from Frank over fifty years ago now. He had also brought Livinia to this ridge to overview the property when he was courting her. He smiled in quiet wonderment at just how happy he had become as an old man.

He sat in the late-afternoon light surveying his small kingdom for many minutes. He thought about his family and the wonderful life he had been delivered through meeting Livinia. He cast a strange thought back to the seemingly cursed Merritt clan and wondered why they had seemed to fare so badly. He thought about the vagaries of life as reflected in his own experience. *Were they so blighted because of some deed perpetrated by Henry or Claude, or were their circumstances so wretched in order to emphasise his own blessings, which were entirely due to my illegitimate act against them.* It was his eternal torment to consider.

As the late-afternoon sunlight brightly illuminated what were his own comfortable possessions, he casually walked back to his former quarters to savour, as he regularly did, the peaceful atmosphere of that hallowed environment yet again.

The old shed quarters remained much as he had envisaged them as a young man and retained the isolated tranquillity that pervaded them when first constructed. They had remained much as he left them when he had moved into the new house he had built for his increasing family. He sat at the desk and fumbled through the contents of the drawers. There were a few old items that were the prizes of his long existence. He had artefacts from old Jack back at the Merritt's, odd items he had collected from sales and, shoved into the back of the drawer, that faded piece of stiff paper that was encrypted with the message that he still did not fully understand. One day he promised himself to investigate its meaning, but not now.

He paused for a moment. *Well, maybe not now. Then again, another puzzling look at it could do no harm.* He extracted it noisily from the wooden drawer. He looked at it uncomprehendingly. On the desk above his line of sight was the only incongruous item from another existence, the picture of his lost son Brendan. He stared at the fading picture sadly.

Other than that deeply melancholy recollection, he felt life had given him more than was fair, much more. He certainly was blessed, at least in this life. *Who knows about the next? Who knows even what is around the corner?* His thoughts strayed to his much-loved grandson, Thomas, who was preparing to return to the fold.

Deep in his own thoughts, John returned to the present and fondled the yellowing stiff piece of cardboard-thick paper that he had puzzled over before. He began to read it again: 'To-day discovered H secret. Money belongs John. There is C £120 grand in folding 4 AJC Already spent lot put this away for J. WTS died no will car to pars H nicked dosh.' It was still cryptic to him and he could only guess at its meaning. *It's clearly Nan's writing. What was the secret she had discovered? Who was WTS? Was that my long-dead father? What money was it that belonged to John? Who was this John anyway?* He turned it over. In the bright light of the well-lit office, he discerned faint pencil marks weaving itself across the soft surface. He reached into the drawer and retrieved a strong magnifying glass.

John stared at the faint bluish pencil scrawl. It was too faint to decipher. He turned it back and forth in his hand. It was a thickish piece and slightly warped. He pulled absently at the edges. He found it peeled away easily, leaving a darker brown stain running all the way around the edges as if it had been glued. A small cutting from an old newspaper fell out onto his lap. He jerked up suddenly to prevent its falling to the floor. He retrieved it from his lap and began to read.

A pall of gloomy shock slowly spread over him as he digested the text of the clipping that had tumbled out of the makeshift home that someone had deliberately made for it decades ago. It read, 'The death occurred yesterday of the well-known racing figure, Mr Wesley Thomas Summers. He was killed, along with his wife, in a car accident on Anzac Parade near the corner of Alison Road. The AJC has expressed its regrets at the loss, as Mr Summers had only recently been awarded his bookmaker's licence to operate at Randwick Racecourse. Mr Summers is believed to have left a considerable estate, following some large and controversial betting plunges on races at both Randwick and Harold Park.'

John sat in despondent gloom as he considered what he had just read. A myriad questions bounced about in his head. *Why had I not discovered this much earlier? He picked up the now-split, thin portions of drab yellow papers that had comprised the once united piece and examined it closely. Who had glued this together? Was it Nan, or someone else? And why? What was the purpose of secreting this long-forgotten snippet of news into the midst of the neatly banded bundles of notes?* John began to try to analyse the steps. The cutting was the first concrete evidence to him of his parents and their demise. It had overtones of an unsavoury nature that John found uncomfortable, firstly over the aspersions cast on his father, and secondly over the estate his father had supposedly accumulated by whatever means.

John sat in the bright afternoon light, regretting that he had bothered to awaken all those old feelings by playing with that piece of paper. In his deep thoughts, he contemplated the character of both his parents. *Oh, how I have missed that relationship.* The need had slowly died over the decades, but he still felt the loss; the never knowing. He wondered how much of his frugal nature sprung from his father. All those snide asides and hidden whispered conversations he recalled from his youth that occurred about him at the Merritts' buzzed about in his head. John tried to remove all these bewildering ideas from his head and return to the concrete present. His mind turned to his grandson, for whom he had specifically bought Auvergne in order that he could return to the fold.

John closed up the drawers and solemnly departed his much-loved former domicile and returned to the big house where his wife awaited him. He sat on the veranda contentedly contemplating the past and the prospects of a fulfilling future. From within his deep idyll, he was aroused by the voice of his devoted wife, Livinia, 'There's a car coming down the drive, John. Are you expecting someone?'

John did not like the unexpected.

At that very moment, Thomas, in faraway Queensland, was loading up his utility. With a slightly saddened heart, he departed for the last time, the property that had been his contented home for more than five years. He drove down the long, dusty gravel track that was its entrance driveway for the last melancholy time. He would head southwest and spend a short time in Camooweal to see one of the girls he had met at the Mt Isa rodeo, and whom he had grown to like, before he began heading south proper, probably via Urandangi. That road was a bit rough but it was a more direct route from

Camooweal south rather than returning all the way back to the Isa and then heading south. He was not particularly in a hurry, but knew John was anxious for him to return and begin his new undertaking. He had a strange feeling as he drove over the flat tableland paddocks into an uncertain future. He hoped he could fulfil his grandfather's hopes and expectations.

www.ingramcontent.com/pod-product-compliance
Lightning Source LLC
Chambersburg PA
CBHW020353120726
47904CB00002B/548